A KIM BARBIERI THRILLER

MURDERER FROM MOSCOW

SID MELTZER

Black Rose Writing | Texas

This is a work of fiction. Names, characters, businesses, places, events, and incidents are either the products of the author's imagination or used in a fictitious manner. Any resemblance to actual persons, living or dead, or actual events is purely coincidental.

ISBN: 978-1-68513-304-7
PUBLISHED BY BLACK ROSE WRITING
www.blackrosewriting.com

Printed in the United States of America
Suggested Retail Price (SRP) $21.95

Murderer from Moscow is printed in EB Garamond

*As a planet-friendly publisher, Black Rose Writing does its best to eliminate unnecessary waste to reduce paper usage and energy costs, while never compromising the reading experience. As a result, the final word count vs. page count may not meet common expectations.

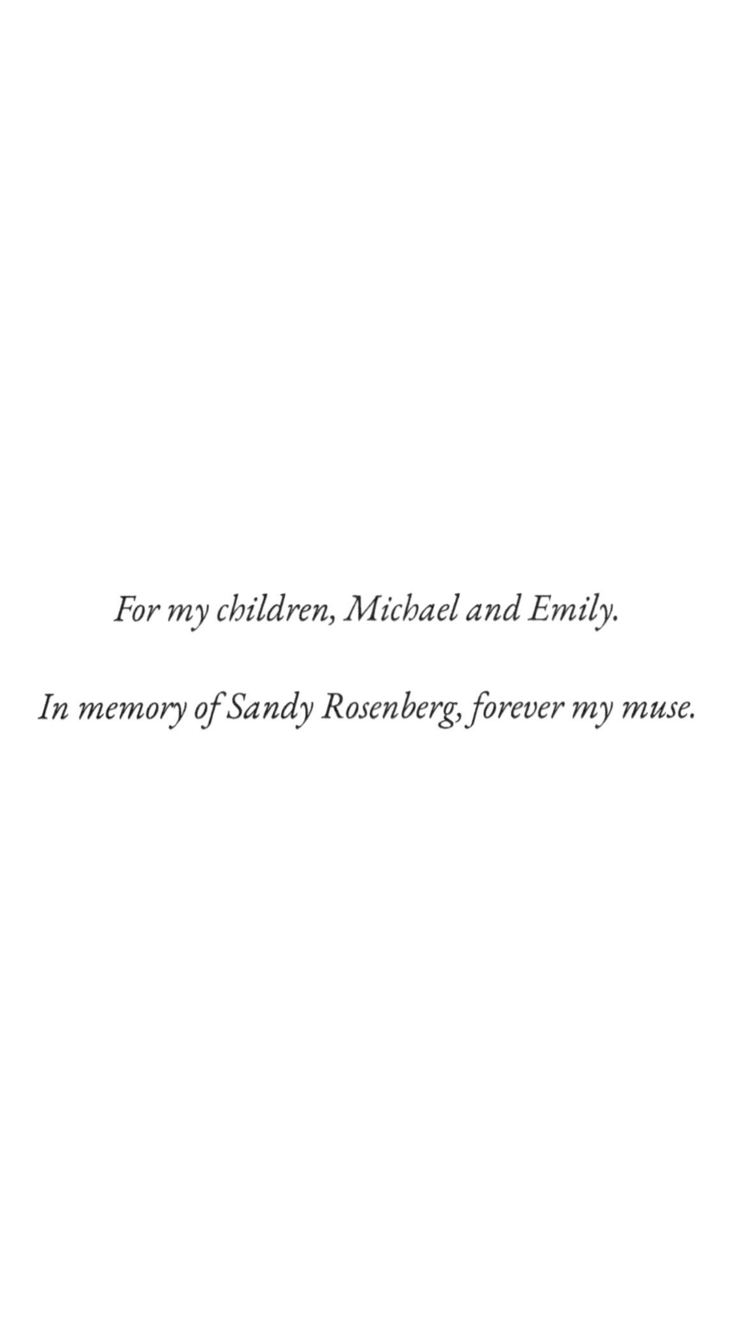

For my children, Michael and Emily.

In memory of Sandy Rosenberg, forever my muse.

MURDERER FROM MOSCOW

CHAPTER ONE

Mokhovaya Street
Moscow
Monday, November 30
5:45 P.M.

Wiping her nose was Olga Kuznetsova's fatal mistake.

After using her right hand to pull open the car door handle, she took out a tissue from her jacket's right pocket and raised it toward her face. Winter was more than a month off, and the weather in the Russian capital had not yet gotten cold enough for gloves and scarves. Less than a second after the tissue brushed against her upper lip, Kuznetsova's brain stopped telling her muscles to keep working. Cut off from the nervous system, muscles all over her body soon went on strike and her body collapsed onto the sidewalk.

After just fifteen seconds, with her diaphragm and ribcage muscles failing, fluid filled her lungs and mouth. Twelve seconds later, she began vomiting. In another forty-three seconds, she was paralyzed from head to toe. Three seconds after that, she stopped breathing and went into convulsions. Sixteen seconds later, Olga Kuznetsova was just a dead body straddling the sidewalk and curb, her legs stretched out beneath the BMW's open door. She never even made it into the driver's seat.

The time between Kuznetsova inhaling Novichok and her death was exactly one minute and fifty-nine seconds. The nerve agent, the deadliest in Russia's arsenal, had claimed its latest victim. As had Bratva. the Russian mafia.

. . .

In the 'CAUSE OF DEATH' field on Olga Kuznetsova's autopsy report, the coroner examining her body entered just one word: 'UNKNOWN'.

At the start of the twenty-first century, the average life expectancy for the average Russian was just over seventy-one years. For investigative reporters who peppered oligarchs with questions they'd just as soon not answer, life expectancy was way below average.

CHAPTER TWO

Sheraton Palace Hotel
1-Ya Tverskaya-Yamskaya Ulitsa, 19
Moscow
Monday November 30
5:55 P.M.

Kim Barbieri wasn't at all sure if the questions she was asking had been the same ones Sergei Petrov was hearing. Or answering.

The Russian interpreter, Annika Zakharova, was a thirtyish, full-figured, slightly nervous-looking blonde with a tiny scar under her lip that Barbieri couldn't help but notice. She had been hired not by her but by her paper, *The Wall Street Journal*. As an investigative reporter in the finance and business arenas, Barbieri had never conducted an interview through a translation filter before. And, to raise the risk of getting critical facts and figures wrong, the interview was being conducted not in person, but on a conference call.

"The penthouse at Fifteen Central Park West in Manhattan? It was bought by Konstantin Sokolov. Correct, Sergei?"

She listened patiently as the interpreter spoke to Petrov in Russian, he gave his reply in Russian, and the interpreter translated his reply into a language she could understand. *There's more back and forth going on between them than my simple 'yes or no' question called for.*

"That's what I read in the papers. Yes."

"The price was seventy-five million dollars?"

After more discussions in Russian between Sergei and the translator, the answer reached Kim.

"How would I know? Konstantin and I don't travel in the same circles. All I can say is that I heard it was over seventy-five."

Barbieri, a tall, slender brunette-halfway-to-gray closing in on fifty, was wearing her travel abroad uniform. Simple white blouse, plain khaki slacks, and canvas slip-on shoes. The only impression she cared to make among Russians was that she was all business, and resistance to her investigation was futile. The sweater, hat, and overcoat she had worn in the taxi, on her way from the airport to the hotel, were not needed once she got indoors. *Russians don't get a lot of things right. In fact, they screw up everything they touch. But they really know how to heat a room.*

Although her hotel suite was in Moscow, she could not tell that from the décor. The dresser, desk, table lamps, even the paintings, could have been in any chain hotel room in South Bend or Amarillo or Milan. She couldn't tell from the suite's smell, either. It had the same antiseptic aroma, essence of Lysol, that seemed to be bottled expressly to give their latest guest a sense that nobody had been there before—at least nobody with anything catching. And that his or her own disgusting residues would be covered up, sprayed away and otherwise annihilated for the next occupant fated to be assigned to that room.

"You've never met him? Sokolov?"

"No. We have never met."

Barbieri didn't really expect Sergei Petrov to give her an honest answer. He was an oligarch–AKA, a wealthy, well-manicured Russian thug in a Brooks Brothers suit. In his country, oligarchs answer to only one man, and that man wasn't the one asking the questions here.

Earlier in her career, as a street-wise crime reporter in New York City and Miami, Barbieri had grown used to putting up with the occasional macho mansplainer. It was just an occupational hazard, this male compulsion to assume that women were ignoramuses who bought any lie that sounded even slightly plausible. And she never once let them get to her.

But now, as a reporter prying into the financial affairs of Russian oligarchs, she dealt with it all day, every day. *Russians. I never met one who wasn't a total asshole.* She had learned long ago how to make macho scumbags blink, and she was afraid this Russian macho scumbag was about to break her winning streak.

"Sergei, I have some documents I'd like you to review. May I come by your office sometime this evening?"

"What documents are we looking at?"

"Real estate transactions. Contracts. I'd rather discuss them with you in person, if you wouldn't mind."

She had told Petrov, when she first set up the interview, that she was doing a story for the *Journal* about the real estate market in New York City. She somehow neglected to mention that her real assignment was investigating money laundering by anonymous Eastern European nouveau riche types who preferred to remain that way.

"Miss Barbieri, interviewing me here would not be wise for either of us, I'm afraid. I will come by your hotel at 9:00 tomorrow."

"You know where I'm staying?"

"Of course, I do. The Sheraton Palace. This is Moscow, Miss Barbieri. If you want a secret to remain a secret, you're in the wrong city."

CHAPTER THREE

117 Aeroporta Proyezd
Moscow
Tuesday, December 1
7:45 A.M.

"Assignment completed."

"Reporter from the *Times*? St. Petersburg, right? Not New York."

"Right. Kuznetsova."

"Cunt."

Oleg Bren and Dmitry Andreyev, two men who really, really disliked reporters prying into their organization's affairs, were standing out on the sidewalk, taking the lids off the coffee containers they had bought moments before from the Aeroporta Proyezd Starbucks. This particular Starbucks was one of the hundreds of American restaurants and shops that had sprouted in Moscow since the capital defected to the West in 1991.

Save for a huge, ugly-ass mole on Andreyev's cheek, the two men were like peas in a gangster pod. Both Andreyev and Bren sported the same mobbed-up Russian look. Both were on the short side, maybe five-five or five-six, and heavy-set, and both were wearing white Oxford shirts, black leather jackets and blue jeans. The only nod to the civilian world around them were their faces, which were clean-shaven to help them blend in with the crowd.

Both Bren and Andreyev were covering their mouths with their hands as they spoke, to avoid being overheard, as well as having their mouths seen by any lip reader lurking nearby. This was Moscow, after all, and being careless around strangers could be harmful to your health. If they didn't intend to make anyone nearby think they were up to no good, this one part of their body language was the tell that would give them away.

"Woman won't be poking her fuckin' nose where it doesn't belong anymore," Bren said.

"How did she find out about the offshore accounts, anyway? We have a mole?" asked Andreyev.

"No other way could she have found out. We'll find him. Matter of time."

The two men began walking up Aeroporta Proyezd, a busy commercial strip lined with upscale stores and businesses, seemingly oblivious to all the other pedestrians streaming past them from both directions.

"How was Kuznetsova neutralized?" Andreyev asked.

"Novichok. New boy. Victim had no clue. Whole thing took a minute. Minute and a half."

"Who was the messenger?"

"Sorry. Need to know only."

"Got it. Plausible deniability," said Andreyev. "Has the *Times* assigned any other reporter to our enterprise?"

"I understand they asked for volunteers. Nobody raised their hand and said 'pick me.' And nobody will, it is safe to say."

"Message got through, apparently. Again. New boy is old reliable. Any product left over? There's a couple of people I'd like to see less of. Huge pains in the ass."

"Sorry. You'll have to find another method. The product was custom made for the target. Not a gram more than it took to kill her."

"Bespoke termination. Nothing left for the Moscow police to find."

"Nothing. Lab guys know their chemistry," Bren said.

"The Kremlin HR department sure knows their shit," Andreyev replied. "Good job, Oleg. The only way they'll learn, these fuckin' reporters."

"They have no choice, Dimitry. Learn or die. Simple."

The two men continued on their way down the busy street, but no longer making any effort to hide their conversation. Business was done. They were just two old friends enjoying a morning stroll, discussing the usual topics old friends discuss. Politics. Kremlin intrigue. Women. Sports. BMW versus Mercedes versus Audi. And women again.

CHAPTER FOUR

Sheraton Palace Hotel
1-Ya Tverskaya-Yamskaya Ulitsa, 19
Moscow
Tuesday, December 1
8:58 A.M.

"Miss Barbieri, your guests are here. May I send them up?"

"Guests? More than one? I was expecting Mr. Petrov only."

"It is Mr. Petrov, along with two men accompanying him."

"Got it. Okay. Send them up."

At nine A.M. on the dot, Barbieri was waiting at the closed door to her suite for Petrov and company to arrive. Standing right behind her was the interpreter, Annika Zakharova, who had joined Barbieri in her suite several minutes earlier.

After hearing a soft rap, she opened the door to find three men about to enter her suite—Petrov and two tree trunks who appeared to be his bodyguards. Both were on the short side, stocky, with a couple of days' worth of stubble on their faces and heads, and the same uniform of pin-striped black suit, purple shirt open to the third button, and a gold pendant hanging from his neck. *Do they call each other in the morning to see what they're wearing?*

"Sergei, please come in," she said, gesturing for the three men to enter. As with the phone interview the day before, the conversation was filtered through Zakharova, who again made sure nothing was lost in translation.

"Nice to meet you in person, Kim. These are my associates, Valery and Gennady. You won't even notice they're here. I promise."

Petrov walked in and sat down on the sofa in the middle of the room, while the two men accompanying him sat in chairs against the far wall, without a hint of an expression on their faces. They were trying hard not to look like they'd be listening in the conversation between their boss and Barbieri. *Do they even speak English?*

The only difference between them that Barbieri could now see was that one—*was it Gennady? Or Valery?*—had a rather large mole on his right cheek. She couldn't tell if either of them was carrying, although it was clear, to her at least, that they were ready, willing and able to beat the crap out of anyone who violated Petrov's do-not-pry zone.

The reporter didn't have to try very hard not to look intimidated by the two goons. She wasn't, not in the least.

She took a seat on the sofa across from Sergei, who matched the photos of him she had seen in her online search. Tall and thin, wearing an expensive-looking suit, with short gray hair and a wary expression on his face.

Seated across from both of them was the interpreter. Hugging her notepad and pen close to her chest, Zakharova was the third corner of a tense, awkward triangle. The fact that they were both Russian seemed, to Barbieri, to make for a stronger bond than the one she and the interpreter had as females jousting with a male.

Barbieri got right down to business.

"Picking up where we left off yesterday, Sergei. You've never been in that apartment building in New York, Sergei? Fifteen Central Park West?"

"No. I was never even in New York City. My work does not take me there."

Barbieri reached into her messenger bag, which she had earlier placed on a small table at the side of the sofa, took out a manila folder, and handed Petrov the two photos it held.

"Never. You're sure about that?" she asked, as Petrov examined the photos one by one.

The first photo was a security camera image of Petrov entering the lobby of Fifteen Central Park West, time- and date-stamped at 2:15 A.M.

on July twenty-seventh of that year. The second was of him leaving the building a little over four hours later, at 6:23 A.M.

"That's you. Is it not? In Manhattan. In the lobby of Fifteen Central Park West."

"I should have known. Where did you get these photographs? How did they end up in your possession?" Petrov did not like anyone knowing more about him than he wanted them to know.

Barbieri ignored Petrov's question, which Zakharov translated as impassively as she could.

"When you were in New York, did you meet Maxim Lebedev?"

"Who?"

Barbieri was growing impatient. Before the interpreter could translate for her, she reached into her messenger bag and pulled out a second manila folder. It was a contract, in English, for the sale of the penthouse apartment in Fifteen Central Park West. On the line for the buyer, there was a single signature. Frank Weston.

"Who is Frank Weston? American?"

"Lawyer in New York," Barbieri replied. "Interestingly, his name is on a number of contracts for apartments there, costing a great deal of money. You know the phrase us reporters use, Petrov? 'Follow the money'?"

"Everybody does. It's from the old Watergate movie. Deep Throat, correct?"

"Correct. All the President's Men. Weston, it turns out, was just window-dressing. I interviewed a few money managers and lawyers to make my way down the money trail, and in this case, I followed the money all the way from him to Maxim Lebedev."

"Him, I do know."

"And the oligarch he represented, though off the record, Konstantin Sokolov?"

She handed the contract to Petrov, who glanced at it and handed it back.

"I came here, to Moscow, to speak with Mr. Lebedev, Sergei. I understand you are the one person who can help me reach him."

Before the translator got a chance to translate the question, Petrov held his hand up to stop her. He turned to Barbieri and addressed her directly. In perfect English, with a hint of a British accent.

"So, my business is not a concern of yours, Miss Barbieri?"

"It is not, Mr. Petrov."

"Good. I know my dealings shouldn't be, as I am... what is the American saying? ...squeaky clean. Unfortunately, Kim—may I call you Kim? — I can no longer help you reach Maxim, as he seems to have disappeared off the face of the Earth. All I can say for sure is that he never left New York." Petrov's tone changed from guarded to friendly, a nod to accepting her word that he was not the subject of any kind of investigation by the *Journal*. He understood that the photos and contract that were shown to him were just Barbieri's way of untying his tongue.

Outside of a small smile, Barbieri did not acknowledge that Petrov had switched from his language to hers, or that he had decided he was no longer a hostile witness. She had already known, from her research, that his English was as good as his Russian. The interpreter Zakharova, who had not known this, kept quiet and put her note-pad in her purse, realizing her services were no longer needed. She remained sitting in her spot on the sofa, though, her eyes darting back and forth from Petrov to Barbieri as each was speaking.

"So, Maxim's not here, Sergei? In Russia? In Moscow?"

"I don't know. We don't know. What I can tell you is that when some people handle money that does not belong to them, they get ideas."

"That happens a lot in the States, too."

"Not more than here, Kim. That is for certain. I'd check with the police when you get back home. NYPD. FBI. They may know something about Lebedev that we do not. By the way, my sources were right about you. I'm impressed."

"I sort of expected you'd have me checked out."

"We did. You've done your homework, that is for sure."

"I always do. It's critical in my line of work."

"And mine. May I ask, how did you get the security camera photos of me? They're files that are supposed to be off-limits to anyone but building management and police. Are they not?"

"They are. But you are not the only one with friends in high places, Sergei. I may run into those friends tomorrow, when I fly back home."

"I understand your interest in finding Lebedev, Kim, but I'd be careful. He does not want to be found, by you or by his associates here in Moscow. Ex-associates, to be precise. Let's just say their interests are not the same as yours. Or mine. Their management style is also not the type that's usually covered by the *Journal*."

"I understand. All I want is to speak with him, Sergei."

"As do I. If they find him first, however, neither of us will get a chance. Kim, these guys care little for me as well. I've managed not to cross them, so far." He nodded toward the two bodyguards. "They're not protecting me from you, Kim."

"By the way, your associates look like they'd be fascinating dinner companions."

"Best to ignore Valery and Gennady. You're better off not knowing anything about them. Or making their acquaintance. They're not brilliant conversationalists, anyway."

"But you need them. Which means you're one of the good guys?"

"If that means being open and honest, I try to be. I am a civilian, if you're familiar with that term."

"I am. It means you don't belong to any criminal organization. You're not in any gang. You're clean, at least as far as the FSB is concerned."

"Correct. Although it's getting more and more difficult to explain that to my friend in the Kremlin. Good luck, Kim."

With that, Sergei rose from the sofa, reached over to shake her hand and walked toward the door, followed close behind by his two henchmen. The zoftig translator Zakharova was next to leave, after checking with Barbieri that there were no more interviews requiring her services.

After the door closed behind them, the reporter began returning her papers and photos to her messenger bag. *If I'm going to find Lebedev,* Barbieri thought as she gathered her things and got ready to leave, *I'd better head back home. I came all this way to find out I did not need to leave New York. How do I explain this to the suits?*

CHAPTER FIVE

Domodedovo Airport
Moscow
Tuesday, December 1
9:45 P.M.

"Brennan."

"Hey, Captain."

"Miss Barbieri! Long time. How nice to hear your lovely voice again."

"Ever the smooth talker, Timothy. We'll talk over old times soon, I promise–but not right now. There's something I need to ask you, on the record."

"Ask away, Kim."

"Anyone on your org chart ever come across a corpse by the name of Maxim Lebedev? He's a Russian national visiting New York City on business, I believe."

It was almost ten at night in Moscow, two in the afternoon in New York. Barbieri was in the airport's international departure lounge, sitting as far as she could from other passengers flying to the United States. Eavesdropping was still the national sport in Russia, so she assumed her cell phone was tapped and she was being tailed.

Still, she tried to not let anyone within earshot in on her business. From looks alone she could usually tell who was Russian—*No Savile Row suit could camouflage trash that white*—and who was American, but why take chances?

Barbieri was not a big fan of long, international, non-stop flights. With all the security hassles and two-hour waits and incredible shrinking seats, the whole thing was just too stressful. She had also never mastered the art of sleeping on planes, which caused her to be drop-dead tired whenever she got back home.

She had taken off her overcoat as soon as she made it to the lounge. The temperature there was a perfect seventy-seven degrees, pretty much the standard for airports across the globe. So, she was now wearing the most comfortable clothing she owned, more appropriate for sitting around and watching TV than representing corporate America in a foreign capital. *My clothes look like they've been slept in, but what do I care? Who do I know in Moscow? And they give me at least a fighting chance of making it home without turning into a zombie.*

The first call she made after making her way through security and checking in for her flight back to New York was to Timothy Brennan, Chief of Detectives in the NYPD. Those two went way back, from her days as a crime reporter for the *New York Daily News* and his as the alpha male of Brooklyn South Homicide. They'd had a thing for a while, about five years before, until she broke it off when she moved to Miami.

When she'd been lured back home by the *Journal*, she got back in touch with him, as she did with many friends and colleagues from days of yore. Although now, she and Brennan were strictly business, determined by mutual agreement to keep things free of hanky-panky. For Barbieri, Brennan was now a source for information only, nothing more, and that was fine with both of them.

"Not off the top of my head, Kim. You're back to covering homicides? I thought you've moved on."

"You thought correctly. I now cover financial mischief exclusively, mostly real estate and tax scams. The *Journal* doesn't do sordid, Cap'n." She still used that rank of endearment from their days as an item. "That's why I'm in Moscow for a story we've been doing about Russians in real estate, so …"

"Moscow? I'm impressed, Kim. We can't build million-dollar condos for the bastards fast enough, it seems. What makes you think this Maxim what's-his-name was murdered?"

"Lebedev. Maxim Lebedev. I don't know that he was, actually. All I know is that he is a Russian national, he was in New York for a closing on Central Park West, and a source in Moscow told me he may have pissed off the Russian mob."

"Of whom there are plenty in New Yorkski. I recall coming across one or two. Lebedev's here? Not there?"

"I was told by my source he never made it back home, which is why his associates here think he is still in New York—dead or alive."

"Okay, Kim. Let me ask around and I'll call you back either way."

"Thanks, Timothy."

"And try to get some sleep, Barbieri. Insomnia doesn't bring out the best in you."

"I will. At least I'll try."

After ending the call, Barbieri looked up at the clock and saw that she still had a good half hour before boarding. She opened her laptop, put on her headphones, and turned on a recording that always took her to a different place. The Royal Opera's performance of *La Traviata*. Getting lost in an opera, especially Italian opera, was one tool she used to have 'me time' while hemmed in by strangers on all sides for hours on end. The other was medication she went nowhere without, one a sedative she'd take only as a last resort, and one for migraine.

She'd gotten a prescription for the migraine drug after her first attack, on a flight from New York to Madrid years ago. And on one other flight after that. But that was well over two years ago. Since then, nothing. She was even okay on her flight to Moscow earlier in the week, which made her hopeful that the last migraine she had was the last she'd ever have.

As she wrote up her notes, Barbieri sat back and wondered what she was now getting into. *Was Lebedev actually killed by the Russian mob? He wouldn't be the first. Did he simply decide to make himself scarce? Is he in*

Witness Protection? Could well be. If the Journal's *investigating all those Russian goons buying up expensive property, the feds might be too.*

She understood that paying all cash for real estate was perfectly legal, but it raised red flags with Treasury agents if there was even a hint of money-laundering. Russian crook puts ill-gotten gains into a bank account, and then moves them to other accounts in other banks in other countries. Repeat as necessary. By the time said crook buys a duplex on Millionaire's Row, his dirty money is now clean as a shiny new kopeck.

One reason Barbieri had jumped from the *Herald* to the *Journal* was to take a break from covering street crime and drug cartels. White collar shenanigans were duller, true, but investigating them called for digging deep into corporate tax returns and financial statements. And sometimes, the dirt she dug up even embarrassed government bigshots enough to get off their fat butts and do something.

She was getting good at that. Finding out why who did what to whom in boardrooms and corner offices, instead of on street corners and dark alleys, was giving her a genuine sense of accomplishment. She thought she was in a good place, investigating shady condo deals, but this Lebedev mystery felt a little like the band getting back together.

Do I really want to get in the middle of a damn murder again? Last one nearly drove me insane.

While that question ate at her, she heard a voice that didn't belong to *Traviata*. It was an announcement coming over the airline's public address system, first in Russian and then in English, that her flight to New York was ready for boarding. She looked up from her laptop to see the passengers around her gathering their things and getting in line at the gate, and started doing the same.

She turned off the music app, saved and closed the Word file, and packed away her computer and ear phones into her messenger bag. Then she carefully performed two pre-flight checks before joining the other passengers crowding the gate.

She reached into the front pocket of the messenger bag to double check for her ticket, and she rooted around in her purse to feel for the zippered case holding her two absolutely indispensable medications. Satisfied that all was in order, she made a silent prayer. *Please, God. Keep me healthy the next eight hours, okay? And don't make me sit next to a Russian. Or if you do, make sure he's taken a shower this week.*

CHAPTER SIX

NYPD Headquarters
One Police Plaza
Manhattan
Wednesday, December 2
2:00 P.M.

Being kicked all the way upstairs to Chief of the New York Police Department Detective Bureau had given Brennan one thing he never really had before. Boredom. That was definitely not what he'd signed up for when he joined the force decades before.

His main job was pushing paper–actually electronic files on his laptop–and moving around men and women under his command as homicides erupted there, and fell here. Chess pieces where it's the bad guys who are checkmated. For a day or two, at least, but sometimes, when a judge decides to follow the law for once, for a decade or two.

His side gig was just as unrewarding. While he enjoyed the full confidence of the Police Commissioner, the one person above him in the One Police Plaza org chart, all the political hacks at City Hall and all the wannabe big shots in all the neighborhoods all over the city seemed to conspire to make his life miserable. Why is the homicide clearance rate only ninety-six percent? Why can't your detectives find these fiends roaming my community? Black deaths don't matter? White deaths don't matter? Asian deaths don't matter?

More than ever, his thirty-eight was a vestigial organ. He'd never fired it at bad actors while he was a detective, nor when he'd been given command of the Brooklyn South Homicide Squad years before, and he sure as heck wouldn't have a chance to shoot anyone now. His underlings had all the fun. Besides, he knew that if the opportunity ever came up, all he'd hit would be a fellow cop, being so out of practice, and a friendly fire report would only bury him in paperwork for all eternity.

Even though he was getting closer by the day to pulling the pin, Brennan remained a cop's idea of a cop. Well over six feet tall and completely paunch-free, still, he had a commanding presence that freed him from having to push his weight around. He was in charge, and nobody dared disagree.

He assigned to himself the job of finding Barbieri's particular missing person, thinking that it'd be almost like real, honest detective work from way back when, before he was kicked upstairs to chess master.

Sitting at his spacious, neat-as-a-pin glass-topped desk in his spacious, sparsely furnished but too-brightly lit One Police Plaza office, glancing up from time to time to look at Chinatown and Little Italy just a few blocks away, Brennan had spent most of the morning making calls to precinct commanders, and his contacts in the organized crime and counter-terrorism bureaus. Nobody knew anything about any Maxim Lebedev.

His name turned up in no arrest records, or missing persons reports or homicide reports or watch lists. Didn't exist. Never was. With no corpse found, there was no murder to solve. Brennan's detectiving turned out to be short-lived.

He called Kim back later that evening, after she'd had a chance to recover from her flight from Moscow, with the not-my-rodeo news.

"Sorry to disappoint, Kim, but Lebedev has disappeared without a trace. I checked with every department here, and nobody in my line of work's ever heard of him."

"Okay, Brennan. Worth a try. I'll stop worrying about it. Lebedev wasn't a big part of the story, anyway."

"Why would it be? Only crimes I've ever seen in the *Journal* were financial. Bank fraud. Embezzlement. Occasional bribery of a public servant."

"True. But murder's still right up my alley. I'm incorrigible."

"Kim, you know what happened last time you got too involved in a homicide, don't you?"

"I almost got myself killed. I sort of recall that, yes."

"You have my number." With that, Brennan ended the call and went back to his day job. Staring out the window at his old stomping grounds, wondering why directing the men under him to do the work he'd rather be doing himself is a good thing.

CHAPTER SEVEN

Wall Street Journal Headquarters
Manhattan
Friday December 4
8:20 A.M.

Barbieri was in the fourteenth-floor conference room, alone, inside the *Journal's* offices on the corner of Forty-seventh Street and Avenue of the Americas. She had never stopped calling it Sixth Avenue, which is how everyone in her family referred to it long after the idiots in City Hall changed its name to something that meant nothing to anyone. *What's next? Cross Street of the Europes? Blind Alley of the Africas? Idiots. The city is run by idiots.*

The space was less a conference room than a war room, designed to help *Journalistas* get their work done and get the news out—harsh overhead fluorescent lighting, bare white walls, a long table surrounded by eight not-quite-comfortable chairs, and four whiteboards. No paintings, no water bottles, nothing to distract anyone convening inside it from the task at hand.

She was organizing her thoughts, and going through her notes, to prepare herself for her first show-and-tell with her boss, Thomas Fitzgerald. Mr. Fitzgerald, she had called him the first time they met, and he had never given her any reason to stop.

The reporter was eager to expose her work, and herself, to someone who knew his way around financial reporting far more than she did. It was a combination of rookie jitters and the desire to learn from a real pro. *Am I as far along as everyone else? Am I as thorough? Am I as buttoned-up? Had anyone dug up facts I need to investigate? Or worse, had missed?*

Her first presentation, if she hit it out of the park, would also allow Mr. Fitzgerald to reassure his reporting team, and his higher-ups, that Barbieri was a solid hire. Although she was new to the *Journal,* she was not new to investigative reporting, and Mr. Fitzgerald had no problem making her a full-fledged member of the team of journalists, forensic accountants, investigators and fact-checkers working on the dirty foreign money story. Sink or swim.

Nobody was going to do her job for her... but her. While she had been concentrating on Russian and Ukrainian buyers, the other members were focusing on Chinese, Arabs and Latin Americans with money to burn. Or bury. While Russians didn't invent money-laundering, they had definitely set the standard for financial now-you-see-it-now-you-don't practitioners all around the world.

• • •

Barbieri knew in her gut that she had risen to the challenge and was about to deliver what had been asked of her. More than what had been asked of her, even. Just an investigative reporter doing her job. But unlike her past reporting—where she usually knocked on actual physical doors to get the details needed to flesh out her story—here she often knocked on virtual, online doors to follow the money. Which wasn't always easy. When an oligarch bought a place, he told only those he could trust not to blab. No reporters, no cops, and definitely no IRS agents. So, he did his best to hide the purchase behind cutouts—banks, law firms, shell companies, hedge funds, and private equity firms—all of which conspired to keep prying eyes from sussing the real master of his luxury domain.

Barbieri had been introduced to this version of a Russian puzzle wrapped in a Russian mystery buried inside a Russian enigma after knocking on the actual door of one lawyer slash middleman. His name had unexpectedly popped up in documents she got a hold of for the first shady purchase she looked into.

At first, Fabian Calabrese, Esquire, was wary of talking to a reporter for the *Journal*, but relented after she swore up and down that neither his name nor that of his law firm would appear in print. She understood full well why he didn't want anyone–especially anyone in the Russian underworld– to know that he was revealing all to the *Journal*. And she was okay with using the interview as a learning experience that would help her navigate the other purchases on her to-uncover list.

After introducing herself and her assignment over the phone, they agreed to meet the next evening, after work, at Fernando's, a posh-by-her-standards establishment on East Fifty-fifth Street off Madison Avenue. When she arrived and looked around for a man sitting alone, she noticed that the place was maybe half-full, and was pretty quiet as restaurants go. Neither loud conversations, nor clattering of dishes, are acceptable at Fernando's.

The maître d' escorted her past several empty tables to the one Calabrese had reserved. She found him already seated, jabbing away on his cell phone, and stopping only when she entered his field of vision. The interrogatee stood to greet his interrogator and gestured for her to sit in the chair that the maître d' had pulled out for her.

As an Italian-American through and through, Barbieri had expected the lawyer to look like the paisanos she grew up with and lived among. Of course, he'd be short, olive-skinned, with black hair and five-o'clock shadow by two-o'clock in the afternoon. But he wasn't. He looked straight out of Teutonic central casting–tall, fair skin, neatly combed blond hair, the only defect apparently a dark beauty mark on his chin. Taken aback as she was, Barbieri didn't let his lack of paisan-ness faze her.

After some mandatory chatting about traffic and the weather, they looked over the menus that had been placed next to their table setting, and Calabrese signaled to the waiter to take their order. Veal scallopine for her and chicken francese for him. Unlike restaurants that had waiters key in orders electronically, on iPads, at Fernando's the waiters wrote their selections like they always had–flipping over to a new page on a small order pad, jotting them down by hand, then repeating them back to the customer to make sure.

After the waiter confirmed their order and returned to the kitchen, Barbieri and Calabrese got down to business. To keep anyone from listening in, they both kept their voices down, even though all the tables around them were empty.

"Here's how I got involved with the Russians, Kim. Back in 2021, an asset manager at Credit Suisse, Seth Howard, contacted me on behalf of a wealthy family," the lawyer explained. "He refused to say who said wealthy family was, only that they wanted to invest tens of millions of dollars, through Credit Suisse, in real estate here in New York. Then he tells me that Credit Suisse had told him that in order to receive this money, he'd have to hire an attorney, yours truly, to set up a special offshore financial vehicle."

"Meaning in another country. To avoid the IRS."

"Cayman Islands. Where funds go to get lost. That was the whole idea behind this whole transaction, not paying Uncle Sam. My firm would receive a sizable fee and we'd give Credit Suisse twenty percent."

"Twenty percent, for doing nothing. Why did he pick your firm, and you in particular? How many attorneys are out there handling that kind of deal?"

Just as he started to answer, he was cut off by the waiter returning with their dishes. After remaining silent as their plates were set down, Barbieri and Calabrese resumed their conversation.

"It's a pretty small fraternity, actually. Maybe a hundred here and in DC, give or take. I guess they asked around and my name came up. I'm a name, which is always good for business. Anyway, I agreed, and was told to set up a meeting with Piedmont Management up in Mamaroneck. Myself, I'd never heard of Piedmont. I go up there and the place looked like a fortress. Or a prison. Thick metal doors, and none of the paintings or fancy décor you see in any other financial company."

"That doesn't sound very inviting."

"No visitors allowed. Exactly. I was suspicious, to be honest, but not enough to prevent me from doing business with them. Way things worked out, one of their guys'd sit on the board of the financial vehicle that I was supposed to set up to get the wealthy family's money. So, I brought on my guy, a consultant named Lester Denmark, as another board member. I asked their guy whose money he was managing, and he refused to say."

"The cast of characters is metastasizing at this point."

"Indeed, Kim. It gets even more secretive, though. The asset manager…"

"Howard, right?"

"Howard. He goes and hires another offshore law firm to do the paperwork for this Cayman investment. Never heard of them, or from them. Complete mystery. I still thought everything was aboveboard, however. But just as a precaution against any financial sleight of hand, I hired Continental Financial Services to administer the vehicle, to make sure that it was fully complying with anti-money-laundering laws."

"Due diligence on your part. You were making sure they weren't doing business with anyone under U.S. government sanctions."

"Both big no-no's in my business. When I got all the papers, a few days later, I happened to notice that some documents were signed by a lawyer by the name of Svetlana Solovyova. Which led me to realize that the guy who I was really investing for was some Russian oligarch. That was my 'aha' moment."

"He could be Ukrainian. Or Belarussian. Not necessarily Russian. And not necessarily illegal, either. But you didn't quit, and you're still involved."

"Not actively. Once the deal was done, I washed my hands of it. Continental had verified that it was all legit. No laws were being broken. No money was being laundered. "

"And you could sleep at night."

"And I could sleep very well at night, Kim."

As Barbieri and Calabrese finished their dinners, they returned to small talk over coffee and dessert. When the waiter returned with their check, Barbieri gave him her credit card, glanced at her watch and realized that it was time to go.

"Thank you for dinner, Kim."

"And thank you for the suspicious purchase master class, Fabian. I can see that there'll be a lot of brick walls I'll have to go around…"

"... Or through."

"Or through, to find the real buyers of the deals we're looking at."

"Better get used to it, Kim. And like you promised, I won't see my name in the *Journal?*"

"I was never here, Fabian."

CHAPTER EIGHT

Wall Street Journal Headquarters
Manhattan
Thursday December 3
8:55 A.M.

At presentations like these, Mr. Fitzgerald had one job to do, which was to poke holes in his new cub reporter's work. Not in a nasty way, of course, nor to make her second-guess her career choice. Instead, his goal was simply to improve both the investigating and reporting sides of her job. It was her own job to make the information she'd dug up totally poke-proof.

When the story finally ran, not one fact could be disputed. The people on the masthead did not look kindly on reporters, or their bosses and editors, whose mistakes forced them to issue a retraction. Embarrassing the paper was a hanging offense, and nobody there wanted any fingers pointed their way.

The important thing, she knew, as she walked her boss through her investigation, was to stick to her mandate of dirty Russian and Ukrainian money pouring into the country. *Don't get bogged down in the fate of Maxim Lebedev. That is just a side-show.*

Before Mr. Fitzgerald entered the conference room, Barbieri had sorted her financial forms, city records, sales contracts and interview notes into eight neat piles, which she placed in a single row in front of her. With all those records to walk her boss through, it had made sense to her to lay them out on a table big enough to handle them all. Hence, there rather than in his office.

I'm ready.

When he came in, at 9:00 A.M. on the dot, he silently took a seat opposite all the folders. Not even a "good morning." It was not personal, not a dis aimed at Barbieri. Mandatory niceties and 'How-was-your-weekend?' were simply not in Mr. Fitzgerald's management toolkit.

Physically, Barbieri and Mr. Fitzgerald were a study in contrasts. The reporter, tall and slender with olive skin and curly salt-and-black-pepper hair still a few years from going all gray, was wearing what she had hoped passed for business casual–loafers, black slacks, and a plaid button-down shirt. There was nothing 'business casual' about her boss, though, who came to this internal meeting dressed for don't-mess-with-me success: Navy blue, well-tailored suit, short, carefully parted hair, black horn-rim glasses and a demand that the only term of address he would respond to is 'Mr. Fitzgerald.' Anyone calling him Thomas, Tom or Tommy was let off with a warning.

Although her boss was about half a foot shorter and twenty years older, Barbieri recalled her impression of him when they had first met three weeks before: Thomas Fitzgerald was clearly someone she could look up to.

Mr. Fitzgerald did not at all look down on Kim. Although he wasn't one to play favorites among his reporters, he had really looked forward to bringing her on board. There was nothing unprofessional about their relationship, though. He was asexual, and she was good. End of story.

As soon as her boss sat down, he nodded at Barbieri, as if to say, 'You're on.' She picked up the top sheet of paper on the first pile and began her presentation.

"Anatoly Kravsky made millions running an illegal betting ring, and he used his profits to buy an apartment on Eight Ten Fifth for one million five, all cash, in two thousand eighteen."

"We can prove both, Miss Barbieri? The betting ring and the purchase?" Mr. Fitzgerald asked.

"No question." She passed the top two documents in the first pile over to her editor, who leafed through them for a good thirty seconds. "I have to tell you that his case was fairly typical of the Russians, who went through a lot of trouble to keep their purchases under the radar. Between each buyer and seller there were intermediaries–financial managers, lawyers, and bankers–who dealt only with each other.”

“Cutouts. So, none of them might have known the actual source of the money,” Fitzgerald said.

“Probably not. If anything went south, nobody connected the dots, or deliberately decided not to, until I poked around.”

“They all wanted plausible deniability. Understandable, I suppose. We’ll have to vet everything to make sure Anatoly’s guilty as charged. Next house of mirrors, Miss Barbieri.”

“Raisa Chernenko, a daughter of a Ukrainian big shot investor named Peter Chernenko. He was charged by prosecutors there with laundering twenty-seven million. She paid three and a half million in cash for a one bedroom in Trump Tower in two thousand sixteen.” She slid that set of documents over to Mr. Fitzgerald.

“Seriously? Trump Tower? Ukrainian?” He went through those documents as well, just to confirm the transaction with his own eyes.

“Not sure the apartment has a gold toilet, but … yes.”

“Let’s just make sure we keep politics out of this. Just honest and impartial reporting.” He returned the Chernenko documents to their rightful place.

“No agenda. Got it.”

“That our only Trump Tower purchase?”

“That’s the only one I’ve found so far.”

“Okay. I’m wondering if this one case could be a distraction we don’t need.”

She nodded as if to say she understood, then moved on to the top sheet of the third pile. “Moving on. Eduard Dvorkin has a record for laundering drug money. Five months after buying a place at Eight Eighteen Park, he was found murdered in Tblisi.”

“Capital of Georgia, correct? Theirs. Not ours.”

“Correct, Mr. Fitzgerald. Theirs. Police named no suspects, as far as I can tell, although it’s not clear they went out of their way to solve the case.”

"We're sure he's Georgian. Not Russian?"

"Correct."

"Close enough. We're also sure he was killed?"

"Bullet-in-the-back-of-the-head, sure. This gets into a whole area that we need to think through, Mr. Fitzgerald."

"I know where you're going, Miss Barbieri."

"The crimes some of these bad guys are involved in go way beyond dirty money. Should we ignore the bloodshed, and just stick to money-laundering? I'm not sure how far we should stray from our lane."

"I'm not either. Miss Barbieri. You covered murders when you were with the *News*, right?"

"Only a hundred or so every year, give or take."

"Nothing exotic? No foreign intrigue?"

"Most were your everyday dishonor among thieves. Or lovers' quarrels. Once in a while, I covered victims of the Russian mob. Or Albanians. They brought their grievances, and their *modus operandi*, with them from the homeland."

"Like the Italians before. Let's just mention that this Dvorkin fellow, if we include him, was killed. Without tying it to the purchase of Eight-eighteen Park. Nothing that could distract from the main point. For now, at least."

"I understand."

"Any more 'early terminations?'"

"Not that I can confirm, Mr. Fitzgerald, but hold that thought." She pointed to the fourth set of papers. "Next, the brothers Klimnikov. Vasily ran a bank in St. Petersburg whose license was revoked. Vladimir paid fifteen even for a brownstone on East Ninetieth, whose assessed market value was half that."

"A real crime family."

"Here's another. Sisters this time." She moved the fifth set of documents to Mr. Fitzgerald. "Svetlana Renko bought a place in Brooklyn Heights assessed at seven fifty for one million, even. Not to be outdone, Katerina Renko paid seven fifteen for a place down the block with a market value of three hundred thousand."

"Is obeying the law optional over there?"

"Seems that way. And they bring that philosophy along with them when they immigrate here." Barbieri then moved over to the sixth pile. "Here we have a gentleman by the name of Lazar Golshtyn, from Minsk."

"Belarus, right?"

"Right. Another abandoned outpost of the Soviet Union. But his crimes took place here. Not there."

"Here, as in New York City?" Mr. Fitzgerald pored over the documents as Barbieri summed up his story.

"Brooklyn. My hometown. Lazar ran three medical clinics that defrauded Medicare to the tune of thirty-seven million dollars from two thousand thirteen to two thousand seventeen. He's now doing thirteen years in federal prison, but before he was put away, he bought a nice little triplex on Park for fifteen five."

"Thirteen years. Welcome to America, Lazar. Who's next?" He nodded toward the seventh pile. "You've given us a lot to work with, Miss Barbieri. Maybe too much. We might have to jettison one or two just to tell a coherent story."

"Agreed. Three more no-good-niks for us to consider. First are Mr. and Mrs. Gennady Zelnikh. Their company was on the Treasury Department's sanctions list. The Zelnikhs took eight hundred and ninety-five thousand in cash from an account called the Zelnikh Living Trust to buy waterfront property in Manhattan Beach."

"Also, Brooklyn?"

"Correct. Also, Brooklyn. Manhattan Beach is close to Coney Island and Brighton Beach, AKA Odessa-by-the-Sea. I'm not sure why, but maybe that's worth looking into. Something in the water, maybe."

"There's a common thread, for sure. What do we know about this living trust?"

"Nothing yet. I'll dig deeper it if this deal makes the cut."

Barbieri reached the last pile of records. "Finally, we have the curious case of Konstantin Sokolov and Maxim Lebedev. This one's still marinating, Mr. Fitzgerald. These two men signed a contract for a place on Central Park West for seventy-five million. But it looks like they were cutouts. Not the real buyers. From what I know so far, the people they were representing thought they were paying over seventy-five. I'm trying to account for the difference, but Lebedev is whereabouts unknown. He's disappeared on me. He's not in New York or Moscow, and my contact in Moscow suspects some foul play. Here, not in Moscow."

"As in…?" The editor made a throat-slashing gesture.

"Termination with extreme prejudice. Looks like it, certainly. So far, Lebedev's just missing. But we know Putin's buddies don't like to be shortchanged. I'd like permission to keep following this up."

"Let me think on that. Can you hold off until I say otherwise? Or at least do it on your own time, not ours?"

"Sure, Mr. Fitzgerald. Absolutely." She made a mental note that her editor had asked her politely—and had not ordered her to stay away.

"Nice work, Miss Barbieri. If everything checks out, we're on our way to some really solid reporting. I'm going to have our forensic team, Miss Barrett and Mr. Gonsalves, go over all your documents. Then we're going to winnow down your eight cases to maybe three or four. The ones that really stand out *and* are easy for our readers to grasp. We don't want to overwhelm them with information."

"Who decides who makes the cut?"

"We all do. The whole team. You're going to walk them through it all over again tomorrow morning. Seven A.M., sharp."

"All eight?"

"Not Chernenko and the last one. Sokolov and Lebedev. Not yet."

"Crime in progress?"

"Let's just say it's too complicated right now. We want to keep our story linear, with no dangling threads. Nice work, though, Miss Barbieri. Lots of meat."

Mr. Fitzgerald abruptly rose from his chair, shook his cub reporter's hand, and walked out of the conference room. As he did so, Barbieri walked over to the door and pushed it shut.

Once she heard the lock click, she pumped her fist and stage-whispered "nailed it" to the empty room.

Because of a bad case of impostor syndrome, she hadn't yet told her old colleagues at the *Daily News* metro desk that she was now back in New York, doing investigative reporting for the *Wall Street Journal*. A real bump in the journalist pecking order. But she was ready now. *Who do I call first? Whose nose do I rub in it, first?*

CHAPTER NINE

Wall Street Journal Headquarters
Manhattan
Friday December 4
7:00 A.M.

The next morning, at 7:00 A.M. sharp, Barbieri gave a repeat performance to her six colleagues who'd been busy investigating buyers of New York properties from other parts of the globe. Even more than with Mr. Fitzgerald, she wanted to gain some cred with a jury of her peers. Based on her first presentation with the boss, she was confident that she'd do exactly that.

Moments before, as each of them filed in, they made small talk with Barbieri and gave her a little signal that said 'you'll do great', or 'no worries.' Mr. Fitzgerald's throwback, impersonal management style hadn't rubbed off on them yet.

There were three men and three women, and Barbieri noted that five of them looked to be about her age, or close to it. Which she took to mean they were all experienced journalists, and that Fitzgerald didn't want to bother breaking in cub reporters. *He's not making me sit at the kids' table. That's good to know.*

They each took their place on chairs across from her, while Mr. Fitzgerald sat by himself, off to the side. With everybody present and accounted for, her boss gave Barbieri the green light to present her findings on the purchases that were still alive, and the team went about deciding which to keep and which to jettison, based only on how well they fit into the 'crooked foreign purchases' narrative.

As she went over each case, she tried to make eye contact with everyone. It was a way to make sure all her team members were buying what she was selling. And judging by their responses, they were eating it up.

This investigation was serious business, and everyone knew the rules of engagement. Don't tear the work down. Make it better. They'd all been in her position on their first assignments, and they'd all appreciated the do-unto-others way their work was vetted. As they deliberated among themselves, their boss was a silent partner. He would only weigh in if any of his team needed to be reined in. None did. Improving each other's work was what Mr. Fitzgerald expected of each of them, and they all behaved.

After a lot of spirited back and forth, and some serious pushback, the team kept the Renko sisters, Dvorkin, Golshtyn, and Zelnikh.

"Good work, Miss Barbieri. Solid." Fitzgerald turned to the others across the table from her. "Any dissents?"

Seeing none, he turned back to Barbieri, who looked visibly relieved. "It's unanimous. Write it up with just those four purchases and we'll see if it works, and make it mesh with everyone else's reporting."

"Will do, Mr. Fitzgerald."

Mr. Fitzgerald got up and headed toward the door, the signal for her teammates to leave with him and get back to their own assignments. As each fellow reporter filed past Barbieri toward the door, they gave her a big smile and either a thumbs up or a mimed hand clapping.

When she was alone. Barbieri sat in her chair and exhaled. *They like me! They really like me! Impostor syndrome, my ass.*

CHAPTER TEN

317 Tverskaya Street
Moscow
Friday December 4
2:45 P.M.

Sergei Petrov's office in the Tverskoy district, just a *kamen's* throw from the Bolshoi Theater, had no other furniture save his own tired office chair, a bare-bones, wooden desk, and a single, hard-backed plastic and chrome chair for a single visitor. Likewise, the old wooden desk itself was sparsely furnished, with just a top-of-the-line Mac notebook, a landline phone, a lined writing pad, and a teacup. That was all Petrov needed to finish his work by quitting time; anything else was a distraction.

Even though he was usually the only person in his office, and the office itself looked like a relic of the Soviet era, he was dressed as if he were in the corporate offices of a Fortune 500 firm: well-tailored Ermenegildo Zegna suit, white oxford shirt, red silk tie, and hand-crafted Beckett Simonon shoes.

He was poring over a spreadsheet displayed on his computer screen when the desk phone rang. Momentarily distracted by the net loss figure in one spreadsheet cell, he continued staring at the screen as he picked up after the second ring.

"Petrov."

"This reporter from America, Petrov? Why was she talking to you?" asked Boris Belyaev.

"Who told you I met with her, Boris?" Petrov replied, closing the spreadsheet on the screen. Belyaev, a crime boss never known to take kindly to anyone meddling in his affairs, now had his full attention. The profit-and-loss figures could wait.

"Why, Sergei?" In Belyaev's line of work, anything other than a simple, straight, truthful answer was unwise. And possibly, quite unhealthy.

"She was interested in Lebedev, not me. Some property he bought in the United States. New York City. Manhattan."

"What about it?" asked Belyaev.

"I don't know. She said her paper was looking into foreigners buying up all the condominiums there."

"Foreigners, meaning us, Sergei?"

"She didn't say. I assume so. But every rich bastard in the world seems to buying up properties in New York and London, so maybe her paper's investigating everyone. Not just Russians."

"Did she have any evidence, Petrov? On us?" Belyaev asked.

"City records. Contracts with his signature. I didn't get a good look at them, but they appeared legitimate," Petrov replied.

"Why did she come to you about a purchase made by Lebedev?"

"She'd heard I knew Lebedev, and thought I could help her get in touch with him."

"How did she know you knew Lebedev, Sergei?"

"She wouldn't say, but she came here, in Moscow, to find him. I told her I couldn't help because I didn't know where he was."

"She believe you, Sergei?" Belyaev asked.

"Seemed to, Boris," Petrov said. "I convinced her I'm an upstanding citizen ..."

"...who'd never associate with the likes of us. Her name is Barbieri, correct?"

"Correct. Kim Barbieri."

"*Wall Street Journal*?" asked Belyaev.

"Yes. Boris," Petrov said, adding, "But if you want to find her, don't bother looking here in Moscow. By now, she's already back in New York City."

"We are there as well. Getting her to back off shouldn't be too difficult."

Belyaev hung up, leaving Petrov wondering if he had said more than he should have.

Would his side of the conversation suggest to anyone listening in that he was conspiring with a gangster? He took it as a given that his phone was being tapped, this being Moscow under Emperor Vladimir. Petrov replayed the conversation several times in his mind, convincing himself that he had not. He said nothing that Belyaev should not have already known, and everything he said was the truth.

Reassured that he'd proven he was still a civilian in good standing, Petrov went back to work. He re-opened the spreadsheet and went back to those vexing profit-and-loss figures. They had changed little in the last ten minutes.

• • •

Barbieri's visit to Petrov three days earlier had come to the attention of Belyaev's associates in Bratva. The Brotherhood. The Russian mafia. They had eyes and ears and guns and knives everywhere they could make a fast buck.

In the old days, under Krushchev and Brezhnev and all the other Soviet evs, Bratva was pretty much small time. The communist state had the power, and the communist apparatchiks in positions of power used them to steal whatever money, property, luxury swag and loyalty they wanted. Bratva members were left to fight over scraps.

Now, with the communists gone and Putin's kleptocrat bandits in charge, the Bratva was making more money than any other organized crime ring in the world. The president himself was one of them, the king of thieves, and his Bratva underlings were getting away with murder after murder. Putin saw to that.

Gang members were making millions in loan sharking, gun smuggling, human trafficking and heroin. And the Bratva goons in power looked the other way, after getting their cut. Putin guaranteed their loyalty, not by being their BFF. He guaranteed it my making them filthy rich. Almost as filthy rich as he was, in fact. As long as his thieves gave him his hefty share of their ill-gotten gains, they were untouchable. And as long as he kept up his end of the deal, he'd stay in power. Simple as that. Back-scratching on Slavic steroids.

All that dirty money needed to be sent out of Russia–to Europe and the United States, mostly–to be laundered and sent back in, nice and clean and untraceable.

This reporter from New York, Kim Barbieri, was getting a little too close for their comfort, and that was a problem. More than that, she was a threat. She was turning over rocks. And millions, billions of dollars were at stake if she turned over the wrong one.

Bratva could never let that happen. Getting her out of the way, though, couldn't be handled in the usual Bratva way. In Moscow, threats to their operations were removed in plain sight. The mob was sending a message, and the fresh corpse left unburied was its calling card. Everybody knew who did it, and nobody dared say a word. It was assassination without subtlety, and it worked like a charm.

Barbieri, however, was in New York. The United States. Where the rule of law still trumped mob rule. Bratva didn't have home-field advantage. And in dealing with her, in New York, Bratva didn't want to send a message. Quite the opposite, the reporter had to be removed from the scene without drawing a whiff of suspicion their way.

She had to be killed with no one aware that a crime had occurred. Which meant the Bratva had to involve the FSB. Russia's Federal Security Bureau, the heir to the dreaded KGB of Soviet days. These guys had been assassinating people inside and outside Mother Russia for decades. They were pros. When the FSB came calling, the death certificate read 'Cause Unknown' and the perpetrator who caused that death was not seen, or heard, or ever found.

It was an execution seemingly without an executioner.

CHAPTER ELEVEN

Wall Street Journal Headquarters
Manhattan
Friday December 3
4:47 P.M.

Confident that her research would stand up well to her everyone's scrutiny, including the team's forensic accountants, Barbieri began writing up and fleshing out her article on Russians turning condo purchases into money-laundering scams. She had done her homework, going through contract after contract and cutout after cutout, to ID the son-of-a-bitch Russian moneybags behind every sale.

She was in her office, or rather cube, in a warren slash corn maze on the fourteenth floor of the *Journal*'s building. On the way to her job interview weeks earlier, she had made a point of peeking, without seeming to, into the cubes clustered outside Mr. Fitzgerald's corner office. Everyone's space was furnished about the same, she'd noticed–a computer, a stack of writing pads, a business phone, and not much else–and she'd decorated her own cubby hole the same bare-bones way. *They really don't want us to feel at home here, do they?*

One thing missing from almost every cube, besides chachkes and family photos, was its occupant. *Everyone must be working from home, or out doing research or interviews.* The few cubists she saw in the office, about the same number of men as women, all seemed to be well-groomed and dressed in some variation of business casual. There were none of the distressed jeans and worn sneakers her colleagues wore at the *News* and the *Herald*. *This is a place for adults getting work done, not for juveniles trying to get into everyone's distressed pants. Perfect.*

The article actually hadn't taken long to complete because she had been already writing up each section in her head for days, starting on the plane back from Moscow. By the time she actually got down to putting pen to paper for Fitzgerald, it was just a matter of coming up with a compelling lede, weaving in just enough detail of each sketchy purchase to make the case for readers with short attention spans, and coming up with an ending that would tie all the strands together, nice and neat.

With all her reporting experience at the *News* and the *Herald*, the 'journalist' half of Barbieri's title was not even close to a challenge. Her stories never had to be rewritten by her editors, no mistakes ever retracted. She did feel challenged by the 'investigative' half, considering that the crimes she was exposing were now mostly financial. And in her mind, she had risen to it pretty darn well. *All my years of writing about violently dispatched corpses at the News and the Herald weren't for naught, after all.*

Her day job done, she emailed the file with her reporting to Mr. Fitzgerald, then went back to thinking about the mystery of Maxim Lebedev. Investigating corporate hanky-panky was in her job description. Crime reporting was in her blood. *Where on Earth did Lebedev go? Was he alive and well, or dead and buried? Or dead and incinerated beyond recognition?*

• • •

The reporter took out her cell from her left-front pants pocket and called up a real estate broker named Martin Leotta, whose name she had gotten through a mutual acquaintance a few days earlier. A lifelong Brooklynite, she had known no brokers who handled the high-end properties on Manhattan's tony East Side, which Lebedev would have been in the market for.

As a major player in that arena, Leotta dealt largely with foreign buyers–Chinese, Israelis, Saudis, Ukrainians and Russians, mostly–who had a few extra million dollars that needed to be parked where their government's auditors couldn't touch them. Just getting their extremely, often violently, ill-gotten gains out of the country was close to a guarantee they'd spend approximately zero days behind their homeland's bars.

Leotta's East Side office was the perfect place to engage them, he believed. As a broker, he had found that living among his clients, shopping where they shopped and dining where they dined, was good for business. Familiarity bred sales. Familiarity bred hefty commissions that allowed him to keep living and dining and shopping among them.

All Barbieri had told Leotta was that she was doing a story on foreign buyers, and wanted some background information on the luxury market. The reporter had reassured him she was interested only in the buyers he had dealt with–not him, personally. The *Journal* was not about to do a hit job on him, she told him. Eager for free ink for his business, especially in the paper his clients were apt to read, Leotta readily agreed.

Noting that the realtor's office on Madison and Fiftieth was maybe a ten-minute walk from where she was at *Journal* headquarters, Barbieri sent Mr. Fitzgerald an email asking him if it was okay if she left the office early. He agreed, adding that he'd send her his edits as soon as he was done reviewing her article.

Between the time she had arrived at her office earlier that morning, and now, the temperature outside had dropped fifteen degrees. And what had been a light breeze became a strong wind that made walking even a block or two totally exhausting. Especially if the person doing the walking was heading into the wind, as she was about to do. Though the light coat she'd left the house with that morning wasn't up to the task, she decided that she'd survive a few minutes outside, and began walking over to her next interview.

CHAPTER TWELVE

Leotta Realty
450 Madison Avenue
Manhattan
Friday December 4
5:20 P.M.

When Barbieri got to Leotta's building, she found that his office was one flight up from street level, and as she had expected, the space matched the condos he was selling. Spare, bright, modern, with zero clutter and less personality.

Leotta himself was a living, breathing version of the same thing. Lean, tall, combed back brown hair atop a perfectly tanned face and the dazzling white teeth of a local weatherman. Wearing a well-tailored Savile Row suit, he was also dressed to impress foreign house-hunters with extra euros and rubles on their hands.

After putting her coat in the closet and getting the pleasantries about their mutual acquaintance out of the way, she sat on the other side of his desk. It was right in the middle of the space, between a spiral staircase on one side and a bank of floor-to-ceiling windows facing Madison Avenue on the other. Barbieri took her notepad and pen out of her messenger bag and got right to the point.

"In any of the sales you've done, Mr. Leotta, have you ever dealt with a Russian named Lebedev?" she asked.

"Martin, please. Maxim Lebedev? I sure have," Leotta replied. "He's bought quite a few of my properties. Five I believe."

"Lately?"

"Not in the past year or so. Hate to lose a repeat customer like that."

"Was he legit? Was there anything about him that made you suspicious in any way?" she asked.

"Not at all. He came across as one hundred percent honest. At least, there was nothing shady about him I could see. Can I be frank, Kim? About the real estate business, I mean?"

"Of course, Martin."

"A good real estate agent can spot a hinky buyer a mile away, and no alarm bells ever went off with Mr. Lebedev. Even if they do, or when they do, I try not to ask too many questions. You know ... pry too deeply into where their money was coming from. If they're Russian or Ukrainian, especially."

"Understood. A buyer's a buyer."

"And a commission's a commission, to any broker. I don't want to drive them to my competitor across the street, who'll just look the other way. As for Maxim, no, I never got the sense he was connected. Or that his money was dirty. Why are you asking about him?"

"He's missing. At least, he appears to be. His name came up in one sale we're looking into."

"Might explain why I haven't seen him in a while. One of my properties?"

"No. Another agent handled it. Martin, can you reveal all the properties he bought through you? Maybe there's something in your records that can help me find him."

Even if he wanted to, Leotta had no reason to withhold anything from Barbieri, or the *Journal.* Records on real estate sales were public information, so she could just get them from City Hall, anyway. Leotta saved her the trouble. He clicked a few keys on his laptop, found the files she wanted, and printed out all the paperwork involving Lebedev's purchases.

"Here you go, Kim," Leotta said. "If you find Mr. Lebedev, can you ask him to call me? Please."

"Certainly," Barbieri replied. "You have new properties you want to show him, I take it."

"Only one. It just came on the market. As long as *you're* here, Kim...?"

"Thanks, Martin. But I'm happy where I am. Williamsburg's the new East Side, or haven't you heard?"

"I have. Everyone's moving there, it seems. Well, if you're ever a little less happy, call me. I'd love the chance to earn your business. Perhaps show you something nice on the old East Side."

"Certainly, Martin." While the agent remained seated, Barbieri got up from in front of his desk, shook his hand, and showed herself out, retrieving her coat from the closet along the way.

When she got downstairs and out on the street, she steeled herself for the walk to the subway station a few blocks away. It was still windy as hell, but at least now she'd have the wind at her back. And the sun had come back out. Not quite a stroll in the park, but nothing she couldn't handle.

CHAPTER THIRTEEN

Midtown Manhattan
Friday, December 3
5:55 P.M.

Just as she was about to climb down the stairs to the Fiftieth Street subway station, Barbieri felt a cramp in her stomach. Again. That organ had a habit of demanding attention at the worst moments, and had decided that right then was as good a time as any to scream for help.

One joy of getting on in years, she'd discovered, was that more and more parts of her body needed more and more TLC, to do all the things they had done without complaint since she took her first breath. It was usually nothing serious–just the occasional stomach cramp or shortness of breath for now–but every few months, it seemed another organ joined the list of body parts that needed rehab.

An old friend of hers, a world class hypochondriac who knew every symptom of every condition by her diseased heart, had warned her that she definitely, probably had a bad case of Crohn's Disease without a doubt, but Barbieri didn't buy it. *Bitch, please. Until my gastro guy says otherwise, it's just a cramp.*

Whether the cramp was a symptom of something more serious, or worse, she was realistic about middle-age-dom. She was determined to not let her ever-expanding catalog of aches and pains take over her life, as they had with so many of her friends. *They all gave in, but I ain't giving up without a fight.*

Barbieri reached into her messenger bag, felt around inside, and pulled out a small bottle of water and a bottle of dicyclomine capsules, both of which she always carried with her. She was about to open the bottle of capsules and take one when she noticed the coding stamped on the label. In the middle of the number and letter codes, which she could not decipher, she made out a very faint 'Discard After 0520'. Not good. *Expired. Shit! I should've checked before I went to work. There's gotta be a Duane Reade near here.*

As a veteran pill taker, she of course had understood that the 'use-by' date on a drug did not actually mean it wouldn't work, or wouldn't work as well, but she could never bring herself to flout the law, or tempt fate, with her health. An excess of caution, perhaps, or just superstition. She put the bottle back in her purse and reversed course, knowing there'd be a pharmacy nearby. *These days there's a Duane Reade on every fuckin' corner. Thank God.*

She found one just a block and a half up the avenue. Upon entering the store, she asked the security guard at the door–a middle-aged, dark-skinned woman, perhaps an Indian immigrant, who didn't look like she'd be much of a deterrent to your average teenage shoplifter–to point her toward the prescription counter. The guard nodded silently toward the back of the store, and Barbieri walked over to plead her case to the pharmacist on duty. Fifteen minutes later, she had her refill and gulped down one dicyclomine capsule right at the counter. Just the act of swallowing it made her stomach feel better.

On the way out, her new prescription medication securely in her messenger bag, she grabbed a container of yogurt from the refrigerator case, careful to check that its expiration date wasn't anytime soon. It wasn't. She got on the back of the checkout line, then opened the container and had a spoonful even before she paid for it.

When the security guard, ever alert for inventory shrinkage, started eyeballing her, Barbieri gave her a shrug and a small smile as if to say, 'I can explain, officer.' The guard gave her the evil eye in return, as if to say, 'Okay, lady, but nothing gets past me', and went back to watching inventory go out the door in the hands of paying customers only.

CHAPTER FOURTEEN

Odessa Laundromat
512 Brighton Beach Avenue
Brooklyn
Friday December 4
11:40 P.M.

"Leotta is taken care of?" asked Vasily Klim.

"Yes," Grigory Gryshin replied.

"Good. Blabbermouth. Who was asking him about Lebedev? Did we find out?"

"Leotta did not say."

"Why?"

"He wasn't asked."

Klim and Gryshin, two semi-retired Bratva lifers cleverly disguised as harmless senior citizens trying to get by on modest pensions, were the only ones inside the empty, darkened laundromat. Still, they spoke in whispers, in case the place was bugged. One. And two, they had to stop talking about every ten minutes, anyway, because their words were drowned out by the noise of the trains screeching and braking, then starting again at the elevated Brighton Beach station platform right over their heads. The station has been a presence–and an extremely loud and intrusive one at that–for everyone forced to live and shop and work under it since it was erected over a century earlier.

The Odessa Laundromat had closed hours before and the lights were out, which meant that they were almost invisible to passersby on the avenue outside. The two Russians were sitting opposite the idle washers on a cheap, uncomfortable plastic bench, which during the day was usually occupied by babushkas who had emigrated to the United States the day before and spoke barely a word of English. If everyone in their insular world spoke Russian or its very close cousin, Ukrainian, why bother learning a language they'd never use?

Klim and Gryshin owned the place, or more accurately, their employer Bratva did, but they were never inside during business hours. The mob had installed a Russian immigrant cutout to actually mind the store, keep the machines running and the customers from complaining. As long as the cutout collected the quarters that piled up hour by hour, day after day, week after week in the washers and dryer coin slots, his employers were happy to keep him on.

Brighton Beach, an old, tired oceanfront community just down the road from Coney Island, was home to countless East European immigrants, most living in decrepit, antiquated apartment buildings that had no washing machines of their own. Giving them a chance to clean their unmentionables was an ideal front for Bratva, a cold cash business generating thousands of dollars a week, with a good ninety percent never making it into the books. It was as good a front as the Russian grifters could ever hope for.

"He wasn't interrogated first, before the message was delivered?" asked Klim. "Who did we send to deliver it?"

"Vasily," Gryshin said.

"Idiot."

"Who assigned him?"

"Borzov."

"Idiot. Any way to find out now who Leotta talked to?"

"Unless there were security cameras, no."

"Were there?"

"No."

"Idiot. Let's go home, Gryshin. Nothing more to talk about. Besides, my wife doesn't like it when I stay out late."

Their big, important business meeting over, Klim and Gryshin then got off the bench to leave. Gryshin looked out the front window to make sure they weren't being spied on by agents of the FBI, ATF, DHS or any other law enforcement types. Satisfied that the coast was clear, he unlocked and opened the door and the two old Russians stepped outside. Gryshin then locked the door behind them and the pair left the laundromat, Gryshin walking in one direction and Klim the other. The subway train above them had let passengers out minutes before, and as the two walked away they fell into step with everyone exiting the station.

Klim was not happy. Although one loose end, Leotta, was cut off, another anonymous loose end remained. The reporter who was sticking his nose where it didn't belong. Which meant that he had to tell his employers that they still had a problem on their hands. These were people who did not like getting bad news. In frauds where millions of dollars in unreported profits were at risk of circling the drain, failure was definitely not an option.

In his world, bearers of bad news were not simply told, 'Better luck next time, Igor.' They were executed on the spot, because a message had to be sent.

He couldn't make Gryshin take the blame. Those two went way back, all the way back to the homeland in Petrograd. Klim owed him that much. Instead, he'd tell his employer that he would figure out how to identify who was asking about Lebedev, and take care of the loose end himself.

He hoped and prayed that would keep the executives in the Bratva corner offices off his back, for a while at least.

CHAPTER FIFTEEN

10 North 10th Street
Brooklyn
Saturday, December 5
4:46 A.M.

In her penthouse apartment in Williamsburg, Barbieri was still in her pajamas, just sitting on her sofa, her hands kept warm by a mug of freshly made cappuccino.

It was just before five in the morning, still pitch-black outside and in. She'd left the lights off, thinking the less stimulation the better. Her only exertion now was squinting her eyes to make out things she'd left lying on the floor the night before, so she wouldn't stumble over them on the next trip to the bathroom that the cappuccino caused.

Maybe it was her approaching the half-century mark, or maybe it was just utter exhaustion, but it was taking longer than usual to get back to her normal schedule after flying all the way to Moscow and back. And then, right after, having to successfully validate her existence to her new employer, as well.

When she'd returned to her hometown from Miami three months earlier, she found a place just a mile or so from her old apartment in the Fort Greene area of downtown Brooklyn. The Williamsburg neighborhood was becoming hip now, just as she'd helped her old one become a few years before, and newcomers there demanded new, sleek apartments in chic-chic glass towers—not old, dowdy apartments in old, dowdy brick buildings.

Supply seems to meet demand overnight when there's big money to be made. So, without too much effort, she'd found a place where she felt she belonged—a large two-bedroom on the top floor of a new building made of irregularly shaped apartments piled atop one another, like alphabet blocks. All jammed between a one-story electronics warehouse on one side, and a big four-story, been-there-forever factory building being carved up into small niche factories on the other. Her own building's architect was no doubt impressed with his latest masterpiece, but clearly didn't give a damn that he had imposed this loud, brash and ungainly newcomer on a block of early twentieth century structures that had survived for a hundred years without it, thank you very much.

The outside wall of her living room was made entirely of glass, offering breathtaking views of Manhattan just across the East River. She had found that observing the city from a safe distance, without actually being sur-rounded by all its chaos and noise and hustle and bustle and panhandlers and crazies, was quite reassuring. Plus, the scene seemed to change minute by minute, with cars and boats and planes off in the distance, journeying from point A to point B and beyond twenty-four seven.

While the amenities were twenty-first century—a rooftop garden, a pri-vate terrace off the living room, sleek Miele appliances—the furnishings Barbieri had brought with her were clearly from an earlier era. She'd never lost her taste for the old-fashioned furniture she'd grown up with, and which somehow followed her home everywhere she called home. Fort Greene, then Miami, and now Williamsburg.

There was probably no other apartment in her hoity-toity building with retro décor that matched hers, and she was okay with that. *I'm not a twenty-something, I'm a forty-something closing in on a fifty-something. Come on in and make yourself comfortable. Or don't. I don't give a crap.*

The reporter walked over to the kitchen, careful to avoid all the obsta-cles lying in wait to trip her up, poured herself another cup of cappuccino, her fourth, then walked back to the sofa and switched on the art deco torch lamp behind her. It was time to put Puccini's *Tosca* on the old RCA turn-table—itself another period piece from her formative years. Even though she'd migrated, albeit reluctantly, from the analog world to the digital, she'd never quite bought into the idea that music could be streamed on demand. *Nobody plays anything anymore. They listen to it, but don't play it. How is that even possible?*

She made sure to turn the volume down as part of her good neighbor policy. The record player had been her father's back when she was growing up, and it was hers ever since he passed. It still worked fine, in between occasional trips to the repair shop, and she saw no reason to get rid of her vast collection of vinyl LPs of her beloved Italian operas. Not German or Russian or French. Only Puccini and Verdi and Donizetti, as well as a few other long-forgotten and barely missed fellow paisanos.

She spread out on her comfortable old sofa and opened her copy of the *Times* from the day before. The paper of record had been part of her morning routine for decades, long before she joined its archrival, the *Journal*, and nothing was going to change that. She appreciated good journalism no matter the source, and the *Times* always showed her how it's done.

After wading through the international and national news from twenty-four hours earlier—and thus not the least bit newsworthy anymore—she scanned the metro section for local items that rarely make into her own paper. Like celebrity mischief. Sports. And the unending New Yorker-on-New Yorker butchery that had been her bread and butter for years at the *News*.

One headline stopped her cold. EAST SIDE REALTOR MURDERED. She did not have to read any further to know whose life had come to such a sudden, violent and ugly end. And she was right, as the first few sentences of the opening paragraph revealed. *Oh, shit. I got Leotta killed!*

• • •

Barbieri put down her mug, grabbed her cell off the coffee table and called Brennan. He picked up immediately. She didn't care that it was well before dawn, and she knew Brennan wouldn't either.

"Kim. You just going to sleep or just getting up?" he asked.

"Not sure, to tell the truth, Timothy," she said.

"You calling about this Maxim fellow, I assume? The body that isn't there?"

"Nope. A certifiably dead body this time. Martin Leotta. Real estate broker on the Upper East Side."

"I got the Investigation Report late last night," he informed her. "Killed in his office on Madison. No arrests. You think they're connected, these homicides? Lebedev and Leotta?"

"I do. And if I'm right, *I'm* the connection. I interviewed Leotta yesterday and asked him about Lebedev."

"And ..."

"Lebedev was one of his best customers. Leotta could afford a closetful of fine European suits with the hefty commissions he earned from Lebedev."

"So, you brought up Lebedev to Leotta. Leotta went and told some bad guys that someone's been asking about Lebedev."

"Then they went and told their higher-ups that someone's stirring up trouble ...."

"... and said higher-ups eliminated one blabbermouth. All in a couple of hours. I think the detectives need to hear from you, Kim. Give me a second to see who caught this case."

"I think you're right." Barbieri sat quietly, just sipping her cappuccino, listening to the clicks as Brennan pressed a few keys on the laptop that never left his side. "Who caught it?"

"Sam McNamee and Diana Curley. Good cops. Know 'em?" he asked.

"I sure do," she said. "McNamee was in the Bronx, and Curley was in Brooklyn with you. Five or six years ago, at least. We had a few dead bodies in common. Cleared just about all their cases, as I recall."

"They still do. I assigned them both to the one-nine a few weeks ago. They'll learn to co-exist, like my guys always do when they're paired up."

"Sort of an odd couple, don't you think? I remember him being kind of schlubby. Overweight and a lousy dresser. And she was...."

"... pretty fit, and buttoned up. Dresses like she means business. I'm not a matchmaker, Kim. Let me correct that. I am a matchmaker, but not for the lovelorn. If two of my men..."

"... or women."

"Or women can spend a whole shift together without wanting to throw their partner off the roof, I've done my job."

"Wouldn't have worked, anyway. I always suspected she was a scissor sister," she said, opening and closing her index and middle fingers as if they were snipping paper.

"A what?"

"Gay. Lesbian."

"Clever. It's not my business who sleeps with who, as long as she closes cases and plays nice with her partner. Which they both already do better than just about any of my other teams. The Department's pretty open-minded about diversity, anyway."

"Which means you are, too."

"Of course, Kim. I ain't rocking that boat. Not when I'm this close to walking off into a really beautiful sunset. You'll be hearing from them later today. Them. I can call him or her them if I don't know if he or she is a him or a her. Do I have that right?"

"You're capable of learning, Captain. I always admired that about you. Just make sure either he or she or them gets back to me. Please."

After ending the call, Barbieri went back to the paper, and saved the best for last. The crossword. Noting that she was actually doing Friday's puzzle, not Saturday's, she was a little disappointed. Way the *Times* worked, the puzzles got harder and harder during the week, and while the Friday puzzle was indeed difficult, it was simply not as challenging as the Saturday one. They were the ones Barbieri really looked forward to tackling. They took longer, and required a lot more mental gymnastics, but that's what made them even more worthwhile when she filled in the last empty square. In ink, of course.

Who cares about pushovers? Formidable opponents are a lot more fun.

CHAPTER SIXTEEN

10 North 10th Street
Brooklyn
Saturday, December 5
3:46 P.M.

The interview with Curley and MacNamee, the two investigators who had caught the Leotta homicide, was set for seven that evening on the Upper East Side of Manhattan. The 19th Precinct station house was smack dab in the middle of the high-rent stomping grounds that Leotta used to preside over.

The station house was maybe a half-hour away on the subway, which meant she had a good three hours of me-time to do whatever the hell me felt like. Accordingly, Barbieri took her sweet time getting ready to make herself ready for her close-up. Absorb three more mugs of cappuccino. Check email, scour news sites that tilt left or right in an understated way, then scroll through Twitter. Repeat as necessary. *I don't for the life of me understand why TikTok and WhatsApp and the other newfangled social media are so popular, and frankly I don't see why I should even bother trying them.*

Barbieri was off duty, but that didn't mean she was totally off the hook with her editor, Mr. Fitzgerald. Only after she started working for him did she discover he was the worst kind of twenty-four seven workaholic, with a reputation for texting his people when they were least expecting it. Still, with the experience she was getting, Barbieri judged that her new gig offered a pretty good trade-off between her career growth and her admittedly stagnant personal life.

So far that day, thankfully, Barbieri had not heard from him. *How badly did I screw it up? Was it so awful that he had to rewrite the whole damn thing himself?* Whistling past the reporting graveyard, she spent the last few moments of her me-time on a lifelong routine. Make sure her make-up was still okay. Check that her articles of clothing matched the occasion and each other. And finally, take whatever medication she needed for the condition of the day. Over the years, as she got older, she found that the last item on the agenda took up more mental space than the other two.

She'd timed it all perfectly. At six-fifteen on the dot, she was ready for her close-up with the two detectives investigating the untimely demise of the broker she'd interviewed only hours before his sudden death.

CHAPTER SEVENTEEN

19th Precinct Station House
East 67th Street
Manhattan
Saturday, December 5
7:00 P.M.

To Barbieri, it was like the good old days... almost.

As a *Daily News* crime reporter who'd covered many of the homicides that a city of eight million could be counted on to generate, night after night after night, she'd interviewed hundreds of cops at the crime scenes and almost as many detectives who started investigating the incidents right after. But, somehow, she'd never made it to the inside of an interrogation room, and never been on the receiving end of an official New York Police Department Q and A session.

The 19th Precinct station house, a century-old building surrounded by modern and not-so-modern luxury high-rises, was just a few upper-crusty blocks from where Leotta was killed. As she entered the building, she couldn't help but notice that just across the street was the Russian mission to the United Nations, a forbidding fortress surrounded by heavy gates, security cameras pointing every which way, and cars with diplomatic plates parked anywhere and everywhere, without regard to 'No Parking' signs.

And that unsmiling, Russian plainclothes agents were hanging around outside the entrance, talking and smoking and texting and smoking again as if they were on a permanent break from their western civilization-undermining work inside. *Are Leotta's murderers right there right now? What do I do, go up to the front door, press the intercom and ask, "All right, which one of you goons did it?"*

She stopped at the station house front desk to tell the officer manning it that Macnamee and Curley were expecting her, and after checking her ID, he pointed her to an interrogation room up one flight. As she took off her winter coat and hat, Barbieri looked for a familiar face among the cops and detectives doing cop and detective tasks like carrying folders, escorting witnesses and victims, and keying in data on their computers. She saw none. Absolutely nobody she knew from her crime reporter days. *I don't know anybody, and nobody knows me. After less than five years? Jeez, girl.*

The two detectives were already in the interrogation room when she arrived, checking their phones and flipping through their notepads. She rapped on the doorjamb, and they each looked up, gave her a big smile, and walked over to the doorway to greet her.

While cops ordinarily had their guard up when talking to reporters, these two had learned early on that Barbieri had always treated them fairly in her stories. She was as close to them as a civilian could be, and they treated her like one of their own. Besides, she was buds with their alpha male, Chief Brennan, and neither of them had any desire to be added to his shit list.

The room was exactly as she'd imagined, recognizable from a steady diet of *Law & Order, NYPD Blue* and a million other cop shows she couldn't stop watching growing up. A rectangular green table with a thick metal ring in the center for securing handcuffs, three simple government-issue gray chairs positioned around it, harsh fluorescent lights suspended from the ceiling. Three walls, all as dull a shade of puke green gray as is humanly possible to make, were completely bare, while the fourth had a wide mirror in the center that she assumed was one-way.

Without too much effort, she could only imagine how much the room must have reeked of cigarette smoke in years past, before smoking became a big no-no in city buildings.

The reporter recognized Curley right away. The female cop hadn't changed a bit since Barbieri had seen her last, years ago. Not one more wrinkle on her face or neck, not one more gray hair on her head. Much to her surprise, though, today's version of Macnamee looked far better than the Macnamee of old. He'd taken off serious weight and was dressed like he actually owned a mirror. Clean white shirt, pressed khaki chinos, and Clark shoes. Barbieri thought for a split second about asking him if partnering with Curley had anything to do with his metamorphosis into stud muffin, but then thought better of it. There was a limit to their friendliness, and she didn't want to push it.

After she draped her coat over the one empty chair, Barbieri and Detectives Macnamee and Curley got the mutual corpses chitchat out of the way, then got down to the business at hand- the recent demise of Martin Leotta.

Because the detectives had just started working together, they had not yet worked out their bad-cop, good-cop interrogation roles. This time, with a friendly witness, Macnamee led, moving his chair opposite Barbieri's, while Curley sat off to the side and took notes as she listened. All police interrogation technique 101 to Barbieri, based on all the cop shows she'd ever seen.

"So, Kim, about your connection to the deceased? Why were you interviewing him, exactly?"

"It was for a story I'm doing for the *Journal*. About Russian buyers laundering money by buying up condos in New York. A Russian named Maxim Lebedev in particular. I'm trying to find him, and I thought one broker he'd used might know where he is."

"He's missing?"

"He is to me. I don't know where he is."

"Leotta. You already knew Lebedev was a client of his?"

"Not for certain, no. I was just fishing, actually. Reporter's intuition, maybe, which occasionally pans out. I was using him to help me decipher the real estate business, and I got lucky. It turned out that Lebedev had bought five places though Leotta, but I didn't know that for sure until I met him."

The reporter coughed into her hand, then reached into her purse and took out one of the throat lozenges she always carried with her.

"I need a second. Excuse me..."

"You okay?" Detective Curley asked. "Take your time."

Barbieri held up her hand, palm facing out, as she sucked on the lozenge for a few seconds. "Okay. I'm good."

"You sure?" asked Macnamee, joining the interrogation. "Okay. What did Leotta have to say about Lebedev? About money-laundering?"

"He wasn't aware of it, actually. Said all his purchases were one hundred percent aboveboard. He just assumed Lebedev was a good customer who came by his money honestly. But Leotta admitted that even if Lebedev was dirty, he'd still do business with him. He wasn't about to let a competitor have a rich client with deep pockets. It's been years since Leotta last saw him, anyhow."

"So, Leotta couldn't help you find him? This Lebedev fellow."

"Nope. But if Lebedev bought five condos through him, he is either very wealthy or just a front for other buyers. Russian gangsters, probably."

"Who prefer to remain anonymous."

"Totally anonymous. If nobody ever heard of them, they'd be thrilled to death."

"Okay. So, you ended the interview…?"

"… said our goodbyes, and I took the subway back home. Next thing I knew, I read about the homicide in the paper the next day, and called your boss. Where was Leotta's body found, by the way? And did the killer leave any evidence behind?"

"His office on Madison," Curley replied. "Impaled on a sharp instrument. Which the killer left sticking out of his chest. Kim, what makes you think he was killed because of your interview?"

"Logic, Detective. One, I may have been the last person Leotta saw."

"Besides the guy killed him."

"Okay. Next to last. Two, Leotta handled Lebedev's purchases. Three, Russians are involved, somehow, because Lebedev. And four, I suspect Leotta may have told someone he shouldn't have that someone's been asking about them."

"That someone being you," Macnamee said.

"Adds up," Curley said. "The Russians over here don't like people prying into their business. Especially the shady stuff. You're reporting about other Russian buyers, right? Besides Lebedev?"

"Right. But not just Russians. We're looking at other foreign buyers, too. But only three or four of the Russians I'm investigating will end up in the *Journal* article we're writing."

"*We're* writing? Plural?"

"Yep. We've got a whole team on this story. That's how the *Journal* does things. I'm not certain we'll be printing the subjects' real names, though. At least not yet."

"We'll need their real names and addresses. Definitely. Any idea if Lebedev knows any of them? Or does business with any of them?"

"I don't. Sorry."

"Okay," Curley said. "There may be something there."

"I'll email their contact info to you guys today," Barbieri assured them. "What about me? Am I next on the hit list?"

"We can't say, yet. We don't know for certain, yet, that it's the Russians killed Leotta. And we don't know that they know about you. So, no. Not right now. What we can say is, if this turns out to be some kind of Russian mafia thing, clearing this case may take a while. Russians we've dealt with have been pros who knew how to get away with murder. Scumbags, but real pros."

"Ones I've come across are, certainly. But they won't force me to go into hiding. Screw that. Ask your boss. He'll tell you I'm not the type to be pushed around by violent men. Especially by violent men. Please let me know if you guys get anywhere."

The detectives looked at each other to see if she'd answered all their questions, and checked their notes. They nodded to each other that she had, then got up to leave. "Certainly, Kim. Thanks for your time."

Barbieri rose, donned her coat and grabbed her bag, checking inside it to make sure she'd left nothing behind, and followed the two investigators into the hallway, down the stairs, and out the front door of the station house. As she'd done on the way upstairs, she looked for a familiar face among the cops she passed, and again found none.

Once out on Sixty-seventh Street, the two detectives zipped up their coats and headed east, toward Second Avenue, and Barbieri headed west, back toward the subway stop on Lexington. Thinking about the fate that had already claimed the broker, and that might come to claim her, one question popped into her mind and refused to leave.

What kind of fuckin' mess have you gotten yourself into this time, you fuckin' idjit?

CHAPTER EIGHTEEN

Willowbrook Mall
Edison, New Jersey
Sunday, December 6
10:35 P.M.

The eight men and women, all Russian, Belarusian or Ukrainian, huddled together near their cars, either Japanese or German or Korean, which were parked facing each other at the most desolate end of the enormous, otherwise totally empty, parking lot.

Though the spaces they were standing in were lit almost bright as day, thanks to the powerful sodium streetlight shining right above them, they didn't expect to be noticed by any shoppers or mall employees at that ungodly hour. Who would care about a bunch of old folks doing nothing more than schmoozing before heading off to their respective happy, split-level, four-bedroom suburban homes?

The evening was chilly, enabling the six men to be dressed in what they thought of as the middle-class, American uniform of the day—garish heavy jackets, black slacks and cheap faux leather shoes. The two women wore theirs as well, bright red lipstick, red down coats, white slacks and Nike running shoes with not a scuff on them.

They had all agreed to meet after two of them, Chernenko and Renko, had been contacted by homicide detectives from the NYPD earlier that day concerning the death of a real estate broker named Martin Leotta. Both had denied knowing anything about the victim. Both had been told that other

Russians who'd recently bought luxury Manhattan condos would be contacted by detectives. And the detectives hinted, strongly, that neither should plan on leaving the country. They were not actually warned not to leave, but that was a subtlety that did nothing to ease their paranoia.

"Who gave them our names? You, Raisa?" That question was asked in Ukrainian, so close to Russian and Belarusian that no translation was needed for anyone in the group to understand what anyone else was saying.

"Absolutely not."

"You, Dmitri?"

"Don't be stupid."

"So, none of us. Which means the informer's someone from outside," said another Russian. "Why would he think we'd have anything to do with Martin Leotta? Much less for killing him? Was he the broker for anybody here?"

"No."

"No."

"Lebedev," said another Russian. "He was the broker for Maxim Lebedev. He told me."

"Lebedev bought several units with him. He did. But why would the informer tell the police we were all connected to Lebedev? Why lie? Is whoever this pig is out to destroy us?"

"Lebedev's just a front. Who the fuck knows who the real buyers are? All I know is that we are all clean. We all paid with our own money."

"Hard-earned."

"Legitimate income."

"They can't prove it's not, the fuckin' police."

"Not so far."

"Mostly legitimate, anyway. So how do we get the detectives off our back?"

"Will they take a gift?"

"Not them. Maybe for some other crime. But not murder."

"This is not Russia."

"Have Bratva take care of it," a Ukrainian offered. His country was just as much subject to Bratva plundering as Russia itself was.

"Worst thing we can do. Kill a police officer. Spend the rest of our lives in American prison with the coloreds."

"Then how about we just give them someone to blame for the murder of this Leotta person?"

"That's an idea."

"Who?"

"Lebedev," one twin offered.

"Lebedev. Good. They're going to blame him anyway, right? He was a client of Leotta. Anybody see him? Or at least know where he lives?"

"I haven't."

"I don't."

"He's disappeared."

"Not here to defend himself."

"Okay. Settled. Detectives come around again, you all say you heard something about Lebedev. Keep them busy for a while."

"What if Lebedev turns up alive?"

"His tough luck if he does."

"Let him rot in prison. Killers like him make the rest of us look bad. Animals. They deserve it."

Satisfied that their scheme would take all their names off the NYPD's list of likely suspects in the murder of Martin Leotta, the eight all nodded goodbye to each other, opened the doors of their respective getaway cars, then drove out of the lot and into the darkened streets of northern New Jersey suburbia.

Ordinary American citizens going about their ordinary American lives. Nothing to see here.

CHAPTER NINETEEN

Odessa Restaurant
1318 Brighton Beach Avenue
Brooklyn
Monday, December 7th
7:35 A.M.

"We've identified the reporter."

"The one asking about Lebedev?"

"Yes."

"You're going to tell me his name?"

"Her. Kim Barbieri. *Wall Street Journal.*"

Vasily Klim and Grigory Gryshin, the pair of Bratva members put out to pasture in New York City, were sitting by themselves, off in a corner of the restaurant, talking barely above a whisper over coffee and an enormous slice of *medovik.*

There was no need, other than their own fear of eavesdropping by the FBI, for them to isolate themselves. Odessa, a garish, brightly lit diner with red velvet covered walls and red velvet covered chairs and red velvet covered waitresses, was just a few blocks away from their money-laundering laundromat in their new homeland, Brighton Beach.

Every other fellow countryman having breakfast there looked and acted very much like ordinary, average Americans talking about their relatives and their houses and their children and their jobs and their cars. They still spoke in Russian, but over time, their lives had become totally American.

"Another loose end. Does she know anything about him? Lebedev?"

"Just that his name was on several contracts. And that he's missing."

"Not dead. Who told her that?"

"She was just in Moscow, and she spoke with a lot of people we know there. Sergei Petrov for sure."

"Petrov. Another fuckin' hanger-on we don't need. Where does Barbieri work? At the paper?"

"One day a week, we think. Maybe two or three. The other days we don't know."

"Telecommutes from wherever she's sent. We know where she lives?"

"Yes. Apartment in Brooklyn. Neighborhood called Williamsburg."

"Williamsburg. Dangerous? Negroes live there? Spanish?"

"Used to, years ago. Now it's been discovered."

"What is the word the Americans use? *Gentrified*. Because all the young, wealthy morons want to live on top of each other again, like their parents did. Until they had enough and moved out to New Jersey or Connecticut somewhere. This reporter from the *Journal*? She lives alone?"

"Looks like it."

"Approved."

"Got it."

"One thing. This won't be assigned to Vasily."

CHAPTER TWENTY

10 North 10th Street
Brooklyn
Monday, December 7th
10:40 A.M.

Why the hell didn't I ask those questions first? Damn!

The edits Mr. Fitzgerald had made to Barbieri's first draft, which had just popped up in her work e-mail, were a combination of minor nits that would take just a few minutes to address, and questions about the dirty-dealing that required some more digging. By her.

Barbieri was working from home, which meant she was dressed as if she was at the office. Even when she was a freelancer for the *News* years ago, she never indulged in the scruffy reporter look that was close to a uniform among her barely age-of-sexual-consent colleagues. And now that she was reporting on captains of industry with the *Journal*, she upped her game even further.

Today, she wore a blue button-down blouse, dark brown pants, and beige suede loafers. *Is it just another sign of middle age, getting dressed like I was at the office? Or is it because it puts me into work mode? Fuck knows. But I know it keeps me focused on the story.*

She poured herself a cup of coffee from the kitchen counter, grabbed her cell and a notepad, and took a seat at the counter. She did business sitting up there rather than sprawled out on the sofa for the same reason.

Positioning herself as if she were at a desk put her in the frame of mind needed to get things done.

Prodded by Mr. Fitzgerald's questions—while torturing herself for not asking them before her boss did—she spent several hours online, poring through records and databases to ferret out more details on all the purchases. And many more hours on the phone politely interrogating each sale's middlemen—the lawyers, accountants and money managers who kept the real buyer's ID from getting out—to connect just a few more dots.

Barbieri dug deep in the usual financial sand boxes until she addressed every one of Fitzgerald's concerns to her satisfaction. And hopefully to his. She even unearthed up new information about her own, off-the-books, topic of interest—Maxim Lebedev.

It turns out that the missing-and-maybe-deceased Lebedev was a party to twelve home purchases with different brokers, not just the five with Leotta. All were in tonier parts of town, according to the City's property records office. *Did the Italian suit model know Maxim was two-timing him? And which broker not named Leotta was he using? Or brokers?*

A few quick calls to likely brokers doing business on the Upper East Side revealed that the other seven apartments were handled by two competing hoity toity brokers, Corbin Laurence and Richardson Ellis.

The signature of Konstantin Sokolov, of Fifteen Central Park West fame, appeared on only three of his newly unearthed purchase documents. The other four were co-signed with a name new to her, Henry Chuan. *He's Chinese? Not Russian? Why?* Rather than take the time to search for Chuan herself, she gave her email address and phone number to an agent at Richardson Ellis, an experienced realtor named Frederick Ashe. She asked him if he wouldn't mind giving Chuan her number and passing along a request to call her. *If this Chuan fellow was well off enough to read my paper, he'd probably get a kick out of seeing his name in it.*

It didn't take long for Henry Chuan to take the bait.

• • •

"Miss Barbieri?"

"Speaking." Barbieri did not recognize the number that popped up on her caller ID, or the name, Xi Li. She could not tell at first if the caller was male or female, or detect any kind of accent, but assumed the call most likely involved work. It was definitely not any friend or colleague of hers, at least one that she was aware of.

The call came just two hours after her conversation with Ashe, and she was still in her work-from-home frame of mind. She got off the stool by the counter, grabbed her notepad, and poured another cup of coffee as he continued speaking.

"My name is Xi Li. Mr. Ashe just called me on your behalf. I understand you have questions about Maxim Lebedev."

Barbieri was momentarily taken aback by the caller affirming his name as Li.

"I do, but for a gentleman named Henry Chuan. The caller ID says your name is Xi Li." She needed to nail down with whom she was talking first, before going on to whether this individual and Lebedev had indeed purchased apartments together.

"That's me. I have both names."

"OK. Thank you for calling... Xi. Or should I call you Henry?"

"Li is fine. Many Chinese have two names. Immigrants, like myself. Confuses you Americans, not us Chinese."

"Okay. Li it is. Can I ask you about the properties you bought with Mr. Lebedev, Li? I believe there were four."

"Yes. Four. There would have been more but they got... what's the word...?

"Suspicious. Sketchy."

"Yes. Illegal or close to it. I get into real estate with someone knows what he doing. Met him through mutual friend, and he seem OK." Barbieri quickly picked up on the fact that his English was not quite perfect, yet was still perfectly understandable.

"We make some nice money buying properties and then renting them out. Real income machines. I'm happy. He's happy. Then two things make me think, not kosher."

"May I ask where'd you learn that word, Li? Kosher?" Barbieri asked, momentarily confused by this Chinese man's use of a Hebrew word. She'd used it all her life, one of the many foreign words that had snuck their way into her Brooklyn version of English over the years.

"You do business here, you learn language." That, Barbieri understood perfectly, being a New Yorker used to speaking with others whose backgrounds were completely foreign to her. Her hometown's always been a melting pot for languages, too.

"First thing suspicious, he start asking me about other places to park our money. My money. Shady, you know? Way he talk about them, they stink of fraud. Insurance scams, Medicaid mills, that sort of thing. Felt like he treat me like a mark instead of a partner. I am not mark."

"Got it. What was non-kosher number two?"

"Right before we sign contract on last property, a condo on First Avenue, he pull out. Tell me his backers want money back. I didn't know he even had backers. He has no choice, he tell me. Then he say, 'I won't be hearing from him for a while.'"

"This conversation was in person? Over the phone...?"

"Phone. That the other thing—his voice. He was scared. Normally he sound friendly, you know? Like we old buddies. But on that call, I hear something else."

"Fear?"

"Fear. Yes."

"Did Lebedev say what he was afraid of?"

"He did. He told me his backers say he cheating. That money they gave him was more than cost of unit."

"Skimming off the top. Did he admit it to you?"

"He say it all was misunderstanding. Cash flow hit a snag, that all. Said they were giving him seventy-two hours to make them whole." Barbieri smiled slightly on hearing the words 'make them whole', a nouveau slang version of 'compensating someone for losing big bucks on the deal'.

"He tell you who these backers were? Or why they were using him instead of buying the property themselves?"

"I ask him, and he say something like, 'better you didn't know.' I did not press him on that."

"What did he mean by 'make them whole'?"

"Give them their money back, how I took it."

"No doubt. Did he say how?"

"Not specifically, He was not sure where he would get money, but he'd definitely get it to them in time. Somehow. His words were what I want to hear. But his voice, though, did not sound so positive."

"Fear."

"Terror more like it. That told me everything about his backers. Picked the wrong people to bankroll him."

"Probably not from Chase. Or Citibank."

"Not probably. I wanted no part of them, that much clear. Then he say, I wouldn't be hearing from him for a while."

"Meaning ...?"

"Meaning he going to have to disappear, that is my guess."

"You're not going to make yourself scarce, too, Li—are you?"

"Why should I? I do nothing except make the same mistake they did."

"Which was to trust Lebedev. Somehow, I doubt they'd show you much sympathy, Li. These scams Lebedev wanted you to go in on? Medicaid mills, et cetera? Do you know if he ever actually invested in any of them? With anyone else?"

"From the way he talked about them, yes. Like he was just getting started, becoming typhoon."

"Tycoon, you mean. You know where? Manhattan?"

"Yes. And Queens. Lot of people spending lot of the government's money. Disneyland East for money laundering."

"Okay, Li. Thank you very much. Can I call you again about Mr. Lebedev?"

"Sure, Kim. But like I say, I doubt I ever see him again."

The call over, Barbieri mulled her next steps. Lebedev had disappeared off the face of the Earth. Barbieri's part of the planet, anyway. There were plenty of records for his real estate empire, which included several home addresses for him. *I should have paid more attention. Damn it! A few calls to a few landlords could've told me he actually lived in none of them.* There were, of course, no records of restaurants he went to, or friends he hung with. He wanted to make himself unfindable by his mobbed-up bankrollers, and he'd succeeded. *If he owes these Russian motherfuckers money, they're going to have a hard time collecting.*

Barbieri was staring down a big, gaping hole, but she knew of one person who could fill it. She picked up her cell, scrolled through her recent calls, and pressed the one with a Moscow area code.

CHAPTER TWENTY-ONE

317 Tvetskaya Street
Moscow
Monday, December 7th
7:40 P.M.

"Petrov."

"Hey, Sergei. Good evening, I think. It's Kim Barbieri. *The Journal.*"

"Kim! Didn't recognize the caller ID. Still poking around Lebedev, are we?"

"Not we. Just me. The *Journal*'s not involved. I'm trying to recreate his life here in New York City, but I'm running into one great big brick wall. He's left not a trace that I can find."

"I don't know that I can help you, Kim. All I know for sure is that he lives, or lived, in a studio off of Fifth Avenue in Manhattan, if memory serves. Which I guess means he has no wife or girlfriend. One thing I know for sure is that Lebedev was not a man about town. From his expense reports, it looked like he almost never ventured out to restaurants, or shows, or ball games. Maybe he just went home every evening and watched reruns of Law & Order, just like any American does these days."

"A homebody with no wife and no life, it seems. Like I said, a brick wall. Do you have a picture of this cipher?"

"There's got to be one on some official site here, and I'll send you a link if I can locate it. I can tell you he was not bad looking, as Russian men go. I wouldn't want you to fall for him, Kim. We're lousy husbands, I'm told.

Gigolos, cheaters, and, of course, drunkards. Some of my countrymen, I hear, drown their sorrows in vodka. Can you imagine? By the way, is it Mrs. Barbieri? Or Miss?"

"Uh, no, Petrov. That information is in some file you guys have on me. Do some more homework for me, please. Make a few calls. Somebody you know must know something about this Lebedev fella."

"Okay. I will. But if Lebedev's mobbed up, I have to back off."

"Understood. Do not-I repeat, do not-put yourself in any danger because of me. Please. This is not worth it."

"No argument there, my friend."

"Thank you, Sergei."

"You're welcome, Kim. I won't put a target on my back, I assure you. Surviving is something I'm quite good at. Maybe it's the Slavic in me."

"Americans have that talent, too. Or at least this American does. Speak to you soon, Sergei."

• • •

The call with Petrov over, Barbieri made her escape. *I've got to clear my head*. She changed from her proper office attire to a warm exercise outfit, complete with fanny pack. She then put buds in her ears and retrieved a small plastic bottle of water from the refrigerator and stowed it in the pack. Her cold-weather outfit complete, she took the elevator down to the lobby, exited her building, and walked at a fast clip over to nearby McCarren Park.

Weather permitting, she usually walked four times around a meandering, one-mile-long path that circled the inside perimeter of the park. And today the weather was indeed permitting, offering a cool temperature that would keep her from overheating, along with zero threat of rain.

When she reached her starting point just inside the park entrance, she pressed the music icon on her iPhone, scrolled down the menu, and selected an obscure opera she'd only recently discovered. *L'ultimo giorno di Pompei* by Giovanni Pacini, performed at Teatro alla Scala.

Italian operas on her cell did their job of letting her leave the here and now behind, but they also left her less aware of her surroundings, unfortunately. While crime continued going way down in Gotham, the city was still the city. Bad actors there were endangered, but not yet extinct. Lowering one's guard, even on a lovely day, in the middle of a park filled with babies and dogs and mommies and nannies, could still end badly if you weren't careful.

CHAPTER TWENTY-TWO

10 North 10th St.
Brooklyn
Monday, December 7th
12:15 P.M.

Where the hell did all these drugs come from? When did I start taking that?

Feeling a headache coming on—a plain old regular one that pounded away, usually, until beaten into submission by Extra Strength Tylenol—Barbieri cut short her jaunt in the park after just one hour. Returning home, she headed straight to the bathroom, where she opened the medicine cabinet and grabbed the bottle of Tylenol. That was her pain reliever of choice when the pain was throbbing away somewhere deep inside her brain.

Once she filled a Dixie cup with water and swallowed the tablet, she took a moment to stare at the inside of the cabinet, as if it was something she'd never really noticed before. It was filled with an array of pills and creams and lotions and tablets that seemed to have taken over her life. Slowly, stealthily. They'd been metastasizing there, right in front of her, yet they were always invisible. Plain as day, but unseen. As it was growing, she'd never really taken stock of her medication cornucopia before.

Tylenol for headaches, Amitriptolin for back pain, and Biofreeze for knee pain, Pepto for stomach pain, Midol for menstrual pain, Azo for urinary pain and Zomig for migraine.

GasX for bloating. Imodium for the runs and Miralax for the stops.

Witch hazel for when her skin started itching, Aveeno when it became dry, and Effaclar when it became oily.

Preparation H for when her hemorrhoids acted up, Robitussin for coughing fits, and Variderm to keep her varicose veins in check.

Covaryx for menopause, and Replens for vaginal dryness. *The old girl's more trouble than she's worth. I haven't let any men I've met lately anywhere near her. Honestly, I don't think I have any use for her anymore, anyway.*

Until that moment, she had not realized that over the last decade or so, she had been taking more and more drugs to relieve this or cure that, just so she could tell herself, and her friends, there was nothing wrong with her. And she no doubt could expect to add even more of them in the years ahead. Getting older did that to people. *You're gonna need a bigger cabinet.*

One by one, working her way from the top shelf to the bottom, she picked up each bottle, box, tube, and spray, and squinted at its code numbers to see if any had outlived its expiration date. That would at least give her a reason to toss any she hadn't used in a while, and might not need anymore. She was savvy enough to know that the date did not mean the medicine wouldn't work as advertised. It just meant the company couldn't vouch for it after that date. But that was not enough for her. *If they won't stand by their drug, why should I take the risk?*

Among all her meds, Barbieri found just one she could toss right away. Midol. It was the one medicine she hadn't been taking recently–and definitely no longer needed. She picked up the box of caplets and tossed it in the wastebasket under the sink. All the other medicines she checked turned out to be still good, their expiration dates weeks away at least, and would definitely still need. Probably. *Add maybe twenty meds. Subtract just one. Golden years, my ass.*

CHAPTER TWENTY-THREE

Federal Security Service Headquarters
2 Bolshaya Lubyanka Street
Moscow
Saturday, December 12
3:15 P.M.

"Captain Nevski."

"This is Andropov."

"What can we do for you, Andropov?

"Support for a mission."

The telephone call to the FSB was made because the assassination being planned could not be carried out by the Bratva alone. That organization lacked the skills, expertise, and resources required for an operation with that degree of difficulty. But certain apparatchiks in the Kremlin were more than willing to provide them–for a modest fee, of course.

"By 'mission' you mean 'termination'?"

"Yes."

"This mission has been authorized?"

"Certainly. At the highest level of my organization."

"I will verify that before we assist you. Who is being terminated?"

"Nobody of concern to the state."

"Understood. A private matter. When?"

"Within weeks. There is some urgency in this matter."

"Understood. Where?"

"New York City."

"Branching out. Interesting. FSB scientists will need the details before they can fill the order."

"What details?"

"Target's height. Weight. Diet. Delivery date. Product is made to order."

"Understood. We'll provide the details."

"We will proceed at that point. Not before. Understood?"

"Understood."

"And we will proceed only after an advance payment for the substantial expenses we will undoubtedly incur."

"Understood."

"Paid in full. One hundred percent."

"Understood."

"Good day, Andropov."

"Good day, Captain Nevski."

• • •

The call to an FSB bureaucrat named Nevski had come from a Kremlin bureaucrat named Andropov. Neither name was real.

The Kremlin is at the very tippie-top of the Russian red-tape food chain, run by automatons who are perfectly fine doing nothing but making the 5:15 home. When a task is being planned—whether the repair of a broken street light or the execution of a nobody trouble-maker—it has to go up the regular chain of command, and then down the regular chain of command. Even bratva hits can be slowly strangled to death by bureaucrats.

When a Kremlin nobody signs off on a termination, the message goes up the chain to a Kremlin big shot, who calls the head of the FSB—the Federal Security Service. The FSB then sends it down its own chain of command to the Chamber—the poison lab, where thousands of R and D science types create the toxins that kill their targets without leaving behind any evidence that could be traced back to the Russian state.

Each dose of lethality is made-to-order, because the assassin will have only one shot at the victim. There are no re-dos in that line of work. Before the scientist chooses the poison and the dose, he considers the dimensions of the target–his height and weight, his type of body frame, and the amount of body fat he's carrying around. He is also given a full list of everything that goes into the target's body. The foods he eats, the liquids he drinks. And the medications he takes, their dosages, and how he takes them. Are they pills that are swallowed, lotions that are rubbed on, or liquids that are injected?

All this goes into choosing the right poison, calculating the right dose, and selecting the form it takes: Liquid, solid, spray or gas, depending on which offers the best chance of entering the victim's body, reaching the right target organ, and sending him on his way to an early grave.

If the dose is too low, there is a risk that the victim might live. That is an unacceptable risk. If it's too high, the victim might go into convulsions or die before the assassin has time to escape. Also, unacceptable. Or the unused dose may be left behind for the cops to find. Unacceptable, as well. These are risks that are simply not tolerated in terminations, and must be minimized if the mission is to be successfully carried out–and not traced back to any apparatchik in the Kremlin.

Like everything else in life, execution is all in the details. If the target is murdered successfully–that is, he is dead, and the killer is neither identified nor caught–the assassin is paid well for his trouble, in vacations or luxury cars or cash or women or dachas far from Moscow. If he makes a mistake, like merely hurting the victim or leaving the weapon behind, he's not. He worked for nothing. Or worse, he makes himself the target of a termination, and is never seen again.

The assassin is merely a cog in the gig economy, and he knows the deal going in. The Russians are good at this. They don't make rookie mistakes. They've been terminating enemies for a long time, inside and outside Russia, and the man doing the terminating is almost never caught. Getting away with murder is what he does for a living.

When assassinating a target, execution is all that matters.

CHAPTER TWENTY-FOUR

Unit 29155, Military Intelligence
Headquarters 161ˢᵗ Special Purpose
Specialist Training Center
Moscow
Sunday, December 14
7:43 A.M.

"Institute for Scientific Research Number Two."

"This is Nevski. You have an assignment."

"May I have the details, Nevski?"

"You'll get them. My client is working on that right now."

"Client. Here, in Moscow?"

"No. U S A. New York City."

The Federal Security Service is a bureaucracy. The goal is set. Priorities are prioritized., decisions are decided upon, resources are allocated, and staff is assigned. The goal is met. At this one moment, on this one call, there was but a single goal: to execute an enemy individual. The agency that the FSB tasked with the assignment was military in name only. The Specialist Training Center was a wholly owned but totally off-the-books subsidiary of the FSB. If any foreign power wanted to find out where Russia's lethal poisons came from, they'd hit a dead end right here.

That this was a high-priority assignment, one that puts all other assignments on the back burner, was established by the position of the caller. Nevski was as high up in the FSB org chart as they come, so there was no decision to be made by the scientists themselves. Their sole option was to accept the assignment. Their only concern, therefore, was devoting the resources necessary to carry out the assignment and get Nevski off their back for a while.

"Special precautions are required. We have to take product transport and assembly into account. I'll have the Chamber prepare to take on this assignment, so that they can accept it without delay."

"That will be acceptable to my superiors, I am certain."

"You understand that in order to proceed, we need precise information about the target."

"I do."

"Please call me as soon as you have it, Nevski. No point wasting our time, is there?"

"Wouldn't think of it."

CHAPTER TWENTY-FIVE

10 North 10th Street
Brooklyn
Sunday, December 14
9:45 A.M.

That morning was the start of a much-needed break for Barbieri. She was off that day, or at least hoped to be, so she'd switched off her workday routine and switched on her do-whatever-I-damn-well-feel-like routine.

It was looking like it was going to be a beautiful, brisk fall day, a little chilly but no wind to make it un-go-out-able, so she wanted to stay out of the kitchen if she could at all help it.

Cooking was not her forte. If she'd inherited the Italian cooking gene from her mom, it was still all but dormant. If not extinct. She put on her seen-better-days sweatpants and sweatshirt, opened the apartment door and picked up the copy of the *Times* that had been left for her by her downstairs neighbor–like herself, a print edition-reading dinosaur–and tucked it into her messenger bag. This being Sunday, the paper was simply too bulky and heavy to carry otherwise. Then she closed the door behind her and walked down the hall to the elevator.

After entering the elevator and pressing the 'lobby' button, she pressed a few keys on her cell and Giuseppe Verdi's *Nobucca* started emanating from her ear buds. Not her favorite, but worth revisiting every year or so. After exiting her building, she walked over to the Starbucks on Bedford

Avenue to pick up her usual cappuccino and croissant, and headed to McCarren Park, just two blocks away on North Twelfth. Once inside the park's gate, she was oblivious to the sounds surrounding her, which were all drowned out by Verdi's arias that continued streaming out of her earbuds.

She discovered, much to her delight, a park bench that was both empty, save for an old, soggy Thai takeout menu, and faced the sun. Perfect. The morning sky was clear, and on days that were a little nippy, as this was, she felt that warming up with the sun's rays directly on her was about as pleasant as it gets.

Sitting down, she sorted through all the paper's sections to find the magazine, which she then opened to the crossword on the next-to-last page, and grabbed her pen from the messenger bag. That ritual accomplished, she took the lid off the cappuccino, unwrapped the croissant and put it on the bench beside her, and uncapped her pen. She then methodically proceeded to fill in square after square of the crossword across, then down—as if she were taking some kind of aptitude test.

Even though it was a Sunday, when the key to solving the puzzle was figuring out the theme as much as filling in the right answer for each clue, she breezed through it without working up much of a sweat. *I should finally write one of these things and send it in. How hard can it be? Even if it wasn't accepted, the puzzle editor guy at the Times would appreciate the brilliance of it, at least.*

Distracted by both the puzzle on her lap and the opera in her ears, Barbieri was totally divorced from the comings and goings around her. She barely noticed all the children racing past her. Nor the two mothers walking their three toddlers to the playground. Nor the four Latino *ancianos* playing dominoes across the way.

For a second or two she did notice a man sitting on a bench facing her on the other side of the park, maybe one hundred feet away. He was big, about six-feet tall, and stocky, wearing a gray baseball cap with no logo of any kind, a black zippered parka over a brown plaid button-down shirt, tan chinos, and blue running shoes. Other than a neat mustache, he was clean-shaven, and had crewcut salt-and-pepper hair. The only thing unusual about him, in her mind, was that she had no memory of seeing him before. *Maybe he's new to the neighborhood. Even newer than me. I'm an old timer, and I just moved here myself.*

Every few minutes, the man looked up from the magazine he was pretending to read to glance at her, and wrote a word or two down on a page hidden inside it.

Finishing her breakfast, Barbieri unfolded the Sunday paper to its full, humongous size and devoured it systematically as she always had, section by section, page after page, beginning with the Business section and ending with the Sunday Review. She took her time, too. She admired good reporting, even from her own paper's chief competitor. A good story, well-written, didn't make her jealous. It made her determined to up her game, and Barbieri was never one to back off from a challenge.

As she devoured the news, the man sitting across the way sat still, his head down, as if engrossed in an article. He did nothing to get Barbieri's attention, and she obliged.

Finally finishing all the sections, she put them back together as neatly as possible and placed them back in the bag, then opened her cell and lowered the volume of the opera she'd been listening to. She leaned back on the bench, turned her face up toward the sun, and closed her eyes. *I'm not in a park in Williamsburg, Brooklyn. I'm in Teatro alla Scala in Milan. I'm not in a park in Williamsburg, Brooklyn. I'm in Teatro alla Scala in Milan. I'm not in a park ...*

Thirty-five minutes later, Barbieri woke up, opened her eyes, and glanced at her cell phone for the correct time. She had stopped wearing a wrist watch since she started carrying a cell many years before. Surprised at how much time had passed, she picked up the paper bag in which she'd put the empty cup and wrappings from her breakfast, and the now neatly folded newspaper, and headed out of the park, back to her apartment. No hurry.

This sudden burst of activity got the attention of the man sitting across the way. As she walked away, he closed his magazine, folded it, and slipped it into the pocket of his parka. He then just sat there, still, legs crossed, seemingly alone with his thoughts. Not a care in the world.

Only when Barbieri was actually outside the park entrance, and out of his line of sight, did the stocky man in the gray baseball cap sitting across from her get up and start walking in the same direction. If his goal was not to appear to be following her, he'd met it. Barbieri kept walking at a what's-the-hurry pace, not realizing she was at the head of a two-person parade back to her home.

CHAPTER TWENTY-SIX

Yoshi Restaurant
146 Bedford Avenue
Brooklyn
Sunday, December 14
8:15 P.M.

"What can I get you tonight, Kim?"

"What do you have that won't kill me?"

"Tonight? Teriyaki Salmon. Three customers survive so far."

"Night is young, Yoshi."

"Nice knowing you, Kim."

Barbieri was sitting in the last seat at the counter in Yoshi, the Japanese restaurant that was her go-to place whenever she was too tired to even think about making dinner. Yoshi was a long, narrow space, with a row of tables for three against one wall, and the counter where the imported Japanese chefs prepared the sushi and sashimi dishes on the other.

That evening, just about every table was taken, as was every other seat at the bar, by twenty-something boys and girls who knew everything and understood nothing.

On the walls were banners with Japanese calligraphy, Koi ponds, Mount Fuji and other examples of authentic Japanese kitsch. Barbieri thought every meal she'd had there was the real deal, though, so it was easy for her to tune out the décor and concentrate on her culinary adventure.

Yoshi Ito owned the place, Barbieri had been one of his first customers when he'd opened the restaurant, and was still one of the most loyal. It was a place where nobody knew her name, as she was a brand-new but no-youngster Williamsburger, except its owner. And that was perfectly fine by her. Over the past few months, their relationship had evolved from formal owner and loyal customer, to not-quite-intimate friends who knew how to make each other laugh when they needed it most.

While heading for her meal to arrive, Barbieri worked her phone, switching back and forth between Twitter, newsfeeds, email and messages. All the while listening to Giuseppe Verdi's *Rigoletto* coming through her ear buds and tuning out the inane chatter from the idiots sitting near her. She was twice as old as everyone else at Yoshi, yet she could multi-task with the best of them. Maybe too much so.

As Yoshi placed her salmon dish on the counter in front of her, she moved to the side without taking her eyes off the screen. If she had, she might have noticed that at one table a few feet away from her, the young Asian couple sitting there when she came in had left, replaced by a man sitting alone. A man with a neat mustache, wearing a gray baseball cap, with a black jacket draped over the back of his chair.

Distracted by the onslaught of the-world-is-ending updates delivered by her phone, and by her dinner, she didn't notice a waiter coming to the man's table, placing a cup of tea and a small dish on it, and handing him a menu. She failed to notice the waiter retreating from the table, then coming back when the man signaled that he was ready to order. She didn't see the waiter take his order and relay it to the chefs working right in front of her. She failed to see them prepare a yellowfin tuna sushi roll and a salmon sashimi and place them in a long, narrow dish and hand it to the waiter, who then returned to the man's table, silently set the dish down before him, and retreated.

Distracted as she was, though, she began after a few minutes to sense one thing. Someone was looking at her.

Barbieri put her chopsticks down on her plate, took her eyes off the phone, and turned her head first to her left, then to her right. Slowly, so as not to draw attention from other diners or alert whomever was watching her she was onto him.

There was nobody. Not the other twerps beside her at the counter, nor anyone at the tables behind her, nor any of the waiters or chefs working all around her. She went back to her dinner, and to her cell. *Get a grip, girl!*

But in the middle of answering an email from an old colleague at the *News*, she suddenly stopped. *What was it? Something's not right.* She connected the two dots that she'd missed just moments earlier. *It was the man sitting by himself. Where have I seen him before? Wait–this morning! That's the guy who sat across from me at the park!*

Barbieri turned and looked directly at him. He wasn't looking at her. He had finished his meal, and was trying to get the attention of his waiter. He spotted the waiter standing off to the side and gave him the 'signing the receipt' hand gesture. After eyeballing the check, he took out his wallet, and as he was doing so, he saw Barbieri looking at him. He gave her a small smile and a nod, as if he were being hit on at a singles bar, as he took two ten-dollar bills out of his wallet and left them on the table. Barbieri watched as he stood up, grabbed the jacket from the back of his chair, and made his way down the aisle toward the restaurant door.

She continued staring at him as he pulled the door handle as if to leave, but then turned back toward her.

Now, they were looking directly at each other; he standing at the door and she sitting at the counter. It was as if it was just the two them there, all alone. The other diners sitting between them, and their waiters, were just props in a sheriff-versus-bad guy drama that they had no clue they were in.

As Barbieri stared at him, and he stared right back at her, he raised his right hand to his neck and put his fingers around it as if he were strangling himself. He raised his eyebrows as his lips formed a small smile. The man then turned back toward the door, pulled it open and left, the door closing behind him. Barbieri sat there, staring. *Was I hallucinating? Did I just see what I just saw?* Nobody else in the restaurant had. They were all dining and flirting and pontificating without a care in the world.

Never one to lose her composure, Barbieri turned back to the counter, took a deep breath, and put her head in her hands. She was used to dealing with shitstains who wanted her maimed or dead, from her freelance gig at the *Daily News*. Threats of bodily harm were the price of entry for reporting about violent crimes by violent criminals. Her job had been solely to observe their world, but sometimes they suspected she'd trespassed.

She believed that now, however, when she was merely looking into financial crimes, the worst that the white-collar criminals appearing in her articles would do is maybe sue her paper for libel. They'd object, in other words, but not violently so.

Her thinking was now clear, and unaffected by panic. Barbieri's initial reaction, outright fear, was being replaced by a steely resolve to kick this guy's ass. Hard. All the way back to Russia, if that's where he came from.

As a crime reporter, she'd faced down plenty of dangerous men, and every single one had ultimately regretted coming after her, because they wound up spending a lot more time behind bars.

They also gave her all the target practice she needed for this latest imported version. Gathering her thoughts, she decided that her next step would be what she had done last time she faced the death penalty: Call in the cavalry. *I ain't gonna wait to call Brennan like last time. That almost got me killed.*

CHAPTER TWENTY-SEVEN

NYPD Headquarters
One Police Plaza
Manhattan
Sunday, December 14
8:25 P.M.

"Kim! This is a surprise. On a Sunday evening, no less."

"I need your help."

"I'm off at nine. Can it wait a half hour?"

"No."

"Where are you?"

"Yoshi. Japanese place near me.

"Location?"

"Bedford Avenue, off North Eighth."

"Stay there."

Barbieri and Chief Brennan had been friends with very frequent benefits, once, but not in a long time. Not since she took that detour several years ago to Miami, after helping him put away a crazy-ass, cold-blooded murderer in Brooklyn.

They still understood each other, though. Still knew how to read between each other's lines, and he heard something in her voice that he hadn't heard before. Except maybe once, years before, when she went out alone to meet and greet that homicidal psychopath in Prospect Park.

He closed his laptop, grabbed his jacket, and rode the elevator down from the fourth floor to the garage in the One Police Plaza basement. Police Headquarters was in lower Manhattan, just across the East River from her neighborhood in Brooklyn, and he got to Yoshi in under fifteen minutes. Traffic delays were not an issue when traffic laws were optional and your car had an ear-shattering siren and a flashing red light to make lesser mortals clear a path for you. It was good to be the Chief, at least when you had no choice but to pull rank.

Between the time he'd left his office, and the time he reached the restaurant, it had rained pretty hard. Brennan parked the car by a hydrant about forty feet from Yoshi's door and rushed over, his left hand holding an old newspaper over his head in a totally useless attempt to keep dry and warm against the near-freezing rain, his right hand on the grip of the pistol strapped to his waist. He got under the restaurant's awning within seconds, but before opening the door, he stopped to calm himself down. Even though it had been years since he last responded to a crime in real time, he knew enough to avoid making a bad situation worse by acting without thinking.

Barbieri, who had been staring at the front door since her call, waved rapidly to him as he entered, got up from her stool, and strode over to meet him at the entrance. She had already paid the bill and had her coat on and zippered up, so they went straight back out the door and ran over to his car, dodging raindrops as best they could. Neither said a word, Brennan understanding instinctively that with Barbieri, getting her away from danger was more critical than talking about it.

Once they were both settled in the car, he drove over to her building, again parked within ticketing distance of a hydrant, and jogged with her to the front entrance. Both now soaking wet and miserably cold, he waited as she tried and failed to enter her apartment code on the lobby door keypad, which would unlock the door. Unlike in her old place in Fort Greene, where she'd lived when they were an item, he couldn't let himself in with his own key.

After two or three fumbling tries, she finally opened the lobby door, and they entered the elevator waiting for them on the ground floor. They reached her floor, and as soon as they entered her apartment–while standing in the hallway with their coats still on–Barbieri began opening up to Brennan about everything that she'd just experienced.

She told him about going to the park, the restaurant, the man she'd seen in both locations, and his charade of strangling her to death. Only after she finished telling all did Brennan help her take her dripping-wet coat off, then his own. She sat down on the far end of the sofa, just staring at the floor.

"The bathroom?" he asked her.

She looked up and pointed with her chin toward the hallway. He left her field of vision for a few seconds as he carried both coats to the bathroom and draped them over the shower curtain to dry. He then quickly came back to the living room and sat down on the opposite end of the sofa. He kept quiet, waiting for a signal from her that she was ready to resume their conversation.

"I got used to dealing with bad actors, Timothy, when I worked for the *News* and the *Herald*. Some of those bozos actually liked the free publicity, even though they were too fuckin' illiterate to read what I wrote themselves. Reporters like me gave them street cred."

"But some of them jamokes took exception to what you wrote, right? You were threatened, as I recall. I also remember that after a few threats, you grew a pair. Gotta say I admired that in you."

"Thanks, Timothy. 'Balls of steel'... I believe those were the words you used. Just what a girl wants to hear. I was indeed threatened more than once, which was just part of the job. But you're right. I stopped losing any sleep over them after a while, and the ass-wipes just wound up getting more jail time. But Russians...?"

"You're assuming he's Russian, and that he's coming after you because of the story you're doing? You didn't hear him say anything, did you?"

Barbieri debated with herself only a moment before answering. "No, I did not. Now, I'm not sure if he's gonna kill me because of the story we've been doing in the *Journal*, or because I've been looking into Lededev's disappearing act. That Russian's purchases are not part of the story, and I've been investigating him on my own time."

"You're freelancing, Kim? Can't help yourself."

"Guilty."

"Does your editor know?"

"About me drawing outside the lines? No, he doesn't."

"You'd better tell him."

"I will."

"Look, Kim, the act this ass-wipe just pulled is not just fun and games. If he is in fact Russian and gets his way, you're going to die, and he wants you to know you're going to die."

"All true. But I saw his face, so I'd recognize him easy."

"Kim, he doesn't give a shit if you could pick him out of a lineup. He isn't like the garden variety shitheads who used to want to kill you. Before leaving the motherland, these guys did time in the gulag-a brutal place. After those hell holes, our own prisons don't scare them much."

"Maybe. He has no clue, however, that I've been here before. I ain't in the least intimidated by death threats, and I never will be. Trust me on this, Timothy. I'm not really afraid of him, or of being killed by him. When I was reporting on gangbangers and mafioso for the *News*, I didn't really mind the fact that I was sometimes putting myself in danger. It was kind of thrilling, in a way, like I was as much as a part of the action as the cops and the perps were. But that grew old pretty quick, which is why I leaped at the chance of working for the *Journal*. I thought that by investigating accountant types and quarterly statements, the only risk to me was being bored to death."

"Not anymore, it isn't. Now, you've put a big fat target on your back, Kim. That thrilling enough for you?"

"Kinda. I'll need a bodyguard, though, Timothy."

"You'll need more than one, and we'll take care of that in the morning. But it might not matter much, because he'll find a way around them. Besides, this guy may not be just a garden-variety thug with a rap sheet written in Cyrillic. He could be special forces."

"You mean like Navy Seals? Delta Force?"

"Even more dangerous, because these Russian motherfuckers have no principles holding them back. They're assassins for hire, killing machines.

Putin sends them wherever he wants just to cause trouble, and they'll murder an enemy without a second thought."

"Only now it's at the behest of crime bosses who pay a lot more than the communists ever did. So which half is this guy?"

"I'd operate as if he were special forces, if I were you. And defend yourself accordingly."

"Hope for the best and prepare for the worst."

"Worse than you or I can imagine. I'll take the second bedroom, Kim."

"Thank you, Captain," Barbieri said as she sidled over on the sofa close enough to Brennan to embrace him. He embraced her first. "Try to get some sleep, Kim. I'll see you in the morning."

After ending their hug, she rose from the sofa and walked over to her bedroom, while Brennan made his way to the spare one. "I'll be right here, Kim. Nobody's coming after you tonight," he said over his shoulder.

"He'd be fuckin' crazy if he did. I think he's just biding his time, waiting for the right moment. Like you just said, these bastards are tenacious."

"Oh, he'll be back, or he's got to answer to his minders in Moscow."

"I'm not running, Timothy. If he comes back, I'm willing to bet that if one of us ends up dead, it will not be me."

"I'm not betting against you, Kim. I never have, and never will."

CHAPTER TWENTY-EIGHT

Wall Street Journal Headquarters
Manhattan
Monday, December 15
7:30 A.M.

"Hey, Mr. Fitzgerald," Barbieri announced, as she gently rapped on her editor's open door. She had been driven from her home to the paper's headquarters by Brennan, who again used his siren and lights to encourage other drivers to let him through–or else.

Brennan pulled up in front of the building on Avenue of the Americas and parked, oblivious to the No Parking, No Stopping, No Standing, No Nothing signs that mere mortal drivers had to obey. He then asked her to stay in the car as he got out, eyeballed everyone walking or standing nearby, and determined that there were no evil-doers ready to smite her.

Satisfied that it was safe, he then escorted her into the building, accompanied her through the security checkpoint and onto the elevator to her floor, and remained by her side even as she opened the glass door to the outer office. Only when she walked past reception, into the office proper, did he let her out of his sight–but not before giving her a hug and telling her he'll be on standby, just a text away.

He then rode the elevator back down to the street, left the building, and drove to his office several miles away, in Lower Manhattan. Not in any hurry to get back to his day job, he left the sirens and flashing lights off as he made his way to police headquarters.

The chess pieces could wait.

. . .

"Have a seat, Kim. I'll be right with you," said Mr. Fitzgerald as he put the finishing touches on an email and pressed send.

"Sofa okay?" his newest hire asked, noting the choice was there or one of the uncomfortable-looking chairs facing his desk.

"That's why it's there," he said, without looking up from the screen. Barbieri walked over to his sofa and sat at the far end.

About one minute after she came into his office, another woman joined them. She was a short, stocky African-American wearing the security department uniform–white shirt, red tie, gray slacks and navy-blue jacket– accented by her steely don't-fuck-with-me demeanor. Barbieri did not recognize her at first, so she glanced at her *Journal* ID badge to see her name and title. Stella Green, Director of Security.

"Kim, Stella. Stella, Kim. My newest ace reporter." Mr. Fitzgerald made the introductions after Green closed his office door, shook hands with Barbieri, and sat on the other side of the couch from her.

"Pleased to meet you, Kim," Green said.

"Likewise, Stella," Barbieri replied. "Although I wish it was under different circumstances."

Turning to Fitzgerald, she asked, "Does my benefits package include bodyguards? I think I need one. I know I need one."

"We know you do, as well," Green interjected before the editor had a chance to answer. "They came after Mr. Leotta. Now you. But they will *not* succeed, I assure you."

"I know they won't. I've gotten death threats before, plenty of them, and I'm still here."

"We don't need another Danny," Fitzgerald added.

Seeing that Green was obviously up on current events, her boss got right to item one on the meeting's agenda. The 'Danny' he was referring to was Daniel Pearl, the *Journal* reporter who had been kidnapped and beheaded in Pakistan a few years before. He'd been investigating jihadists there, and to the terrorists, American reporters were a legitimate target. Pearl was Jewish, too, which meant that his Jihadist killers got bonus points for taking him off the battlefield.

"No, we do not." On hearing the name of Daniel Pearl, Green looked down and wiped at her eyes to keep a tear from forming. She was clearly struggling to keep her composure.

"I have to be honest here, Mr. Fitzgerald. I don't think it's our dirty foreign money story that's put me on their hit list, or just that I talked to Leotta."

"Then what was it?"

"It was that I asked Leotta about Maxim Lebedev."

"Who's Maxim ...?" Stella asked.

"Lebedev," Fitzgerald said. "He's one of the Russian buyers we were looking at, but we decided not to include him in our article. He's disappeared on us, anyway. On Kim. He's dead, probably."

"Then why would the Russians want to come after you, Kim?"

"Because I decided to find ..."

Fitzgerald jumped in before Barbieri finished her thought. "It doesn't matter whether she was wandering off the reservation, Stella. We protect our own, particularly when it's terrorists who want you dead and buried."

"I agree, Mr. Fitzgerald. Completely," Green replied, then turned to face Barbieri. "Kim, we're assigning a security team to protect you."

"Bodyguards."

"Not in our lexicon, but yes. Security professionals embedded with you twenty-four seven. Even with them, let's not take any chances. For the time being, you're going to be working from home full-time."

"The security team. Who are they? They work here?"

"They do work here. You'll probably recognize them when you meet."

"Got it. So, I'm under house arrest. Nice. Isn't there another way, Stella?"

"It's your new reality, Kim. You can go as far as Starbucks for coffee, or a diner close by for lunch, as long as the team goes with you. Pick up groceries, or better yet have them delivered. That's about it. The security team will escort you back and forth."

"No more field trips to Russia?"

"Maybe when we've eliminated the threat. And we will eliminate the threat, I assure you. We have to be extra careful, at least until we figure out what those Russians know about you, Kim," Green explained.

"Cop friend of mine told me the Russians won't give up trying."

"They might not, but we'll make damn sure they won't succeed."

"We need you alive and well," her editor added.

"How many bedrooms?"

"In my apartment? Two. One's my office, actually."

"Not anymore. You live alone?"

"I do."

"Not anymore. You now have a roommate. Two roommates, in fact. You have a car?"

"Nope. I take cabs and the subway everywhere, and Uber once in a while."

"Okay. If you have to go the corner to pick up a pack of cigarettes or a container of milk, they walk with you. No exceptions. If you do have to go anywhere that's beyond walking distance, they take you in their vehicle. No exceptions. Understood?"

"Understood, Stella. Yes, ma'am." Barbieri knew Green meant every word, and would not take well to having her threat management skills questioned. Or to minimizing the danger she herself was now in. This was not a moment for bravado, false or otherwise.

"If they want you dead, Kim, it may not be because of Lebedev. It could mean we're onto something with this story," Thomas Fitzgerald added. "The more we expose their crimes, the more pissed off they'll get."

"And the more dangerous they'll get."

"Danny Pearl."

"Danny Pearl. We didn't protect him–enough, anyway–and we let the terrorists turn his wife into a widow. Now you're going to go home and write your ass off, Kim…"

"… with an escort," Green interjected.

"Go home, Kim. I'll tell everyone else on the team you're safe and sound." Fitzgerald turned to Green. "Stella, would you excuse us?"

"Of course," the Director of Security replied, gathering her papers, rising from the sofa and walking out into the hall. As soon as she was out of earshot, Fitzgerald's demeanor switched from boss to protector. He got up out of his office chair and sat down next to Barbieri on the couch.

"Kim. I don't care why they're after you. The money-laundering, or Lebedev."

"I should have listened to you, Thomas." She saw his gesture as permission to drop the 'Mr. Fitzgerald' rule.

"Perhaps so, Kim, but it doesn't matter now. Water under the bridge, in my opinion. If it was, in fact, your snooping around about Lebedev that's got them riled up, it's only a matter of time before the article comes out. And I expect that'll make them want to kill us all, me included. Especially me, I'd like to think."

"And then the paper will have to protect the entire team. I'm not in trouble with management?"

"Not at all, Kim. Protecting our reporters is mission critical around here. It's the new normal, as far as everyone here's concerned. For now, Kim, go to your office and get your things."

Barbieri rose from the couch, shook Fitzgerald's hand, and walked out into the hall toward her own cubicle. As she made her way, she was joined by a security officer she didn't recognize at first, because he was out of the usual company uniform that rendered them invisible day to day. Instead, he wore chinos, a black form-fitting tee shirt and running shoes, and carried a duffel bag. The officer looked to be about thirty and was clearly in excellent shape. Fit and alert, and not to be messed with. While she was glad to see him, she wondered whether he was enough, by himself, to hold off the Russian mob.

"Miss Barbieri."

"Kim, please. You my hero?"

"More like your shadow. You'll get used to me. Us."

"There's more than one of you, I was told."

"We come in a set, and my partner will meet us at your building."

"Got it. Why the bag?"

"Tools of the trade. I'll do a show-and-tell for you later."

"Oh, goody. You carrying?"

"Can't reveal that."

The cops Barbieri had dealt with at the *News* and at the *Herald* never made a big deal about being armed. Their weapon was just another tool in their tool belt, like zip ties and two-way radios, with one big difference. It was never fired, and almost never pointed at anybody.

What had always been drilled into them was that if a cop ever drew his weapon, he'd lost control of the situation, and he'd better have a good reason for doing so. Until that's determined after a thorough review by Internal Affairs, and the shooting was found to be justified, he rides a desk.

Instead of heading to the Fiftieth Street Rockefeller Center station, which she'd used every day, twice a day, when she went to the office to work, Barbieri was led by the guard out the side entrance on Forty-seventh Street.

"Where are we going?"

"Your commute just got easier."

He escorted her to a black Chevy Suburban. the beast big shots are always photographed coming out of, waiting at the curb along with other limos, taxis, Uber cars, and food carts that catered to the hundreds of employees who fill up all the office buildings in midtown Manhattan.

The guard opened the rear door, eyes darting all around him, held it open as Barbieri slid into the back seat, then carefully closed it. He then made his way around to the other side of the car, opened the driver's side front door, then stopped again to look up the street, then down. Satisfied that they weren't being tailed, he sat himself down behind the wheel and closed the door.

"This thing bulletproof?"

"No, ma'am. You're safe as long as you stay inside, though. That's all I can say."

"Stop with the 'ma'am', please."

"I'll try. Some clients prefer being called 'ma'am' and 'sir.' This is not my first day on the job."

"I see that. As long as we're going to be buddy-buddies, would you care to introduce yourself?"

"Carl. Reynolds."

It was clear he would say no more. Conversation would only distract from his mission, which was to get her from point A to point B in one piece.

Reynolds was not one of the ordinary guards who checked out anyone going through the security gauntlet in the *Journal* building's lobby. He was a well-trained, military-grade pro, and his only job was to keep alive the client he'd been assigned to protect, whether that meant taking a bullet or turning a murder attempt into a suicide mission. He did it well, always finding the right balance between protecting his clients and letting them live their life as if he wasn't there.

Barbieri was not exactly pleased with the arrangement, but she understood completely why it was necessary. She was never one to back down from a bad situation, but her employer was taking zero chances. She didn't take her resentment out on Reynolds, of course, knowing he was just doing his job,

"Mind if I smoke?" Reynolds took a pack of cigarettes from his shirt pocket and looked at her in his rearview mirror.

"I do. Sorry. I'm allergic." She looked in the mirror, but saw only his eyes looking back. That was a white lie. She wasn't allergic to cigarette smoke, or any other allergy trigger for that matter. She just couldn't stand the smell of it.

"No problem." For the next thirty-seven minutes, they rode in silence, Reynolds behind the wheel and Barbieri sitting behind him, as they made their way from midtown Manhattan to her home in Brooklyn. The ride, which was stop-and-go despite being against traffic in the middle of the day, gave her plenty of time to think about what had happened to her since the night before at the restaurant. *Me? Now I need a bodyguard? W T fuckin' F?*

CHAPTER TWENTY-NINE

10 North 10th Street
Brooklyn
Monday, December 15
9:30 A.M.

Even as the company Suburban stopped at the curb in front of her building, Barbieri turned her body toward the passenger side door and moved her hand to grasp the handle. Before she had time to pull it, though, Reynolds shifted the gear into park, turned back to face her and said, "Wait here, please. Do not open the door."

His tone was even, conversational, more parental than threatening, but she took it as a command from the alpha male of the situation she'd found herself in. With his self-confident, I'm-in-charge-here demeanor, Reynolds had learned early on that there was rarely any need to raise his voice.

Accepting that she was in a protective bubble she didn't dare break out of, Barbieri turned back into her seat and sat absolutely still. Reynolds left the engine on and turned his head back toward the windshield.

The reporter noticed a man and a woman coming towards the Suburban, both young and fit like Reynolds. Both had their down jackets open, and from what she could see, they were both wearing the same security uniform underneath and had gun holsters at their waist, tucked behind their belts. Only the woman, however, was carrying a company duffel bag like Reynolds had.

Barbieri had always had nothing but admiration for strong women. She herself was one damn strong one who had always more than held her own among her alpha male peers. But there was something about having one in her home, sharing her kitchen and bathroom, that made her a little uncomfortable. *My other roommate's a woman? Will we be competing for Reynolds' affection? This should be interesting.*

As the two guards reached the driver's side window, Reynolds pressed the button to lower hers, and Barbieri heard him and the other male exchange a couple of words she couldn't quite make out. They were both speaking softly, and urgently, in some kind of security agent double secret code. Then, Reynolds grabbed his duffel from the front seat and made his way out of the vehicle, with the other man moving over a bit to give him room to maneuver.

The woman, who had been standing silently off to the side closer to the back seat, then opened the passenger side rear door, offered Barbieri her hand to help her climb out, and closed the car door behind her.

As the other guard stood watch over the Suburban, Reynolds and his partner escorted Barbieri toward the building entrance, keeping her between them to hide her as much as possible from view, and kept their eyes peeled for anything suspicious as she punched in her code on the keypad.

Once the lobby door opened for them, they faced the elevator just inside the entrance. It was a small, narrow building, with the elevator shaft taking up most of the ground floor. The lobby was empty and quiet. Barbieri pushed the elevator button and the guards, as they were waiting for it to come down, kept looking around the lobby and the street outside for anything that didn't belong. Nothing set off any alarms. Nothing didn't belong.

The elevator doors opened and, satisfied they weren't being followed, the guards and their client took the elevator up to her floor. When the elevator reached it, they got out and walked in over to Barbieri's apartment, with the guards walking slightly behind, silently, as only she knew which door was hers. There were only two apartments on each floor, so there was a fifty-fifty chance they would have been wrong, anyway.

After she opened the door and all three were inside the apartment, Barbieri turned on the lights. She then glanced at Reynolds' waist and spotted the holster she had not noticed before. *They're both carrying. Everyone's got a fuckin' gun but me.*

The two guards strode over to the living room windows and inspected them to make sure they were locked, then lowered and closed the blinds. It was still light outside, but why take chances? All business, no chit-chat. They then did the same to the floor-to-ceiling glass door to the patio off the living room. The potential access points from outside now secure, the two bodyguards checked the doors and windows in her bedroom and the second bedroom slash home office, the bathroom and all the closets. Their movements were perfectly choreographed after years of working together. Efficient and thorough and done. No monsters hiding in their client's closets or under her bed.

"Clear."

"Clear."

"We're in the penthouse, right?'

"Top floor, I'll admit to. Not 'Penthouse.' That ain't me."

Reynolds then pressed several number icons on his cell, waited a moment, and said "Clear" to the person the other end. For the third guard standing by outside, that was the signal that he was free to return to their office at *Journal* headquarters.

"Access to the roof?" her female guard asked.

"Not from here. From the stairway in the hall. Neighbors go up there sometimes, but usually only in nice weather. Whenever they're up there, you can hear their footsteps on my ceiling."

"Ever hear anyone else walking up there when the weather's not so nice? Repairmen? Con Ed?"

"Once in a while, but nothing strange."

"Any burglaries in the building?"

"Haven't heard of any."

"OK. We'll check it all out later today or in the morning."

With the threat level looking just about non-existent, the two security guards took their coats off and took seats on the sofa opposite Barbieri, and

Reynolds felt free to make the introductions. The female guard reached out to shake Barbieri's hand.

"I'm Connie. Connie Shelton."

"Kim. Welcome to my home, Connie."

"Nice to meet you, Kim." She nodded toward her duffel bag. "Where should I put my stuff?"

"Stella told me you'd also be staying here. How long do you guys think?"

"That's all to be determined. Depends on how things develop. Mind if I take the second bedroom? Carl? Okay with you?"

"Sure. Sofa looks comfortable enough," Reynolds answered.

"By the way, Carl. You were going to tell me about the tools of your trade."

"Right. I did. It's pretty standard stuff." Reaching into his own duffel, he took out his inventory one by one. "Besides a change of clothing, I got a flashlight... walkie-talkie in case Connie and I get separated... pepper spray... night stick... extra set of keys... zip tie handcuffs. Most of this equipment I've never had to use, though."

"Likewise," Shelton added. "They're all weapons of last resort. Gandhi got the whole non-violence thing from us." Tapping her noggin, she added, "Fact is, by using what's up here first, rough stuff ain't ever needed."

"You two have obviously worked together before. Am I right?"

"We're partners, yes," Shelton replied.

"Same with the cops I used to cover." She gestured toward Shelton's weapon.

"You ever had to point that at anybody?"

"No."

"Not yet, anyway. Not in our job description," Reynolds added.

"Again, same with the cops," Barbieri said. "Perps knowing you're carrying is enough to make them reconsider their chosen profession."

"Our job is *not* to get in any situation where they're needed. If we do, we've failed," Reynolds said.

"Got it. So, make yourselves at home, my new best friends. Two things, though. I've got almost nothing for you to eat. At least right now. We'll all go to the supermarket tomorrow, if that's okay with you. By the way, I hope you guys can cook. Because I can't."

"We'll manage, Kim. There a deli nearby?" Reynolds asked. "Coffee place?"

"Maddy's. Right around the corner on Bedford."

"Then, we're good. We won't starve, at least."

The guards refrained from commenting on the décor, which was from another era. Literally. She had decorated her twenty-first century home with early twentieth century furnishings that followed her wherever she had lived. The sofa, the table and chairs, the lamps were all straight out of old black-and-white photos of middle-class Brooklyn A-listers. That was Barbieri's style. *If guests have a hard time dealing with the contrast, they can leave.*

"The second thing? No smoking, right?" Shelton asked, taking a cigarette from behind her ear.

"No, Connie. Sorry," Reynolds answered for their client. Shelton tucked the cigarette back behind her ear.

"So, how do we do this? Without killing each other, I mean?" Barbieri asked.

"Stay out of each other's way."

"Or ignore us."

"Got it. You're my new roommates, and neither of you are here."

"That about sums it up. Seriously, Kim, we've been here before, and nobody's feathers were ever ruffled."

"Okay. I'll adjust. So, what do you guys really think? Your boss isn't watching you. Am I vulnerable here?"

"You're vulnerable everywhere, Kim, even here. Your home is where the men who are after you know you'll be. They do their research before they go in for the kill. We're just improving your odds of not waking up dead."

"By decreasing their ability to get close enough to attack you. They might murder us instead, of course..."

"Guess that's what you signed up for, right? All right then, I'm now living in a safe house."

"A *safer* house, more accurately. You are not totally safe." Barbieri got up from her chair and took two steps toward the window.

"Please don't, Kim. Try to avoid all the windows, if you can, and please stay off the patio. We don't know what firearms they have, or whether they're in buildings on the next block that face this one. But we do know they're excellent snipers."

"Understood." Barbieri stopped where she was, looked at Shelton and turned toward the kitchen, where she turned on the tap, filled a carafe, poured the water into a coffeemaker, and set it to start automatically before she got up the next morning.

"Espresso OK in the morning?"

They both nodded.

"If it's OK with you, I'm going to go to lie down. There's room in the hall closet for your coats, I think. Sheets and towels are there," she said, pointing to an old wooden cabinet in the hall that must have held food or tools in an earlier life. "And blankets. Carl, you'll have to do the best you can with what I've got. Sorry."

"No need to apologize, Kim. I'll survive, I'm fairly sure. But it's only eight o'clock. Is it us?"

"Nope. It's me. This whole thing is stressing me out, and I need some quiet time. I'm going to finish the story I'm working on for another hour, maybe, and send it to my boss. Then beddy-bye. What are you two planning for me in the morning?"

"Just to never let you out of our sight."

"That shouldn't be too hard. Tomorrow's my day off, assuming my boss doesn't ask me to rewrite anything. So, I... we... will do weekend stuff. Groceries, like we said. Bookstore, maybe, or just hanging around. With your permission, of course."

"You'll be on a short leash. I believe Stella made that clear."

"Totally clear. I get it."

"But wherever you go, we'll stay out of your way."

"While never leaving my side. Got it. A few years ago, the NYPD assigned cops to protect me. Undercover. They tried to blend into the background and failed miserably, because I made every one of them."

"We're both trained in the fine art of blending into the background, Kim. If we find we have to be right next to you, we'll give you a heads-up. Later on, when we're all back home..."

"... safe and sound..."

"... we'll compare notes."

"See if there's anything we can do to improve your odds next time." Barbieri turned toward her bedroom. "Until tomorrow, though, I'll be out of your sight. 'Night."

At that, Barbieri walked into her bedroom, and closed the door behind her. As she wrote and rewrote her follow-up story on the Russian real estate scams, she reminded herself that she was never one to follow orders blindly, especially from controlling men. Nobody told her what to do unless she gave them permission beforehand. But this... this was a whole new level of control she'd have a hard time getting used to. *Now I've got a woman watching over me, too. And they're in my home. I can't fuckin' escape. Like it or not, these two are in control. Not me.*

CHAPTER THIRTY

10 North 10th Street
Brooklyn
Tuesday, December 16
7:15 A.M.

Barbieri sprung out of bed the next morning and went straight to the bathroom in the hall, out of sight of her new best friends in the living room.

When she was done there, she returned to her bedroom, looked in the full-length mirror to make sure she was decent—or as decent as her old, worn, red flannel pajamas would allow—then walked out into the living room. She'd expected to see either Reynolds asleep on the sofa, or both he and Shelton having coffee and checking their e-mail, but she found herself alone, in the dark, as the window shades were still pulled down. *Shit! Where are those guys? They left me by myself? Wait. They went out to Maddy's to pick up something to eat! Nothing to worry about. I'm safe. I'm sure of it. But shouldn't Reynolds have stayed here while Shelton went out? Or vice versa? Shit!*

Then she heard something behind her that set off the alarm system in her brain, a metal-on-metal clicking noise coming from the door to her apartment. She turned around at the sound of the door lock opening, which she'd never really noticed when it had been she who was doing the unlocking. Her eyes widened in fear as the front door opened, and light from the hallway flooded her living room, but to her relief, Reynolds and Shelton walked in and shut the door behind them.

"Hey, Kim."

"Where the fuck you guys go? I didn't know you left." As long as they were roomies, Barbieri thought they wouldn't object to her salty language. She was sure they'd heard worse.

"We didn't go far, Kim. Just up to the roof to assess access to your terrace. We tried not to wake you."

"You did a good job. I didn't hear one footstep over me in the bedroom. Fuckin' ninjas, you two. So, can you get to my terrace from up there?"

"I'd say, no. It's close to impossible to climb down from the roof."

"'Close to impossible' is not the same as 'impossible.' Full stop."

"You're right, Kim. Let's say there are too many risks for them to try it. Like being seen, for one. The roof is wide open, all three hundred and sixty degrees. If he comes after you again, it won't be from the roof. Probably."

"Some other access point, maybe, but not from there."

"Probably."

Shelton, noticing that the coffee machine was still on, grabbed a clean mug from the dish drainer, poured herself a mug-full, then walked over to the living room window and opened the shades. There, she grabbed her industrial strength binoculars and went on the lookout for evil-doers, switching back and forth between the binoculars and her naked eyes. The window looked out on the street, but the top floor was too high to offer a good view of any suspicious characters walking nearby, and the view of the building entrance straight below her apartment was cut off entirely.

Reynolds grabbed a mug of his own, but rather than look out a window, he sat on a stool at the kitchen counter and opened his laptop.

After grabbing an apple from the fruit bowl on the counter, Barbieri joined Shelton by the window.

"You guys are here every day, twenty-four seven, right?"

"Not for long, probably. We usually switch off with other guards every couple of days. One of our men'll rotate in, and Carl or I will rotate out. Keeps us vigilant, which keeps you alive."

"You mean I've got to train new bodyguards all over again? Shit."

"Not for two weeks, at least. Depends on what we tell our boss. But when we rotate out, it'll be just one person at a time. Either Carl or myself will always be here, and we'll make sure the replacement knows the drill. You have our word on that, Kim."

Satisfied, Barbieri walked over to the front door and turned the dead-bolt, an act that caused Reynolds to leap up and rush toward her.

"Hold it, Kim! Don't unlock that!"

"I was just getting the paper. This is when my neighbor usually leaves it for me. I should have told you. Sorry."

"I'll open it." With that, Carl turned the knob, opened the door, and stuck his head out to look up and down the hallway. Only then did he look down to see the *New York Times* lying on her doormat. He picked it up and brought it inside.

"Here you go." Reynolds gave her the paper, then walked over to the counter, closed his laptop and took up a position by the other window facing the street.

"Sorry, Carl. I've got to get used to this." She then walked over to the cabinet, turned on her battered old stereo, and put an LP of Puccini's *Tosca* on the turntable. She had several recordings of that opera, but this one, a performance by the Royal Opera, had become her favorite.

"I hope you don't mind. You told me to act like you're not here."

"We don't. Just keep the volume down in case."

"In case my assassin's a total klutz. Got it."

"*Tosca*. Okay, as Italian operas go. Not Puccini's best." Shelton was being provocative, but in a teasing way. She glanced at Barbieri's collection of vinyl, which had been made obsolete decades before. And at her battered old record player, which was almost a museum piece. They were both doomed first by CDs, then by Alexa. "I see your home entertainment system matches the décor. There's a theme here."

"Pre-twenty-first century, that's the theme. I have a problem letting go. Just, okay? Connie? *Tosca*?" In that instant, the relationship between her and Shelton evolved a bit. Whatever ice there was, their shared appreciation of Italian opera broke it. Barbieri always gave people in her life, male or female, bonus points if they were fans. These days, among the colleagues she worked with and friends she hung with, they were pretty rare.

"Somehow, I didn't think you were the type, Connie."

"I am. I always dreamed of being a diva when I was little, taking bows and getting bouquets. Real girlie stuff. Until I found out I can't sing to save my life. The singing lessons my mom and dad made me take would never change that."

"Now you're in security, protecting damsels in distress."

"My other dream. That one came true."

"Don't knock it. Opera's a tough business." She pointed to her collection of LPs. "Be my guest. Pick any album you'd like to hear."

"I was hoping you'd say that. I peeked before, and they're mostly Italian. A few token Germans. But otherwise, all Italian."

"That's an improvement for me. It used to be one hundred percent Italian. Every single one. I was extremely prejudiced, or perhaps just small-minded."

"Also, you have a lot of operas I didn't know existed. Who the hell is Pacini?"

"Giovanni Pacini. He wrote *L'ultimo giorno di Pompei.* It's got everything, Love, betrayal, adultery, revenge and a volcano."

"Let me guess. Pompeii."

"Yep. Mount Vesuvius. I started collecting recordings of operas nobody's ever heard of, by composers nobody's ever heard of. Most of them, the world's better off without them, to be honest. To me, they're totally unlistenable, but one or two you might even like."

"May I...?" Without waiting for their owner's reply, Shelton walked over to the bookcase holding the collection and sat cross-legged on the floor in front of it. She then started pulling out one sleeve after another, reading the front and then the copy on the back, and returning it to its rightful place.

"Here's another nobody. Montemezzi."

"*L'Amore dei Tre Re.* You might like that one, if you're into strangling and poisoning your relatives."

"That thought's occurred to me, more than once."

While the female guard studied the collection, Barbieri plotzed down on the sofa, tucked her legs beneath her, and devoured whatever she could get from her cell phone–texts, email, news, tweets–without falling into the trap of constantly refreshing each page. That finally done, she got herself another mug and began the *Times* crossword… always the first order of the day.

"When are we heading out to the supermarket, Kim," Reynolds asked.

"I'd say one, maybe a quarter after. That okay with you two?"

"Yup," Shelton said.

Shelton and Reynolds gave her as much space as a city apartment allowed, aware that it may not be enough for a woman used to living alone. Reynolds went back and forth between refilling his coffee mug and manning his post by the other window facing the street. They were not concerned with the windows in the two bedrooms, which all faced the back windows of the apartment building next door. High rent did not mean no New York views.

The guards were on the lookout for anything suspicious. Which car parked outside was not there the day before? Did anybody walking nearby look like he didn't belong? Was the Con Ed repairman in the Con Ed truck parked down the block an actual Con Ed repairman in an actual Con Ed truck?

From their vantage points by the window, neither guard could see the front door of Barbieri's building, or the sidewalk right in front. They could not see the man, wearing a black jacket, brown pants, and a gray baseball cap, who walked up to the entrance about 11:45 later that morning. They could not see the man press a button on the intercom panel by the front door. They could not see the man wait a moment, then press a second button after getting no response to the first. They could not see the man then wait a moment and press a third button. They could not hear the buzzer that opened the lock on the lobby door, nor see the man open the lobby door and go into the building.

CHAPTER THIRTY-ONE

10 North 10th Street
Brooklyn
Tuesday, December 14
10:47 A.M.

A few minutes before eleven in the morning, the reporter and her bodyguards were busy doing nothing in particular, with another justifiably-on-the-scrap-heap opera, *Iris* by Pietro Mascagni, playing in the background. Shelton and Barbieri listened silently, while Reynolds blocked it out with his headphones, listening to a podcast he found a little less harmful to his health.

When Barbieri's cell phone rang, she turned the record player off, then took the phone out of her back pocket, looked at the screen and recognized the name on the caller ID. But before hitting the 'accept' button, she looked at the two guards and gave a thumbs-up sign. They both nodded, and she hit the button and said, "Karen. Just thinking of you." She listened a few more seconds, and said, "Don't go anywhere. I'm putting you on mute."

She turned to Shelton and Reynolds. "Change of plans. Friend of mine wants to meet me for lunch."

"In the neighborhood?"

"Just a few blocks away. A pretty good burger place you might actually like."

"You won't know we're there. Neither of you."

Barbieri took the phone off mute, and said, "Sure. Burger Meister. Twelve-thirty? See ya then." She pressed the 'end call' button and headed over to the bathroom, and out of view of her minders.

"Forgot all about Karen. We hang maybe once a week, spur-of-the-moment kinda. Supermarket will still be there when we get back, I promise. So, how do we do this, guys?"

"We leave the building together," Shelton explained. "The three of us. And then Carl and I drop back a little. We'll follow from a distance, maybe ten, fifteen feet behind you. Standard Operating Procedure we've followed a thousand times."

"No deaths or dismemberments so far. People think we're just a couple, and ignore us," Reynolds added. "But if we see anybody get too close, we'll put ourselves between you and him in a hurry. Otherwise, like I said, just act like we're not there."

"Okay. Can I tell Karen?"

"About us? That's not a good idea."

"Got it. This is a biggie, though. We'll need about ten minutes to get there. So, we leave in fifteen."

"We'll be ready."

Thirteen minutes later, in the living room, Barbieri heard an 'ahem' coming from the direction of the front door. She had gone back on the couch, feeding her cell phone addiction, and glanced up to find her two bodyguards waiting for her with their jackets and hats already on. Despite the near-freezing temperature, Reynolds' coat was left open, Because of the near-freezing temperature, Connie's coat was zipped from her knees to her chin.

She got up off the sofa, then grabbed an empty plastic bottle off the kitchen counter and filled it with tap water. On the way to the front door, she pulled her light brown, well-used, walking around jacket out of the hall closet, Karen being a friend she did not need to impress, and put the water bottle in her messenger bag.

Before she could reach for the lock, Shelton raised her finger as if to say 'let me', and opened it first. Reynolds stood behind her as she looked up and down the hallway. Seeing nothing, she turned back to Reynolds and nodded. He nodded back, and they all headed out of the apartment and walked in silence, single file with Barbieri in the middle, to the elevator. The elevator car already happened to be on their floor, and they went non-stop to the lobby. There they made their way toward the front door, again in single file.

A few seconds after leaving the building, Barbieri kept up her steady pace, but the two guards slowed down a little to put some distance between themselves and their client, who seemed unaware that she was now walking by herself. As soon as she was about ten feet ahead, though, the guards picked up their pace to match hers. They were now walking at the same speed, with the guards always ten steps behind her.

Shelton and Reynolds were in position, waiting for trouble. Their two sets of eyes looked ahead of Barbieri, and to her right, and to her left. They repeated the same visual check, eyeballing anything and everything that could be even remotely amiss, again and again.

They did not have eyes in the back of their heads, however. If they did, they would have seen the man who'd left her apartment building ten seconds after they did. The man who was following them, and Barbieri, drawing no notice from passersby walking by him or past him. A huskily built man wearing a black jacket, brown pants, and a gray baseball cap.

CHAPTER THIRTY-TWO

Burger Meister bar and restaurant
188 Bedford Ave
Brooklyn
Tuesday, December 14
12:20 P.M.

As Barbieri and her posse-for-hire made their way down the street from her building, the man in the gray cap stayed safely behind. Out of sight. Joe Blow. Just another face in the mid-day crowd.

On weekends, even on not-so-warm-and-beautiful December days, the streets in her neighborhood were crowded with shoppers, errand-runners and hanger-outers given a forty-eight-hour pass for good behavior from their office or school. All these pedestrians made it harder for her body-guards to keep up with Barbieri, because that meant more people finding their way between them and her. But it made things a whole lot easier for the man in the gray cap. The crowded sidewalk served as a sort of camouflage for him, making it a lot more likely to observe her without being observed by her escorts.

At the first corner, as they waited for the light to change, Barbieri took the bottle of water from her messenger bag and had a sip. Although it was chilly out, she needed to hydrate sooner than she'd expected. When the light changed, she put the bottle back in her bag and all three then crossed the avenue to the far corner, with Barbieri in the lead.

When the man following them got to the corner, he went right, to the other side of the street, then crossed the avenue so he was now parallel to them on the same street, but still safely outside the guards' field of vision. He was now in the middle of a parade of other pedestrians strolling slowly, or window-shopping, or striding purposefully as if they had places to go and people to see. Assassin tradecraft one-oh-one: How to make yourself invisible.

For Barbieri, the next light remained green, so she and her bodyguards continued walking at the same pace. As did the man in the baseball cap across the street and slightly behind them. Barbieri continued down the street until she arrived at Burger Meister. She stopped and looked ahead of her, where she expected her friend to come from, as Reynolds and Shelton stopped to window shop, seemingly, at a consignment shop two storefronts, maybe seventeen feet, from the restaurant. Barbieri checked her watch.

The man in the gray cap, still across the street, continued walking. Tradecraft told him that the guards, now stopped, would no longer be looking just ahead and to the side, but behind them as well. Three hundred and sixty degrees of caution. The threat to their client's safety and well-being could come from any direction, they knew. The two guards did exactly what he'd expected them to do. He did not expect them to notice him, walking in plain sight among all the pedestrians walking up and down the street. He was not surprised that they apparently didn't because he knew his job as well as, or maybe better than, they knew theirs.

Barbieri, still standing in front of the restaurant, raised her hand and waved when she saw her friend Karen walking toward her from down the block. The woman, who looked about the same age as Barbieri, was dressed about the same, in a well-worn jacket and old running shoes. She met Barbieri in front, where they gave each other a quick hug and a smile, then walked inside the front door. The two guards looked up from window-shopping and saw their client and her friend leave their line of sight. As did the man, just across the avenue, whom the guards did not see.

Thirty seconds later, Reynolds and Shelton walked into the restaurant and were escorted to a table three tables away from the one where their client and her friend had been seated. Barbieri glanced at them as they passed, unnoticed by her friend, but otherwise didn't pay them any mind. Her minders draped their coats over the back of their chairs, then sat down, quickly scanned the menu, called their waitress over, and ordered. It was their lunchtime, too, and dawdling was not in their repertoire.

They glanced at Barbieri and her friend, and at the other customers, from time to time, but otherwise just enjoyed their lunch. Burger deluxe, medium well for him, turkey burger and chicken tortilla soup for her. They had a sixth sense for danger, and there didn't seem to be any among the many hipsters there.

Outside the restaurant, the man in the gray cap leaned against a tree about thirty feet from the restaurant, and waited. Nobody walking toward him from either direction, or past him, paid him any mind. He was a man waiting for his wife, or a father waiting for his daughter, or a nobody waiting for nothing in particular. Move along. Nothing to see here.

He waited for forty-five minutes, staying in one place, almost still, without drawing attention to himself. To passerby, he didn't seem to loiter for no apparent purpose. Then, he saw Barbieri and her friend come out of Burger Meister, followed a few moments later by the two bodyguards.

He would have told the security team, just as a professional courtesy, that they do not need to be so vigilant, as he was still in the surveillance-of-the-target stage of his assignment. Not the assassination stage, which would come soon enough. That would be implemented after he reported to his superiors what he'd observed about the target, and after they then came up with the weapon best suited to ending her existence.

He watched as the two women made small talk for a few seconds, gave each other a hug and an air-kiss, and went their separate ways, Barbieri apparently retracing her steps toward home. Seconds after she began her walk back home, he noticed the two guards follow her. As they made their way back to her apartment, so did he, the three of them completely unaware that a man assigned by the Russian mob to help plan Barbieri's assassination was as close as thirty feet away.

When they entered her building, and were outside his field of vision, the man in the gray cap continued walking past them as if he didn't have a care in the world. His mission was complete. He'd learned what he needed to learn about the target and her team of one male and one female bodyguard. It was time to report his findings.

CHAPTER THIRTY-THREE

10 North 10th Street
Brooklyn
Tuesday, December 14
1:15 P.M.

After they got out of the elevator on her floor, Barbieri and Reynolds waited in the hall, just outside her apartment door, as Shelton opened it and entered first to have a look-see. The guard went to the two bedrooms, where she opened both closet doors and looked under both beds, and to the bathroom, where she pulled back the shower curtain, before turning back toward the front door and calling out, "Clear!"

Barbieri and Reynolds took off their winter coats as they went inside, and put them in the closet on their way over to the living room. After adding her coat to theirs, Barbieri sat down on the sofa, her two minders taking chairs opposite her.

"Thanks for not ratting on us, Kim," Reynolds said.

"It came pretty easy, actually. I don't think I've ever kept anything from Karen before. I mean, ever. Which means you've turned me into a pretty good liar. A better liar than I thought I was, for sure."

"Having you lie by omission, we'll cop to. Anyway, it's pretty impressive, Kim." Shelton added. "Nice place, Burger Meister. Well worth a trip back there when this is all over."

"It'll be on me, friends. So, what do you guys think? Am I safe now? *Safer*, sorry. We didn't see the Russian guy, right?"

"Right. We didn't. But that doesn't mean he wasn't there," Reynolds replied. "It just means that if he was following us, and I suspect he was, he did a good job of blending in. These Russian agents know what they're doing."

"He changed his clothes, maybe dyed his hair," Shelton said. "Eyeglasses, or a beard, or putting lifts on his shoes to make him look taller. He could make himself totally unrecognizable to you, without too much effort"

"He could've been walking with somebody else. Another man, or a woman. And whatever he looked like today, he'll look different tomorrow. That's their modus operandi," Reynolds added, evaluating their adversary with his partner in front of an audience of one.

"My guess is he was alone, and made two discoveries. First one was, he saw that you now have bodyguards. One male and one female. So, he knows you've told your employer and maybe the police about the threat. And second, at that moment, just now, he was being cautious and held back. There would be plenty of time to go in for the kill later."

"Assuming he was acting alone," Reynolds added. "If he wasn't, it means they're much more determined to kill you. And that makes it much harder for us to ensure they don't. Either way, he's in no hurry right now. He's probably just doing surveillance, like she said, to see if you're ever vulnerable. Or ID locations where they can find you where you least expect it."

"Or when we're likely to let our guard down," Shelton added. "They know every target of theirs has one or two weak points they can exploit."

"He's like anybody doing any job. He doesn't want to make this any harder on himself than it needs to be. And he's not suicidal."

"He wouldn't have learned much today, anyway," Barbieri said, "other than I'm not a vegetarian. So, what now?"

"Now we sit and read, or watch the news, or go on tinder, or make some tea, or play another opera... anything you'd do when you have nothing to do."

"Except go out on the terrace. That's off limits. You guys going to allow me any privacy?"

"Outside of your bedroom and bathroom, nope. Sorry," Shelton replied.

"You go back to living all by your lonesome when we neutralize the threat," Reynolds added.

"You mean when he's dead?"

"Maybe not even then."

"What the hell does that mean?"

"It means that if we take this shithead out, who's to say his boss won't send another?"

"In which case, I'd rather let the motherfucker try and get it over with right now. Get him out in the open and kill him first."

"You're more confident about that than we are, Kim. But if they want you dead, the Russians don't care how many attempts it'll take. Or how many of their own have to die to make it happen."

"Then we have to kill enough of them to make them care, won't we?"

"Not 'we', Kim. It's me and Connie in harm's way. Out here in plain sight. Our lives are on the line, too. Maybe as much as yours."

So, who's protecting who, here? I thought it was just you two keeping me alive.

"You're right. These gangsters may have no choice but to take you both out to get to me. I humbly apologize. So, what now? Witness Protection? Does that even exist when the Russian mob is after you?"

"Worth considering. It'll put us out of work, but there's always another client with a target on his back."

"Uh, no. I'm not the hiding-in-the-desert-for-the-rest-of-my-life type."

CHAPTER THIRTY-FOUR

Unit 29155, Military Intelligence
Headquarters 161ˢᵗ Special Purpose
Specialist Training Center
Moscow
Saturday, December 17
11:11 P.M.

"Institute for Scientific Research Number Two."

"Nevski. I have the details you requested."

"On the termination you requested. I'm listening."

The surveillance that had been ordered on Barbieri was a success. The operative had given his superior a description of the target solid enough to pass on to the scientists creating the poison that would bring her life to a sudden, and painful, end. He could relay an estimate of her body mass, which would help them determine the dose of the poison needed to kill her. And a description of her diet, which would help them determine how it would enter her body, and what form it would take–pill, gas, liquid or lotion."

"The target is five feet, nine inches tall, approximately."

"Male?"

"No. Does gender mean anything?"

"It might to the Institute. What about her weight? Obese? Thin? Average?"

"Estimated fifty-seven kilograms. Sixty possibly."

"That helps. Age?"

"Fifty, fifty-five. Maybe a little younger. Hard to tell for sure with women who don't like anyone to know their actual age."

"Anything about her diet? What foods does she like?"

"Basic American shit. Ground beef. Baked goods. Coffee. Carries a bottle of water everywhere. She had Japanese seafood the other day. Salmon I believe. Beef today, based on the restaurant my operative observed her entering. Hamburger restaurant. That's all he's witnessed so far."

"Good, Nevski. That is enough for us, I believe. I'll get back to you if it isn't."

"OK. I'll have the operative continue surveilling the target and report anything additional that he finds."

"Yes, you will."

"One more thing. The target now has bodyguards. Two that we know of. One man and one woman. They will have to be neutralized before we attack the target."

"By neutralize you mean...?"

"Use any means necessary to ensure they do not interfere with our mission."

CHAPTER THIRTY-FIVE

10 North 10ʰ Street
Brooklyn
Monday, December 20
6:30 P.M.

As Barbieri was making a salad for herself in the kitchen, she heard the familiar you've-got-a-message 'ding' on her cell, which she'd placed on the counter within easy grabbing distance. As a reporter, she'd learned early on to never let it out of her reach. Glancing down at the display, she saw the message was from Brennan.

She turned to Shelton and Reynolds, who were intently staring at their own phones. "Hey guys. It's a friend of mine. Timothy Brennan. He wants to come over and see how I'm doing."

"Homicide. NYPD. Right? You know him?" Shelton asked.

"I do, very well," the reporter said. "We bonded over corpses back when I covered bad guys doing bad things at the *News*. He ran Brooklyn South Homicide then. If there was a dead body in his part of the borough, we'd run into each other at the crime scene, especially if the homicide was so weird his detectives needed adult supervision. Which happened a lot. Now, Brennan's Chief of Detectives for the whole damn city."

"All of New York City? And he's checking up on you? I'm impressed," Reynolds said.

"I grew on him. Okay if he comes by?"

"Don't see the harm. Sure." With that, Barbieri replied to his text and put the phone back down on the counter.

"He should be here in maybe half an hour."

"If I may ask, Kim. This is no homicide. What's his interest here?" Reynolds asked.

"Strictly personal. I told him about the Russian stalker. First person I called, actually."

"He's just a friend, though?"

"Yep. And my personal cavalry." Barbieri saw no need to reveal to her bodyguards that she and Brennan had once been friends with frequent benefits. "When I was at the *News*, I interviewed a lot of scumbags. Real pieces of shit. Whenever one of them threatened to maim the messenger, meaning me, he took care of it."

"Adios, scumbag," Shelton said.

"Adios for good, if the scumbag had half a brain. One time, Brennan helped me catch a killer who'd murdered a complete stranger at the movies. Or maybe I helped him. The killer got away, and we set a trap for him, me and Brennan and some plainclothes cops under him. Idiot fell right into it and he's now locked up forever. So, Brennan was the first person I talked to right after I was threatened by this Russian asshole. I mean right after, like, in seconds."

"I can see why. Brennan'll probably give me and Carl the third degree, to see if we're worthy."

"He's just concerned. When he was a Captain in Brooklyn, I remember he assumed everyone works for him, and reports to him, and needs to be reamed out by him."

"Last thing Carl and I need is to be reamed out by a guy doesn't sign our paychecks."

"I'll make that clear. If Brennan throws his weight around here, I'll tell him I'm in good hands. He'll back off."

· · ·

The downstairs buzzer sounded at seven-thirty, about a half-hour after she'd expected him.

"That's him," Barbieri said as she walked over to the intercom by the front door and pressed the intercom.

"That you, Timothy?"

"It is."

On hearing Brennan's voice, she buzzed him into the building and waited by the front door of her apartment, listening to the elevator's motor as he was delivered up to her floor. When it came and she heard the doors open, she automatically reached for the doorknob, but stopped. By then, she knew not to open the door by herself. At the sound of the doorbell, she looked through the peephole and turned back to Reynolds.

"So, open the door already," he ordered. Permission granted, Barbieri unlocked the door and gave her guest a peck on the cheek as he crossed the threshold.

"You're late, Timothy. Where was the stiff? Staten Island?"

"Sorry to disappoint, Kim. Some shithead little snot from the Mayor's Office needed to lecture me about police work." Brennan was wearing the same office attire he wore just about every day forever. Brown sport coat, white shirt, red tie and khaki slacks. He put his briefcase down just inside the front door, walked over to the two bodyguards standing in the living room, and reached out his hand first to Shelton, then to Reynolds. "So, you're the people keeping Kim alive. I'm Timothy."

"Connie. Nice to meet you."

"Carl. We do our best. The boss frowns on us meeting homicide detectives in an official capacity, after the fact."

"Not what they're paying you for, deceased clients. So, you guys got everything under control, I assume?"

"We do. Kim's under guard round the clock. She's never out of our sight. And we believe that just by being here, we scared off the Russian perp who threatened her. Or perps. That's not clear yet."

"Right answer, but I wouldn't let your guard down if I were you, ever. Military? Police?"

"Air Force."

"Army MP."

"So, you know what you're doing." He turned to Barbieri. "Right, Kim? Your team knows what they're doing?"

"Appears they do, Brennan. I'm still alive and well. Nice of you to stop by, though."

"I'd send my own men if I had any to spare." He turned to Shelton and Reynolds.

"Let me tell you, I've met many Russians in an official capacity, and they're relentless bastards."

"We're prepared. I could name a few tough mothers who've regretted threatening our clients."

Brennan checked his watch and then got up to leave. As he grabbed his briefcase and headed for the door, he turned back to the guards and their client.

"Look, guys. I am absolutely fine with the job you're doing. I can tell my lady friend here is in excellent hands. But I sometimes get a little... what's the word...?"

"Overbearing," Barbieri offered. "Paternalistic."

"... overly concerned when the client's a buddy of mine. Kim, am I out of line here?"

"Timothy, we're good. Go home and take your long arms of the law with you."

He and Barbieri embraced with a small, just-a-friend hug, then he turned to Reynolds before heading out the door. "Anything you need from the Department, let me know." He shook their hands, first Reynolds' and then Shelton's, and gave them each his card as he did so. "I know people."

CHAPTER THIRTY-SIX

300 East 55 St.
Manhattan
Thursday, December 24
1:37 A.M.

"Nine-one-one. What's the emergency?"

"There's a man lying on the sidewalk. I think he's dead."

"Location? Where are you?"

"Corner of Fifty-fifth and Second."

"Manhattan?"

"Yes."

"Any sign of violence? Weapon? Blood?"

"No. Not that I can see."

"Okay. What is your name, please?"

"David Calabrese. I live near here."

"Okay, Mr. Calabrese. We're sending an ambulance over, and a patrol car. Can you wait there, please?"

"Yes. He's Chinese."

"The victim? Asian. Okay. Officers are on their way."

The body in question was lying face-down on the sidewalk, between a fire hydrant at the curb and the side of an apartment house. The scene was lit only by a weak streetlight, which illuminated all the things that humans leave as they pass through a city street. Cigarette butts, an overflowing trash can, a brownish stain of God-knows-what on the curb, and an empty plastic shopping bag. All were accompanied by the aroma of urine, left there either by pet dogs or homeless humans. There had apparently been no attempt to hide the body, although it was partly hidden in the shadow of the building wall.

The NYPD officers beat the hospital's EMT team to the scene by a minute and double-parked at the corner. That early in the morning, there was no real traffic they'd be blocking. When they got out of their radio car, one officer went over to the victim and examined him to confirm that he was deceased, as the dispatch call suggested, or was in fact still alive. His partner walked over to interview Calabrese, standing on the sidewalk fifteen feet away from the apparently lifeless body.

After determining that the victim was indeed dead, the first officer went through his pockets to find his wallet and look for any identification. Calabrese told the second officer he could not say anything more about the victim, or anything at all about the attack. He was just passing by, he explained, on his way home from seeing his girlfriend, when he came across the victim lying on the sidewalk, partly hidden by a trash can.

Seeing that the witness would be of no use to the homicide detectives who caught the case, the officer took down his phone number and address, and told him he could go back home. The detectives will contact him if necessary.

Drawn to a crime scene like moths to a flame, drivers going past slowed down to stare at the body and the officers, and several pedestrians gathered on the opposite corner to gape—and maybe to validate their opinion that their city was becoming way too dangerous to live in.

At that point, the ambulance arrived, and two EMTs, a white male and an Asian female both in their forties, immediately rushed over to the victim. They took his pulse, checked his breathing and listened to his heart with a stethoscope, and confirmed that he had no pulse, was not breathing, and his heart had stopped. The victim was indeed past tense, with no hope of being resuscitated.

After the officers informed them that there was no sign of trauma, the EMT team performed a close inspection of the body, from head to toe, to see if there was any obvious cause of death that the officers may have missed. When the female first responder inspected the victim's head and neck area, she discovered a small puncture wound behind his right ear with just a tiny drop of blood coming from it, as if his killer stabbed him with an ice pick.

"He's dead, right?" The first officer asked anxiously.

"Yes. Probable homicide," the female responder replied.

"What did we miss? You see a wound?"

"Right here," she said, pointing to the hole behind the victim's ear. "Easy to miss."

"What's his name?" the male responder asked. "Did he have any ID?"

"Chee Li. Zee Li, maybe," the officer said, handing the victim's driver's license over to him. "Not sure how you pronounce it."

As the EMT team placed the body of the victim on a gurney, and then lifted and slid the gurney into the back of their ambulance, the two cops wrote up their report on their iPads and got back into their patrol car. Their job was done, the murder victim on the sidewalk headed to the morgue and the murder mystery kicked upstairs to the homicide squad.

The responding officers drove off into the night, ready for the next crime scene the nine-one-one dispatcher dispatched them to. The onlookers gathered at the corner stopped gawking, and went back to their homes and businesses ready to tell anyone who'd listen about the murder victim they'd seen, just lying on the corner of Fifty-fifth and Second.

And with the first responders absent, the homicide victim taken away, and the onlookers gone, Fifty-fifth and Second once again returned to its natural state... an ordinary street corner marked by litter and stains and butts and odors, with no stories to tell.

CHAPTER THIRTY-SEVEN

436 Hylan Boulevard
Staten Island, NY
Thursday, December 24
11:43 P.M.

One of the first things Chief Brennan learned about getting kicked to the very top of the stairs was that there were no boundaries between work and home. Murderers murdering murder victims at all hours of the day saw to that.

All homicides inside the boundaries of New York City happened on his watch, because his watch lasted twenty-four hours a day. It didn't matter if he was at the movies, or having Christmas dinner with the family, or falling asleep in front of the TV on Christmas Eve. Dead people, and the bad people who made them take their last breath, had zero regard for his personal life.

After a fourteen-hour day of meetings with the brass over him, with commanders under him, and with community groups lobbying him to do this and scrap that, he was lying in bed in the sleeping alcove in his studio apartment reading that day's collection of Incident Reports–the first record, and definitely not the last, that the NYPD makes of crimes and accidents that its officers respond to.

Although homicides had gone way down in the thirty years since his days as a rookie cop, the reports made for interesting reading. And not just for their gory details–he had long ago become jaded about the diverse manifestations of intra-species violence–but because they helped him iden-tify where his homicide detectives are not needed, and redeploy them where they are. That, to his chagrin, was ninety percent of his job. The other rea-son he'd made them his bedtime stories was that they were usually so boring he could count on them to lull him to sleep.

He glanced through the first page, noting the names of the victims and the circumstances of their death, but nothing popped out. There was a drug addict named Wiley Taylor in the Village, who got into a disagreement with his dealer about the bill. Nothing new there.

Next up was the murder of a Long Island City bodega owner named Jamal Muhammad, who'd caught some unidentified teenager scarfing down a package of Hostess Snoballs while strolling up and down the aisles pretending to think about what condiments he'll be needing for the dinner he was preparing. Big yawn.

And there was Brianna Henratty, a twenty-three-year-old commuter from Babylon who was pushed in front of a railroad train by a homeless woman as it pulled into Jamaica station in Queens. She was bisected, cut in half at the waist, as the train ran over her. Horrible as that was, he'd seen much worse. Part of the job. Another day, another two halves of one hom-icide victim.

But it was the first victim on the second page that caught his eye. He was Chinese, which was enough to raise his eyebrows. They were among the more law-abiding types, almost never on either side of violent crime. Until recently, that is, when bigoted idiots and mental cases started blaming them for out-of-control pandemics, egged on by a bigoted mental case in the White House.

The victim was a successful real estate investor, which meant he had money and maybe influence. He was found dead on the street outside his apartment building on East Fifty-fifth Street. Another red flag, because homicides were quite rare in the high-rent, and therefore heavily patrolled, Upper East Side. The area was usually saturated with cops, because East Siders had the ear of the city's powers that be.

But this guy was not hit with a brick or knocked out by a punch to the face, like in other hate crimes. Instead, there was a small puncture wound on his neck, which was presumed to be the cause of death. Which meant a professional killer, or some kind of mob hit, was the culprit still at large. Here was a real life, honest-to-God front-page-of-the-Post murder mystery. Brennan could only hope.

The Chief circled the victim's name, Xi Li, and promised himself he'd look into it in the morning. It'd give him something to do, he hoped, besides move live bodies around to help close the cases of dead ones.

CHAPTER THIRTY-EIGHT

Unit 29155, Military Intelligence
Headquarters 161ˢᵗ Special Purpose
Specialist Training Center
Moscow
Friday, December 25
1:37 A.M.

"Institute for Scientific Research Number Two."

"Good morning. This is Nevski. I am reporting in once again about the assignment overseas."

"Excellent. What are your findings?"

"The target is a woman, five feet nine inches tall, forty-three kilograms. As I reported earlier. Unremarkable diet. Meat, fish, cake, coffee."

"Anything new to add, Nevski?"

"One thing we noticed is, she drinks constantly from a bottle of water."

"Good. A potential delivery route. Tap water? Or purchased? Poland Spring, Evian?"

"We do not know yet. Is that important?"

"Perhaps. It could affect the vehicle."

"I'll check."

"OK. Medicines?"

"What about them?"

"We need to know which ones she is taking. How they're taken. How often? Time of day."

"We don't have that yet. I'll order some research."

"You do that. We'll start on the product in the meantime. When it is produced, we will adapt it to the delivery system based on your findings."

"Goodbye."

"Wait. On the same topic, have you learned anything about the bodyguards?"

"They have not been the subject of surveillance themselves, as of yet. We know only that they protect our target. There is one male and one female, as I mentioned. Both are in their mid-thirties, and both look fit. Other than that, we have nothing to help us decide how to neutralize them. We will get you more detailed information that we can act on."

"Sleep well, Nevski."

CHAPTER THIRTY-NINE

FSB Safehouse
345 East 28th Street
Manhattan
Friday, December 25
8:55 P.M.

"Yes?"

"We need you to pay a visit."

"To?"

"To the target's residence in Brooklyn. Not every room. Only the bathroom, specifically, the medicine cabinet."

The man conducting surveillance on Barbieri had been getting some much-needed R and R at the FSB's safehouse, an ordinary row house on an ordinary block in an ordinary Manhattan neighborhood. Russian agents were trained not to draw attention to themselves when they were sent there, and they drew none. Zero. They were just ordinary, middle-class New Yorkers wearing Lands' End jackets and Nike shoes and Levi's jeans and Gap sweaters, carrying Target tote bags or Morton Williams shopping bags.

Neighbors across the street or down the block paid no attention to the comings and goings of the residents of 345 East 28th Street, Manhattan, other than giving an occasional nod 'hello'.

The Russian espionage leaders in New York understood that, as with any skilled operative who consistently delivered, there was always the risk of burnout if they pushed him too hard. They also understood that getting a replacement anywhere near as skilled as him from Moscow was hardly a lock.

It was a simple case of not enough supply and way too much demand. Surveillance was being carried out all over Europe, Africa and Asia, and every chief of operations in every city demanded only the best agents. Moscow, unsurprisingly, had a far smaller supply of 'best' agents, than of 'good enough' agents. The agent assigned to Barbieri did not hesitate.

"Medicine cabinet. Got it. Why there?"

"That's the one part of our ingestion work-up that's still missing."

"Not familiar with that term. What is an 'ingestion work-up.'"

"Ingestion. Look it up. We need to know about *everything* that goes into the target's body, not just what she eats and drinks. You already gave us that. We also need to know what medicines she's taking. A person her age often has many conditions, some serious, some not, and is probably taking a different medication for each one. Maybe a couple of medications. It's how Americans are trained, American women in particular.

We need to see each label. We need to know the dosages as well. We need to know whether the medicine is a pill, or capsule, or liquid, or spray. If it is taken orally, we need to know whether she takes it with food, or without food."

"We also need to know what creams she rubs on, and whether they're in a tube or a jar or some kind of pump dispenser. Whatever medication she is taking, we need to know whether she takes it in the morning, or in the afternoon, or before she retires for the night."

"I am not familiar with a lot of the names of these labels."

"You don't need to know their names. We do. Just make sure the photographs are clear enough to read every detail on the label."

"Easy enough. This assignment suggests a follow-up one. When the product is ready for quote unquote ingestion, I'll have to go back in again and replace one medicine she's using with our poison, won't I?"

"You're catching on. Can you get in?"

"Two factors. Means of entry, and opportunity."

"Your problems. Both of them. Find a way in. And find an opportunity to go in. We don't care when or how. She's got to leave the apartment some time, and when she goes, her two bodyguards always go with her."

"I understand."

"Good. Just go right to the bathroom and take pictures of everything we need. Then send them to us. It will take you only five minutes. Ten, tops."

"Email or text?"

"Neither. Use the secure FSB network."

"Understood. I should check the refrigerator too. People keep medicines there."

"Good thinking. We need the pictures by tomorrow."

"Tomorrow. Got it."

"Do not fail."

"I never have."

"Yet. Merry Christmas."

CHAPTER FORTY

10 North 10ᵗʰ St.
Brooklyn
Friday December 24
11:55 P.M.

The dirty Russian money story finished and submitted, Barbieri realized she still had work to do ,and picked up her cellphone.

Reynolds was still in the living room, sitting on the sofa watching Trevor Noah demolish another board member of the who's who of hypocrisy, while Shelton was in the second bedroom, presumably fast asleep. It was almost midnight in New York, seven in the morning in Moscow. Her call was answered on the first ring.

"Petrov." Her new best friend in Moscow was in his kitchen, preparing his third cup of tea of the morning, when his phone rang. He did not recognize the caller ID at first, but that mystery lasted only the few seconds it took to hear her voice.

"Hello, Sergei. It's Kim Barbieri from the *Journal*. I need a favor."

"Why should you be any different, Kim? What kind of favor? And why are you calling Christmas eve, for God's sake?"

"Get in the Christmas spirit, Sergei, please. I need a big favor."

"Anything I can do to help, Kim, I'll do. Within reason, of course."

"There's a guy who's been threatening me in New York. We think he's Russian."

"We?"

"Me, the police, and my bosses at the *Journal*."

"So, he's not fooling anyone, or even trying to. I imagine he takes exception to the story you interviewed me for. Shady real estate transactions and money-laundering, as I recall."

"That's what we suspect."

"Kim, money laundering is our national sport. Everyone's second job is keeping their money out of the tax collectors' hands. How can I help you over there, though, when I'm way over here in Mother Russia."

"Ask around, Sergei, and see whose feathers we're ruffling. Name names, please. The individual who's threatening me is probably not smart enough to know anything about money laundering. He couldn't even tell you what it means. I'd bet. He's just a dumb goon someone in the Kremlin sent on a mission to kill me."

"I agree. If I poke around, what makes you think they won't come after me, too? And I need not remind you I'm much easier to kill than you are. I live here, and I don't want to walk around with a target on my back."

"I understand, Sergei. I do."

"Respectfully, Kim, I don't think you do. This is a suicide mission you're asking me to go on. These people are fanatics."

"Okay, Sergei, I had to ask. You know that, right?"

"I do, unfortunately. Look. Here's what I can do, Kim. I won't ask anyone anything, because it's just too dangerous. But I will keep my ears open and let you know if I learn anything. That's the best I can do."

"That's good enough for me, Sergei. Thanks."

"You are welcome, Kim. One more thing, though. Does anyone know you're calling me? Anyone at the *Journal*? Police?"

"No. No one."

"Keep it that way. I already got grilled about you after you interviewed me, and it was not a pleasant conversation."

"How'd they find out?"

"It does not matter, and I will never know. Kim, everything's a state secret here. Nobody leaks anything, or they're dead. Nobody knows anything, or they're doomed. This is Moscow. Christmas spirit doesn't exist here."

CHAPTER FORTY-ONE

512 Brighton Beach Avenue
Brooklyn
Sunday, December 26.
3:00 A.M.

"Loose end?"

"Eliminated."

"Witnesses?"

"None. It was late at night. After midnight, I think. Nobody outside except that one loose end."

The laundromat was, once again, empty save for the two retired Bratva members. Gryshin had gone in first, six minutes earlier, unlocking the front door and then locking it again behind him. Waiting several feet away from the front window, he saw Klim sticking his face against the glass, trying to see if anybody besides Gryshin was there. There wasn't. Gryshin unlocked the door to let him, then relocked it.

Their coats still on, the two men sat on hard plastic chairs that were attached to each other, so they both faced a row of idle washing machines. The fluorescent fixtures on the ceiling were all out, and the only light hitting the two old men came from a street lamp down the block. Nobody outside could see them, much less hear them, as they discussed a skill that they were both quite familiar with. Assassination.

"Method?"

"Bullet behind ear. Twenty-two-caliber."

"Dead before he hit the ground, I believe their saying goes. No blood. Good. Who did we send?"

"Vasily."

"Idiot got it right this time? He deserves a promotion."

"He's learning."

"Maybe. He's still an idiot. I'll notify the administrator in Moscow."

"Good news is all Moscow wants to hear, definitely."

"It'll buy us time, anyway. All good news ever means to them is they'll put off sending a hit team to execute us, too."

CHAPTER FORTY-TWO

10 North 10th Street
Brooklyn
Monday, December 27
6:30 P.M.

"What's on tonight's menu, Kim?"

Even though it was almost dinnertime, Barbieri had given zero thought about what she, Reynolds and Shelton would be feasting on that evening. It completely skipped her mind.

They had just gotten back home and settled in for the evening, when Shelton broached the subject. All three had just assumed their usual positions, Barbieri at the counter and her two guards on the sofa, and assumed their usual routine of staring at their computer screens and robotically refreshing all the information on it.

As much as Barbieri had wanted to play something by Puccini or Verdi at that moment, she decided not to. Shelton seemed too preoccupied to listen. And she didn't want to press her luck with Reynolds, who clearly wasn't a big fan of Italian opera, famous or forgotten.

"Shit. Hadn't given it any thought, Connie. Let me see what I can cobble together that won't land us in the ER," she said, getting off the sofa and walking over to the kitchen. She checked the freezer, then the refrigerator, then the pantry.

"Looks like we have a choice, kids. Order in or go out. I ain't got nothing remotely edible."

"Some hostess you are, Kim. I'm okay with going out," Reynolds said.

"Better than staying in again, for sure," Shelton added.

"So, it's unanimous. You guys been to Rocco's yet?"

"Italian?"

"As Italian as I am."

"Food like your mom used to make?"

"Not even remotely. But no restaurant I've ever been to can say that. Deal with it. They're maybe a ten-minute drive from here. Leave in half an hour?"

"Dinner at eight. I always loved that movie," Shelton offered.

CHAPTER FORTY-THREE

10 North 10th Street
Brooklyn
Monday, December 27
7:43 P.M.

When they left her building for Rocco's, all bundled up against the winter chill, they climbed into the Suburban the same way they usually did: Reynolds in the driver's seat, Shelton riding shotgun, and Barbieri in back, behind the driver's seat.

Although all three had stayed fully alert en route from building to vehicle, none of them noticed the man lying in wait for them just down the block. The man in the gray cap. He was sitting in his car perhaps a hundred feet away from her building, hunched down out of sight, his side and rearview mirrors precisely positioned to give him a view of the building entrance and the bodyguard's Suburban.

He had had no way of knowing they'd be leaving her apartment for dinner, but he'd made certain he'd be ready if they did. Tradecraft, again.

When the Suburban drove off down the block, the Russian didn't get out of his car right away. He waited ten minutes, lying low as the FSB had trained him to do, to make sure they didn't drive right back because one of them had forgotten his wallet, or his keys, or his phone. Or realized that he needed to go to the bathroom. All he needed was five uninterrupted minutes to carry out the assignment, which he would almost certainly have if he were patient enough now, and quick enough once he jimmied his way into Barbieri's apartment.

With the coast clear, the man walked over to the front door of her building, stopped in front of it and waited, a little off to the side. It was 7:56 P.M. He had rehearsed an act he'd been trained to do whenever someone came toward the door from inside the lobby, or from the street outside it. He would rummage through his pockets looking for keys, a frustrated expression on his face. It was a common enough predicament that inevitably drew pity from urban cliff-dwellers who'd sometimes found themselves in the very same situation.

And in apartment houses, it was not at all uncommon for tenants to believe strangers lived in the same building, especially if they looked OK, on the assumption that nobody knew everyone else living there. Which they invariably did not.

The man in the gray cap had every reason to expect that one resident would eventually buy his act and let him inside. Three tenants didn't buy his act for a second. But an older man, taking his dog out for the last walk of the evening, did three minutes later. It was now 7:59 P.M.

Once inside the lobby, the man walked over to the mailbox wall to confirm Barbieri's floor and apartment number. He then got in the elevator, slipped on a pair of latex gloves he'd kept in his jacket pocket, and pressed the button for the top floor.

When it landed on her floor, he took a few steps into the hallway, and waited. There was no telling when someone would decide that right then was a good time to go out for a pack of cigarettes. Hearing nothing, he tiptoed over to Barbieri's apartment door, checked the lock, took out his set of jimmy keys and inserted one of them into it. With a few twists, he was safely inside, unseen and unheard. It was now 8:01 P.M.

Once inside, he turned on the hallway light, took out his cellphone from his jacket pocket, quickly entered his passcode, and pressed the camera icon. The latex gloves he was wearing, to keep him from leaving prints behind, fit so snugly that they had no effect on his ability to press the phone's screen icons and keys.

The camera now ready, he walked over to the kitchen, where he opened the refrigerator door. Inside, on the two shelves, were a bottle of orange juice, a container of milk, a loaf of bread, and a half-eaten wedge of cheese. There were no medicines at all. It was now 8:02 P.M.

With nothing in the kitchen worth photographing, he turned off the light and followed the hall leading to the bathroom. Turning on the light switch, he saw the bathroom had a mirrored medicine cabinet above the sink to his right, next to the bathtub. The toilet was directly under a frosted glass window in the back, and there were two glass shelves on the wall to his left, one about a foot above the other. He started his photography assignment with the medicine cabinet.

Opening the door, he found a jumble of small boxes and bottles on the bottom shelf, mostly with names he did not recognize. Tylenol, Biofreeze, Pepto Bismol, Midol, Miralax. Cepacol, Clinique, Sudafed, Replens. He turned them so the labels faced out and took a picture of all of them.

On the shelf above, next to her razor and two tubes of lipstick, were three pill bottles and one box with prescription labels. He could make out only the name on the box. Zomig. The pill bottles he couldn't read.

He took a picture of the bottom shelf as he found it, then faced all the medications so their labels faced him. He took that photo, then put all the bottles back in their original position, or close to it, using the photo he had taken moments before as a guide. 8:06 P.M.

He then took the same steps with the top shelf.

The medicine cabinet done, he turned his attention to the glass shelves to his left, which held a box of tissues, a box of swabs, a container of talcum powder, and several tubes of lotions and creams. Their names were more familiar. Q-Tip, Aveeno, Johnson & Johnson, Eucerin, Neutrogena. He took a single photo of them all, then turned around and opened the shower curtain, which hung from a rod about six feet above the rim of the tub.

On the back rim of the tub were two matching plastic bottles with the same name, Clairol, which he assumed were shampoo and conditioner. He took their photo as well, then carefully closed the shower curtain. It was now 8:08 P.M.

Assignment completed, he then shut the bathroom light, turned off the camera on his phone, put the phone back in his jacket pocket, and walked briskly to the front door, glancing back for a second to confirm that all the target's belongings were just as she had left them moments earlier. He put the left side of his head close to the door, listening for unwelcome noises coming from the hallway. Hearing none, he then opened the door, stepped into the hallway and shut the door behind him.

He walked over to the elevator and pushed the button to summon the car to his floor. The elevator, which had stopped one floor below, took just a few seconds to reach him and open its door. The elevator was empty. On the way down, he made sure to take off his latex gloves and put them back in his jacket before the elevator got to the lobby. He then walked out to the street, walked down the block to his car, got in, and drove off. It was now 8:11 P.M.

Mission accomplished. The whole thing took only one minute longer than he'd planned for, from the time he entered the building to the time he got back in his car. He was happy about completing his assignment on time, not caring that his employers weren't around to notice it. The only thing left to do now was encrypt the pictures he had just taken, then send them back to the homeland, which he would do at the next red light.

CHAPTER FORTY-FOUR

NYPD Headquarters
One Police Plaza
Manhattan
Wednesday, December 29
8:17 A.M.

Chief Brennan made a habit of getting into the office a half-hour early every day, at least. If he didn't, he knew, he'd never have a minute of peace to enjoy his ritual coffee and an everything bagel, and skim through that morning's *Daily News*.

After that brief respite, the phone calls and emails and meetings and texts and conferences–the bullshit he hated enough to make him want to turn in his shield and his gun–would start to make him think about ending it all, once and for all.

The *News* often had stories about homicides that had occurred over-night, after he'd left the office the evening before or too late to be included in his Incident Reports. If any were worthy of his attention–an organized crime hit or a nasty fallout between page six celebrities– the paper gave him a heads up when the press, or the mayor's office, came calling.

He was sitting at his desk, dressed in his go-to uniform of white shirt, red tie, khaki slacks and sports jacket, with the laptop still unopened, his coffee still hot, and his bagel unwrapped and ready to eat.

Buried among the usual stories about scandals and evictions and sub-way vandalism, one story caught his eye. It was about a body, which had previously taken the form of a living, breathing adult male, that had been found inside his apartment in Chelsea, near the Flatiron building just a mile or so north of where he was sitting.

Although it did not appear to be a homicide needing investigation, two things about the case made him pay attention. The victim had apparently been dead several weeks before the body was discovered, and he was identified as a Russian national named Maxim Lebedev.

The first call he made was to Barbieri.

"Captain."

"Kim. The Russian you badgered me about? Lebedev?"

"He's turned up!? Holy...!"

"The article in your old paper says his body was found last night."

"I can't say I'm surprised, Timothy, as I suspected he would end up dead. Does it say if it was natural causes or foul play?"

"It doesn't. But as of now, it doesn't look like homicide. It could be suicide, but he's been dead for weeks, so who knows? I'm going to call the Medical Examiner this afternoon, after they have time to complete the autopsy."

"Where was the body found?" Brennan eyeballed the story before answering.

"Um, Seventeen West Twenty-second. Apartment building."

"Off Fifth. I think I've been in that building. That where he lived?"

"It looks that way."

"Who found him? Does it say?"

"It does not. As you and I both know, it's a good bet that the landlord or super found him. A single man living alone, no contact with other tenants in his building, and no visitors to speak of. After a few weeks of not being seen, or once the corpse ripens a bit, people get curious and tell the doorman or the super. Somebody."

"Especially the busybodies who keep track of everyone's comings and goings. Every building is overrun with them. Keep me posted about the cause of death, Brennan."

"You'll know the second I do."

. . .

Chief Brennan called the Medical Examiner's office later that afternoon.

Never comfortable pulling rank unless playing nice wasn't working, he asked to speak to the pathologist who performed the autopsy on Lebedev, rather than the Chief Medical Examiner himself. As a bureaucrat in good standing, he understood that information gotten right from the source was often more revealing than getting it from someone just reading a report prepared by a peon several links lower on the food chain.

After Brennan was patched through to the pathologist, Doctor Sylvia Mercante, he was told about the steps she had taken, and the condition of his various organs and body parts and systems, all to reassure him that no corners were cut. Only after these preliminaries were done did Mercante get to the precise cause of death.

"First, there was no evidence of foul play. I saw no evidence of blunt trauma, or damage caused by a bullet, or penetration by a sharp instrument. We ruled out strangulation and poisoning, as well.

"Suicide?"

"No evidence of a self-inflicted wound that we could discern."

"So... natural causes, Doctor?"

"That's where I'd put my money, Chief. But the question I tried to answer was, which specific natural cause, of which there are many. Was it a heart attack, or diabetes, or COPD, or Alzheimer's, or some other condition? I cannot say for sure, not right now, anyway, but one thing we can be certain of is that Maxim Lebedev had cancer."

"Cancer, Doctor? Seriously?"

"Without a doubt, Chief, because we found evidence of lesions in his lungs."

"But not enough of them to say that lung cancer was his cause of death?"

"No, sir. There may well have been another cause, to be sure. Most bodies we see have evidence of multiple comorbidities, any of which could be the immediate cause of death. Bodies that are obese can also present with signs and symptoms of diabetes. Victim of breast cancer can have evidence of hypertension. Anemia and hypothyroidism, also. Bodies often have evidence of two or three conditions, especially in older folks."

"Understood, Doctor. And lung cancer? What are its comorbidities?"

"COPD and diabetes are fairly common. Coronary artery disease, too. But in any given death, which condition is the guilty party can be pretty hard to determine, of course. Sometimes, where it's not clear, we just assign one usual suspect, and leave it at that. Then it's on to the next victim."

"So, it's sort of like a multiple-choice test where every answer is correct."

"Unfortunately, yes."

"Do we know if he was being treated in New York? For the lung cancer, specifically?"

"No, Chief, we don't. Sorry."

"So, with one Maxim Lebedev, we determine it is death by natural causes, without identifying which one?"

"That's not all unusual in this line of work, Chief."

. . .

"Cancer?"

"Cancer, Kim. Lebedev definitely had lung cancer. It may not have killed him, but he did indeed have it."

A second after ending the call with the Medical Examiner, Brennan had called Barbieri. Knowing his ex-squeeze as he did, he knew there'd be hell to pay if he kept her waiting.

"So, you have nothing to investigate?"

"Not for now, at least, as deaths due to natural causes are out of my jurisdiction. I told the Medical Examiner to let me know if they ever come up with anything nefarious on Lebedev, so..."

"Okay, Timothy. Thanks. I've got to speak with my boss about this."

. . .

Barbieri's next call was to her boss, Mr. Fitzgerald, to reassure him she was one hundred percent focused on her *Journal* reporting.

"Lebedev is dead, as I suspected, Mr. Fitzgerald, from natural causes. He had lung cancer, but whether it actually killed him is not definite."

"Let us assume his death is unrelated to his real estate deal, Miss Barbieri. End of story."

"So, it appears. The pathologist who performed the autopsy in the Medical Examiner's office has ruled out homicide, and said there's no forensic evidence he killed himself. But the timing still stinks, Mr. Fitzgerald. I wouldn't be shocked if there's more to this."

"Neither would I, Miss Barbieri. But at least you can move on to another story we're planning to do."

"What would that be, Mr. Fitzgerald?"

"The online art business. Get up to speed on NFTs for the next week or two, and we'll get you started."

"I'm not familiar at all with that. What's an NFT?"

"Non-Fungible Token. About all I know about NFTs is that they involve digital art."

"There's digital art now? Like a painting? Anybody commit murder to get one, or get himself killed because he owned one?"

"Sorry to disappoint you, Miss Barbieri, but NFTs don't seem to inspire bodily harm of any sort."

"Business with no violent crime involved. How novel."

"You're a quick study, Miss Barbieri, as you've already proven. We have no reason to think you can't handle this one."

"Thank you, Mr. Fitzgerald."

CHAPTER FORTY-FIVE

10 North 10th Street
Brooklyn
Saturday, January 2
11:15 A.M.

Wait a minute. Fungible? What the fuck does that even mean? And how do I explain that to our readers?

Barbieri was on her living room sofa, in her flannel pajamas, staring at her laptop in between sips of cappuccino. Shelton and Reynolds, fully caffeinated and dressed for work with their pistols tucked inside their belts, were both at the kitchen counter scrolling through apps on their cell phones. Other than the occasional noise from cups hitting the counter and rear ends shifting position, the room was silent. By mutual agreement, and without dissent, Barbieri and Shelton had declared it an Italian opera-free morning.

Taking a break from worrying about the Russians, she chose that morning to get up to speed on the whole non-fungible tokens craze in the digital art business. Fitzgerald had asked her to learn it, and she was determined not to let him—or herself—down.

In her old job, as a crime reporter with the *Daily News*, she became pretty adept at dumbing down her copy to the paper's readers. Way down, to a sixth-grade reading level. Why write 'exceptional' when 'great' will do? Or 'implementation' when 'use' will do? *Those bozos who read my paper were working class, if that. The hardest thing they ever bothered to read were the directions on the side of a box of Cheerios.*

The *Journal's* readers were a bit more of a challenge. They were well-educated, well-off, and well-read, and expected only the precise terminology they needed to assess the markets and invest wisely.

Barbieri had certainly proved she was up to the job in the Russian real-estate story. But that was dollars and cents, the non-fungible facts and figures she'd begun mastering the first time she bought a lollipop at the candy store. This NFT information was cutting-edge computer science, and she'd never bothered mastering anything about that beyond booting her laptop up and shutting it down.

So, instead of dumbing subjects down for her readers, her job at that moment became dumbing NFT-ism down for herself. Then become smart enough about it to convince Mr. Fitzgerald, and the paper's readers, that she knows whereof she writes.

She started by googling 'fungible', and followed the digital bread crumbs from there.

Fungible. That means whatever you're talking about can be replaced. Ok. You don't want an apple? Have a pear. They're interchangeable. So non-fungible, logic tells me, means it cannot be replaced. It's not interchangeable with anything else. Easy enough. Why don't economists just say 'unique', then? Who are they trying to impress?

Putting 'token' on the end of 'non-fungible' takes that idea a step further. The token means whatever you're talking about can't be replaced, changed, or even copied. Like it's written in digital stone.

The digital stone is called a 'blockchain'. Can't these nineteen-year-old tech wizards speak plain English?

Okay, looking up 'blockchain'… that's computer code that can't be hacked or changed. There's no other record like it anywhere on the planet. And once it's created, you can't mess with it. So, what's that got to do with digital art that pops up on your computer?

OK. I got it. An NFT is the digital art version of a Social Security number. It's unique. It can't be changed. It belongs to just one work of art. So, it's proof of ownership of that image. Voila.

When you buy the digital art, you're actually just buying the token that's attached to it, like an electronic stamp. Anybody can google the image. But it's owned only by the buyer of the NFT. Like buying just the signature 'Picasso' on 'Guernica', or 'Da Vinci' on the 'Mona Lisa', means you own the whole damn painting.

Okay. NFTs have penetrated my thick skull. Can I take a nap now?

After she made that mental breakthrough, Barbieri spent the next few hours taking a deep dive into NFTs and digital art, with both the computer technology and its technical language becoming less and less foreign to her with each article she read. She knew she couldn't call Mr. Fitzgerald, however, until she graduated with honors from student to master.

• • •

"Thomas Fitzgerald."

"Hey, Mr. Fitzgerald. It's Kim. I'm up to speed on NFTs and digital art."

Later that afternoon, as soon as she felt she'd nailed the NFT arena, Barbieri had called her boss. Somehow, she knew he wouldn't mind, as Saturday and Sunday were just weekdays to him.

"Excellent, Miss Barbieri. I had no doubt you would."

"So, what's the assignment you have for me?"

"For now, just explaining it all to me. We're keeping you on the money-laundering story, at least for now. That's news we have to get out ASAP. The NFT story is more of a feature article we're planning, the kind we do to bring our readers up to speed on new technology. There's no hurry."

CHAPTER FORTY-SIX

Patriyarshie Ponds
Moscow
Saturday, January 2
1:17 P.M.

Foreign owners of Park Avenue homes:
We follow the money laundering January 2.
By Karen Smith, James Brookings, Franklin Herzog and Kim Barb-
ieri.

Many of New York's most exclusive residential properties are being bought by Iranians, Chinese, Russians, Ukrainians and other foreign nationals, and an alarming number of these transactions involve laundering by the buyers of their ill-gotten gains. That is the primary finding of the *Journal*'s analysis of 274 recent high-end real estate transactions involving foreign buyers.

That was the opening paragraph of the article that had caught Pytor Simes' eye that afternoon, in his home in Moscow. It was on the first page of the online, Russian language edition of that day's *Wall Street Journal*, the American business and finance newspaper that had become required reading for a small share of elite Muscovites—those looking to become obscenely wealthy without having to resort to bloodshed.

Wearing $375 worth of freshly ironed Ralph Lauren jeans, $200 worth of Nike Dunk Low running shoes, and $320 worth of a black Lingua Franca crew-neck sweater, the 30-year-old Simes could be easily mistaken for a Silicon Valley venture capitalist rather than the corrupt businessman he actually was. He did not have to read any further to realize that the article was not good news for his operation. It was not just what the article revealed that alarmed him. It was also the byline. He did not recognize the first three reporters' names, but the fourth jumped out at him. Kim Barbieri.

Simes closed his laptop and grabbed his cell. He spent a few seconds writing and sending off a terse text message to his business partner, then grabbed his coat and laptop and headed out the door. Simes needed to meet with him at the office.

When he arrived twenty-two minutes later, Pyotr Ustinov was already there, sitting at his desk, peering at his laptop's screen open to the same *Journal* article.

Despite being a single room on the fifth floor of a grim Soviet-era walkup, the office was furnished with state-of-the-art glass and chrome furniture, all glaringly lit by track lighting. On the walls were reproductions of paintings by Picasso, Magritte, and Kandinsky, and on the end-tables were well-cared-for indoor plants.

While Simes' and Ustinov's corporate titles were conventional, their division of labor was not. As the Chief Executive Officer, Simes was the public face of the company, the one who dealt with bankers and regulators. Integrity mattered, and he did his best to make sure outsiders saw that in him.

Unlike Simes, Ustinov was not even an employee of the company. He was a freelancer sent by Bratva to make sure the cash flow kept flowing to Bratva's coffers. Ustinov did the dirty, day-to-day work when threats and violence were needed to close a deal or enforce a contract.

The twenty-first century Russian interpretation of corporate responsibility did not stand a chance when the responsibilities of the Chief Bludgeoning Officer included death threats, revenge and extortion. And Ustinov certainly looked the part, with a three-day growth of stubble on his face, and a black leather jacket attempting, but failing, to cover his thick, burly torso.

Simes took a seat at his desk, across from Ustinov's, opened his laptop, and went back to the *Journal* article he had started reading at home. When he finished, he turned to Ustinov.

"They got the details right," Simes said to his CBO. "How did they know about that sale?" he asked, more to himself than Ustinov.

"Anyone we know speak to these reporters?" Ustinov asked.

"Not all of them. Just one. The person this Barbieri woman spoke to. Petrov."

"Petrov? He couldn't have said anything. He doesn't know anything."

"Maybe. Though he's capable of putting two and two together. That doesn't even matter, because Petrov could've helped her investigate our transactions without even knowing it."

"Inadvertently. So, what do we do?"

"You're going to contact your employers, and you will ask them to pay Petrov a visit, Pyotr. Now, before he can do any more damage."

"Understood."

"Good. Take care of it. I don't want to hear anything more about this matter, except that it's resolved." Ustinov closed his laptop and headed out the door.

"It will be. Have no doubt."

"I don't." As Ustinov opened the door to leave, Simes went back to his laptop and opened a new word processing document. "Until I hear from you, I'll make myself useful and craft a letter to post on our website. The *Journal* article is a complete fabrication, written by hack American writers with an anti-Russian axe to grind. The usual bullshit when you have not a single fact on your side. I'll think of something."

CHAPTER FORTY-SEVEN

10 North 10th Street
Brooklyn
Sunday, January 10
3:39 P.M.

Even though Lebedev's death appeared to be from natural causes, the natural cause most likely being cancer, Barbieri thought it was more than a little intriguing that a Russian whose finances she was investigating suddenly up and died. *What's the Russian word for 'coincidence'?*

Back in Miami, when she was reporting on Cuban drug dealers, bodies turned up all the time, each clearly a violent death. Murder was a negotiating ploy, maybe the ultimate hardball tactic, where the party of the first part made his terms crystal clear to future parties of the second part.

But among buyers of multimillion-dollar homes in New York, not so much. If there were threats, they were made in a much more civilized manner. Fitzgerald had suggested to Barbieri that she should let Lebedev's disappearing act go, or at least stop doing any digging on company time. She followed her gut instead and kept doing it on her own. *I am an investigative reporter. Accent on investigative. Do some investigating. GOYAKOD, idiot!*

Years before, as a crime reporter for the *News*, she had picked up a lot of police lingo, the shorthand cops used only with each other, not civilians. Mastering their lingo, and using it only when called for, was a way for her to bond with the uniformed men and women she covered. The particular turn of phrase cops used when they had no leads on a crime that had been committed, and no idea where to turn, was, 'Get Off Your Ass And Knock On Doors.' GOYAKOD.

Ask around, snoop around, and poke around. Make the perpetrator nervous by locating the one busybody who has information on him. Somebody somewhere saw something, and it was the detective's job to find that someone and get him to say something. If you get off your ass and knock on enough doors, you're bound to get lucky.

Lebedev himself had been a great big black hole. To begin filling it in, she decided to knock on a few doors in his apartment building in Chelsea. For a reporter looking for dirt, there's nothing like a nosy neighbor eager to dish it.

• • •

"Guys, pack your bags and put on your hats, coats and mittens. We're going on a field trip to Manhattan. I've got to interview some witnesses."

"Sure. Now?"

"Ten minutes. But I need a favor, a big favor. Please give me some space here. For the interview itself, I mean. I'm interviewing people for a story I'm on, in an old apartment building in Chelsea, on West Twenty-second off Fifth. You'll escort me to the lobby and up the elevator, and escort me back here when I leave, but when I'm in the apartment itself..."

"Got it. Confidential."

"It's more than that, Carl. Witnesses rarely open up to reporters when there's an audience. In my experience, they'll keep their guard up, because they're afraid of revealing too much. And absolutely petrified of the wrong people discovering that they're revealing too much. They're much more forthcoming when it's just the reporter, by herself."

"We can't protect you under those circumstances, Kim. Our boss, and yours, would go ballistic."

"Not when I'm inside his apartment, true. But this has nothing to do with the guy you're protecting me from. Totally different story."

That was a lie, but Barbieri felt she had no choice but to deceive her minders. If she told them the truth, they'd either forbid the interview, or tell the paper their reporter went AWOL on them. Reynolds and Shelton conferred for a minute, then came back to her.

"Okay, Kim. We'll give you some room. But we want you in and out as quickly as possible. And your cell stays on the whole time, in your hand, not in your bag."

"I knew you'd come around, my friends."

• • •

"Who is it?" asked the man's voice coming from the speaker just outside the building entrance.

"Kim Barbieri. I'm with the *Wall Street Journal*. May I come up?"

"The *Journal*? You sure you got the right apartment?"

"I need to speak with you about your neighbor who died recently. Maxim Lebedev."

"Oh. OK." At that, Barbieri heard the buzzer that unlocked the lobby door, and let herself and her bodyguards into the building. All three had been bundled up, and all three took off their coats and hats the second they entered the lobby.

"Half an hour, Kim," Shelton reminded her

"Understood, Connie."

Reynolds and Shelton walked with her to the elevator, and when the door opened, went into the car with her. When it arrived on the neighbor's floor, Barbieri got out and the two guards watched her leave their field of vision, then rode back downstairs. They then exited the lobby and paced back and forth just outside the building entrance, ready to rush back in at the first sign of trouble.

The guards observed no one go in or leave who looked suspicious. Just an older woman with an empty laundry cart, a teenage girl with her eyes glued to her cell phone, and a twenty-something Asian man, a dog walker leading six pedigree curs back to their rightful owners.

The guards began patrolling the area in front of the apartment build-ing, between the lobby door and the service entrance about thirty feet away. After a minute or two, Shelton reached into her bag and got out a cigarette, while Reynolds took his phone out of his pocket and started scrolling through his emails. In the tug-of-war between vigilance and attention-defi-cit disorder, vigilance lost out.

"He was a nice man, Maxim," said Harry Shapiro, who lived just down the hall from Lebedev. Harry had opened his front door, and was in the hall waiting for the reporter when she got out of the elevator. He was an older gentleman, perfectly groomed and elegantly dressed in a suit and tie, as if he were heading off to Wall Street for a big, important meeting with big, im-portant wheeler dealers. But he clearly had nowhere to go that morning. Or any other morning, for that matter, since he'd pulled the plug on his career decades before.

On entering the well-lit living room, which Shapiro had furnished with the same elegance and taste as he displayed with his attire, Barbieri walked over to the brown leather sofa and sat down, keeping her coat on her lap and her cell phone in her left hand.

"Mind if I sit down, Mr. Shapiro?" Without waiting for his okay, she took out her notepad and put her pen to it, ready for the information he'd be providing. Shapiro took a seat opposite her, on the matching leather chair he normally used for reading the financial sections of the *Times* and the *Journal,* and for dozing off afterwards.

"Harry, please. Maxim and I didn't have a lot in common, but he always had a 'hello' when I ran into him in the lobby, or down in the laundry room."

"That sounds neighborly enough to me. Did he have any hobbies that you know of? Friends?"

"None that I saw. It's one of those things about a building like this, where people live on top of one another, but nobody knows anything about anybody else. Privacy matters more than anything here. It's how you keep your dignity, or at least pretend to."

"So, there's nothing that stands out with Maxim?"

"There was one thing. He was always well-dressed, at least until recently."

"Like you are right now, Harry." Barbieri clicked on her pen and started taking notes.

"Sure. You know what they say—admiration is seeing your own qualities in someone else. Maxim, his hair always looked like he just got a haircut, and his shoes were always shined, which made him stand out from the usual slobs who live here. But about three months ago, he started looking different. He wore the same clothes all the time. Dirty and unkempt, like he didn't care how he looked. He walked outside at all hours, and he even stopped saying 'hello' to me."

"A different person. Any idea why, Harry? Medications, maybe."

"You mean was he sick mentally? I can't say, can I? Ask the drugstore on the corner about that. They might know. Just about everyone in the building goes to them." Barbieri jotted down another note to herself on the pad.

"I definitely will. You've been a big help, Harry." Sensing that this neighbor had told her all he knew, Barbieri put her notebook and pen back into her messenger bag and rose from the sofa. Shapiro stood up as well.

"Nice meeting you, Miss Barbieri. Will you let me know when your article is going to run? Please. Sometimes I don't have the time to read the whole paper. I mean, the *Journal*'s an excellent paper, but you know what business is like these days."

"Sure thing, Harry. Definitely."

Barbieri walked over to the front door and left Shapiro's apartment, still holding her coat in her arms and her cell in her left hand, but instead of heading straight to the elevator, she stopped and checked her watch. She had a good ten minutes before she had to return to her security team.

She then walked past the elevator to the stairwell, went down one flight, and made her way to the door of the apartment directly below Lebedev's. She made a mental note of the name typed on the nameplate and knocked on the door. Hearing no response, she took a business card out of her wallet and wrote a note on the back.

As she was about to slip it under the tenant's apartment door, though, the elevator door opened and a middle-aged man came out, jiggling his keys as he walked toward her. She noticed he had a few days' growth of beard, but was otherwise neat–and unthreatening–in appearance.

"May I help you?"

"Mr. Flanagan?"

"That's me."

"I'm Kim Barbieri, with the *Wall Street Journal*," she said, as she handed him her card. Ed Flanagan eyeballed the card, and its owner, then shrugged and unlocked his door.

"I was wondering if I could talk to you about your upstairs neighbor." Then she corrected herself. "Late upstairs neighbor."

"Mr. Lebedev? Poor bastard. Sure."

As they entered, Barbieri again took out her notepad and pen from her bag, and walked with him over to his living room. His apartment, unlike Shapiro's, seemed to be furnished half by Ikea and half by the Salvation Army. Nothing matched, yet everything somehow seemed to go together, anyway.

"Why'd you call him a poor bastard?"

"Is that politically incorrect? Sorry if I offended you. If I were a shrink, I'd use the term 'seriously depressed.' As in, about as depressed as I've ever seen, and I've been around enough mentally ill people to recognize the symptoms. Sit down anywhere, Miss Barbieri. Mi casa, et cetera, et cetera."

She sat on one end of his sofa, while he sat two feet away on the other end.

"Thank you, Mr. Flanagan."

"Ed. Can I get you anything?"

"No. I'm good. Can you elaborate?" she asked, ready to jot down anything worth noting.

"He and I were friends, sort of. Almost, anyway. More like a cultural exchange kind of thing. A few months after he moved in, I started going for walks with him, and we'd talk about Russia, where my mother's side of the family is from. Or politics here, which can be tough for a foreigner to understand. Everything was fine until it wasn't. Last few months, he's getting a little testy with me. He was obviously sad, but about what he never said. Lots of little things that add up to depression, from what I could see. I tried, really tried, to stay on good terms with him, but it got too much for me. He closed himself off."

"Ed, do you think he was depressed enough to take his own life?"

"That I couldn't say. I know next to nothing about psychiatry. So, they never found a cause of death, the city?"

"No. Not one hundred percent, anyway. You know if he saw anyone? Or took any medication?"

"For depression? Not that I'm aware of. Maybe it's a Russian macho thing, not to show weakness."

"What about for medical problems? You know if he had anything, maybe diabetes, heart disease, cancer...?" Barbieri was fishing, a tried-and-true way to get someone to say the magic words you want to hear.

"He never mentioned anything to me about his health, which is unusual because it's topic number one with people our age. Why is the *Journal* interested in him, anyway? Was he some kind of finance whiz?"

"Not that I know of, Ed. His name just came up in some reporting we're doing, and I'm following it up." That too was a carefully crafted evasion. She was, in fact, following up, but not on behalf of her employer.

Barbieri checked her watch, and saw that she had been inside the building, and out of view of her bodyguards, for pretty close to a half-hour. She was also on a different floor than the one they'd last seen her on. Any longer would be practically begging Reynolds and Shelton to barge into the building and conduct a noisy floor-by-floor, door-to-door search for her.

"Ed, thanks for your time. You've been very helpful." Barbieri got up, took Flanagan's hand in hers, then left his apartment and took the stairs down to the lobby, donning her coat between landings. On leaving the building she waved to her bodyguards, phone in hand, pacing outside the entrance--a gesture meant both to telegraph that she was unharmed and to show that she'd obeyed their instructions to hold on to her cell for dear life.

On seeing their client, they waved back. Shelton snuffed out her cigarette and opened the passenger side door of their SUV, which Reynolds had left double-parked right in front of Lebedev's building. Reynolds switched off his cell phone and got into the driver's seat.

"Twenty-nine minutes. I'm still alive. You guys are killing it," she said, as she got close to the Suburban.

"Some gambles pay off. How'd the interview go?" Shelton asked. "Was he... what was the word you used... 'forthcoming'?"

"He was indeed. In the service, you guys ever say 'get off your ass and knock on doors'?"

"Nope."

"I heard it on cop shows a couple of times, but I've never said it."

"Maybe it's a New York thing. Anyway, knocking on doors paid off just now. Care to stop and get something to eat? I'm buying."

"No. sorry. We'd both feel better if you were back home. Taking another risk is just asking for it, and we'd all be pushing our luck."

"Understood. I'll order Japanese for us later."

Barbieri got into the vehicle, Shelton closing her passenger door as soon as she settled in, and she and Reynolds climbed into the front seats. On the way back to Brooklyn, what she'd just learned about Lebedev from the two neighbors kept bouncing around her brain. *Maybe it wasn't cancer that killed Lebedev. Maybe he killed himself. If he committed suicide, what does that mean for the money-laundering reporting? And what kind of pressure might drive him to take his own life?*

CHAPTER FORTY-EIGHT

10 North 10th Street
Brooklyn
Sunday, January 10
5:27 P.M.

Before Barbieri and her escorts arrived back at her place, they made a pit stop at Yoshi's restaurant to pick up a container of yellowfin tuna sashimi for her, and a couple of bento boxes for them.

To leave her bodyguards totally free to act in case of danger, Barbieri carried home the shopping bag with their orders herself. After entering the building and riding up to her apartment together, Reynolds and Shelton hung up their jackets in the closet, then went to their respective corners in the living room to check their phones for the ten thousandth time. Before doing the same routine, their client went straight to the kitchen counter to unpack the shopping bag, take the lid off the three plastic takeout trays, and put them on the counter along with forks, napkins, and chopsticks.

She set her plate of sashimi in front of her on the counter, but before she sat down and positioned the chopsticks in her hand, her phone rang. Seeing a phone-number she did not recognize, she looked over at Reynolds for guidance.

"Know who it is, Kim?"

"Nope. But I get calls from strangers all the time. Occupational hazard for reporters."

"Of course. Answer it."

Barbieri pressed the 'accept call' icon and put the phone to her ear, under the watchful eyes of both Reynolds and Shelton.

"Mrs. Kim Barbieri?" It was a thick Russian accent.

"This is Miss Barbieri. Not Mrs."

"I am Vasily Klimnikov. What you wrote not true."

"Everything's been fact-checked, Mr. Klimnikov. Double- and triple-checked, in fact, as long as you're asking."

On hearing a Russian name, Reynolds walked over from the sofa and made an expression as if to say, 'problem?' and stage-whispered for her to put him on speaker. She did.

"No. Not true. Lie. I have papers."

"What papers are those?" Shelton and Reynolds joined her at the kitchen counter, eating their respective meals alongside Barbieri as she argued with the Russian.

"How you say... contract. Look at Maxim Lebedev, Mrs. Barbieri. Not me." Barbieri didn't bother correcting him this time. Through the thick accent she detected slurring, as if Klimnikov had been under the influence. *Don't the motherfuckers ever stop drinking?*

"What about Maxim Lebedev?"

"I say enough. Not legimitate." Barbieri caught that the word had been mispronounced, and couldn't help but correct him.

"Not legitimate, you mean. You have the contract in the records? Let me see them."

"Not possible. Retract."

"We're not retracting anything, Mr. Klimnikov, until we see proof there's something we need to retract. The article stands. If you dispute any facts, I suggest you call the *Journal*. Not me. In fact, Mr. Klimnikov, you are not to call me again."

"Or what, Mrs. Barbieri?"

"Or you will be arrested. Harassment's a crime here."

"Arrest me. I sit in prison cell. It will not protect you."

"So, now you're threatening me?! When you're on speakerphone?! How fuckin' dumb are you?" Barbieri lost the professional *Journal* demeanor she'd recently gained and reverted to the way she handled threats from thugs back when she was a crime reporter. Insults and threats were the only words some people, like this Klimnikov character, understood.

"I do not care who listen, miss."

"Then you really are one stupid son of a bitch, Klimnikov. You wanna hurt me? You wanna kill me? Bring it, bitch!" At that, she pressed the 'end call' button and looked first at Reynolds, and then at Shelton.

"Who's Klimnikov?" Shelton asked.

"Vasily Klimnikov. One of the Russian buyers we investigated."

"Not sure he understood the nuance you brought to the phrase, 'bring it, bitch.'" Connie said.

"I don't really care if he didn't, Connie. That's how I usually dealt with sleazebags who wanted me dead, back in the day, and I lived to tell the tale."

"Regardless, I wouldn't lose any sleep over this bozo, Kim," Reynolds added. "He told you his name. I'll email Fitzgerald right now, and that'll be the end of it."

"How'd bozo get my number?"

"That's really easy to get these days. Scumbag's totally blotto, anyway. By tomorrow morning, he won't remember he called you."

"Maybe. You're probably right, Connie. But I'll call Brennan just the same. He'll have some cops pay Vasily a visit."

"Good idea. He'll probably warn all the other Russian scumbags that harassing you is not in their best interest."

"Speaking of which, you guys ever had a client poisoned? Or OD on you?"

"Nope. No mysterious deaths on our watch."

"How about suicide?"

"Nope. At least, not while we were on the job. I can't speak to after our assignments ended with them, however."

"Any Russian clients? Have you had them? Or clients you protected from Russians?"

"Alas, no. None before you. Where are you going with this, Kim?"

"Right now, nowhere." Without even starting her dinner, she grabbed her laptop and headed out of the kitchen and into her bedroom slash home office, as her two minders went back to their meals and their digital addictions. "I have to do a little research on the *modus operandi* these Russian scumbags use when they want their victims to disappear. I'll give you guys my book report as soon as it's finished."

CHAPTER FORTY-NINE

10 North 10ᵗʰ Street
Brooklyn
Sunday, January 10
6:15 P.M.

As soon as she closed the bedroom door behind her, Barbieri plumped up some pillows, got into a cross-legged sitting position on the bed, and booted up her laptop. This time, sitting on her reality-based ass and knocking on virtual doors.

How did Russian gangbangers get rid of their enemies? She'd seen a ton of murder victims when she worked for the *News*, and ninety-nine percent of the time cops could tell exactly how the guy was killed. There was usually a knife wound in his chest, or a bullet hole in his stomach, or a bloody two-by-four lying near a bashed-in skull.

The only mystery left for the cops to solve was, who wielded said knife, gun, or blunt instrument? And even that wasn't usually much of a mystery, given that ninety-nine percent of the time the perpetrator was not a paid-up member of Mensa.

The other one percent, where the police had no clue as to what caused the victim's sudden exit, was usually the work of people who were good at hiding it. They were professional assassins, political or criminal or otherwise.

Lebedev was Russian. Russians wanted him dead. She poked around online and it wasn't hard at all to discover Russian hitmen's tricks of the trade.

She found the occasional bullet to the brain, or icepick in the eye, but it was their use of poisons that got her attention. Russian assassins seemed to be the Seal Team Six of chemical warfare against non-combatants.

These animals put ricin in the tip of an umbrella and poked a victim in the leg with it. *Ricin. That's how Walter White killed that woman at the end of Breaking Bad. Poured it into her tea.* They put poison on a letter they knew the victim would read. They used an air gun that spewed a cyanide cloud, and another that sprayed bubonic plague. They put polonium in a victim's teacup, or fed him a rat poison called thalium.

They created lethal bacteria. They exposed victims to mercury, lead and arsenic to induce psychiatric conditions like depression. They put poison in a jewel box they knew the target opened every morning. They rubbed a gel on the victim's arm that caused her to have a heart attack, and injected a poison that caused her to have a stroke. They even turned the extract of a flower into a lethal weapon.

These guys are just a bunch of thugs. How the hell did they concoct all this stuff? And how the hell did they get it all inside their victims' bodies?

A few more minutes online gave her the answer. *God bless the internet and tattle-tales.* The most recent poisonings, the ones that made headlines in Europe and America, all had one thing in common. The President of the Russian Federation, a gentleman named Vladimir Putin. Not Vlad the Impaler this time, but Vlad the Poisoner. Anyone threatens Putin's wealth or authority, and he gets sent to the emergency room or the morgue. The Federal Security Service, the FSB, had a top-secret lab that made all these lethal concoctions, and the officers who managed them all had a price. This was Russia, after all.

So, the Russian mafia had help. Expert help, from Russian apparatchiks in the Kremlin.. For a few rubles under the table, the officials could deliver a dose, along with easy-to-follow instructions on the best way to administer it. All the lab needed was to know was the victim's size, and what foods he ate. They'd custom-make the poison, making sure the dose was not a drop more or less than was needed, and in a form that was guaranteed to enter his body and make its way to the heart or brain or lungs or any other organ it was engineered to destroy.

So, Lebedev could have been poisoned, and the poison could have made him depressed enough to take his own life. But which poison? There were so many.

All she knew about them was what she had just looked up in the last hour or so. Even more frustrating, a lot of information about them was top secret. Nothing much was written about them, in order to prevent terrorists and rogue states from going into the lethal poison business. Fortunately, the reporter had a source who knew a hell of a lot more about these lethal weapons than she did. *I'll call her in the morning. We're both up way past our bedtime.*

Her chemical weapons 101 tutorial done, Barbieri went back into the kitchen to pick at her by-now-lukewarm Japanese food. As she got the coffeemaker ready for the morning, she thought of what to tell her new best friends about her Poison 101 crash course.

"How'd the research go?" asked Reynolds. "What did you find out about our Russian friends?"

"Plenty. And it's plenty scary. In a nutshell, the Russians are world champs at making poisons on an industrial scale. I'm talking tons of different poisons, made from a ton of different formulas. Unfortunately, though, the stuff that's posted online uses lots of chemical and biological jargon the government clearly doesn't want me to understand. But I have a work-around."

"Let me guess," Shelton said. "You have a source?"

"Yep. A good one"

"And with you, this source will be... what's the word you used...? Forthcoming."

"I can guarantee she'll be forthcoming. She knows poisons inside out, and I think I can get her to confess all."

"I assume you'll need to be chaperoned to your appointment with this source."

"You assume correctly. Don't know where, yet, though." The coffee-maker all set for the morning, Barbieri headed back toward her bedroom. "Good night, comrades. Don't let the bedbugs bite. Ivan probably figured out how to make them inject you with ricin."

"Ricin? Wasn't that used to kill…?" Shelton asked.

"It was indeed, Connie," Barbieri interrupted. "Seriously. If these ass-holes somehow get past you to reach me, don't touch any empty vials they left lying around. I don't want any company."

"Thanks for the heads up, Kim. Sleep tight."

CHAPTER FIFTY

10 North 10ᵗʰ Street
Brooklyn
Monday, January 11
9:16 AM

"Dr. Fletcher."

"Hi, Doctor. This is Kim Barbieri. Remember me?"

"Reporter with the *News*. Sure. You interviewed me once about a homicide. Stabbed in the heart, as I recall. A surgeon couldn't have done it better."

"In the aorta, actually. I interviewed you about the autopsy you performed on the victim, and you were incredibly helpful."

"I try to be. That was, like, four years ago, Miss Barbieri. Five, maybe. What can I do for you today? No good deed goes unpunished, as they say."

Back when Barbieri was a *Daily News* crime reporter, Dr. Fletcher was a forensic pathologist at the New York City Medical Examiner's office. Meaning she helped establish the exact cause of death of homicide victims, as opposed to your run of-the-mill deaths by natural causes. They had spoken from time to time when murder victims had to undergo an autopsy, and Dr. Fletcher had since retired and begun teaching a pathology course at the University of Connecticut. Which is where Barbieri caught up with her. No one ever stays hidden in the world-wide hide-and-go-seek web.

"I'm with the *Journal* now? Moved up in the world."

"*Wall Street Journal*? Good for you, Miss Barbieri!"

"Thanks. I'd like another crash course from you, Dr. Fletcher. On poisons."

"As in giving a victim a substance that will kill him? I've had some experience with that murder weapon, I admit."

"That's what I wanted to hear, Doctor."

"So, what do you want to know?

"Everything. Poisoning 101, to be frank. Maybe too much for a phone call. I'd like to pick your brain over dinner, if that's alright with you?"

"It always is, Miss Barbieri. As luck would have it, I happen to be in the city tomorrow for some meetings, which I usually leave close to starvation. I should be through by six, six-thirty. If that works for you, pick out a decent place downtown and I'll meet you there."

"I already have. Hunan Gourmet, on Pell. I assumed Chinese is okay with you. Is it, Doctor?"

"Always. I know the place. How about seven?"

"Perfect. See you there."

CHAPTER FIFTY-ONE

Hunan Gourmet Restaurant
Manhattan
Monday, January 11
6:56 P.M.

When Barbieri and Dr. Fletcher met for dinner at the agreed-on Chinese place, which had been recommended to her by friends, she'd brought an escort. Actually, two, both of them alert, focused, armed and ready to leap to her defense.

All bundled up against the cold, Barbieri and her bodyguards had left her apartment at precisely 6:17, rode the elevator down to the lobby, strode out of the apartment building and made their way over to the Suburban parked just two cars down the block. By 6:19, they were all inside the vehicle and buckled in their assigned seats–Shelton in the driver's seat, Reynolds in the front passenger seat, and Barbieri in the back–and at 6:20 Shelton pulled out of the spot and drove off.

The expected rush hour traffic into the city hadn't materialized, which happened from time to time for no apparent reason, so they arrived at Hunan Gourmet ten minutes early. While Barbieri and Reynolds waited outside for her guest to arrive, Shelton went inside and arranged with the host for a table for two against the back wall of the restaurant. She had been prepared to show the host her *Journal* ID to persuade him to free up that table, as well as the table right next to it, but it wasn't necessary. The place was half empty, which was often the price of staying open on Monday evenings.

When Barbieri nodded to Reynolds–the pre-arranged signal that Dr. Fletcher had arrived–at seven on the dot, the guard went inside to join Shelton. Moments later, Dr. Fletcher and Barbieri were escorted over to a table just a few feet from them, with no occupied tables between them to obstruct their view.

As the two women walked past the guards' table, Barbieri made the mistake of giving them a wave so small that she'd hoped the Doctor wouldn't notice.

"Who are they?" Doctor Fletcher noticed.

"Couple of friends from the 'hood. Pay them no mind. They know not to bother me when I'm working." After they had both removed their coats and hats and were seated, the host handed them each a menu and walked back to his post by the cash register just inside the front door.

"How do they know you're working?"

"This." Barbieri took out her cell phone from the messenger bag hanging on the back of her chair and placed it in the middle of the table. Dr. Fletcher then looked around at the other diners, and at the meals they were halfway through, and asked, "*Here* you want to interview me about lethal poisons, Miss Barbieri?"

"Kim, please. You have something against Chinese food, Doctor?

"Linda. I'm off-duty. Love Chinese, and Szechuan's my favorite cuisine. But Kim, we're eating."

"Trust me. I can handle gore almost as well as you can... remember?"

"I do indeed. I know you've seen enough of it at crime scenes. You've walked through the valley of the shadow of death a thousand times, and always managed to come out without even a paper cut."

"Psalms twenty-three dash four. I'm impressed, Linda."

"Don't be. It used to be posted somewhere in the Medical Examiner's office. Can we order first? I'm fuckin' starving," Dr. Fletcher said. "I've been lecturing idiots all day, and the food they brought in was inedible. Vanilla sandwiches. Barbarians."

After they both scanned the menus front to back, and were ready to order, Barbieri signaled to the waiter. He was an older gentleman who, they soon discovered, spoke no English at all. Like he'd been off the boat only since that afternoon.

Not getting anywhere giving him the names and numbers of the dishes they wanted, Barbieri and Dr. Fletcher simply pointed to them on the menu with their index fingers. That the waiter understood. He squinted at their menus, scribbled their choices down on his notepad in Chinese, and slouched off toward the kitchen to so inform the cooks.

Dr. Fletcher was just as Barbieri remembered her, from years before. Bright lipstick and colorful pendant earrings, and a warm, wonderful smile... the last thing she had expected from someone dissecting cadavers all day. When the waiter brought their dishes–spring rolls to share, General Tso's chicken for Barbieri and beef with broccoli for her guest–they waited until after they'd each had a few bites before addressing the topic at hand.

"So... poison. What do you want to know?" Dr. Fletcher asked.

"Everything. Just let your stream-of-consciousness stream away." She picked her phone off the table, pressed a series of buttons to set it to record, and placed it back on the table, right between them. "Mind?"

Sensing that Barbieri and her guest were comfortably settled in and not going anywhere, Reynolds and Shelton both ordered their meals as well. But instead of concentrating on their cells, here they both kept their eyes peeled on everyone else in the restaurant. Diners enjoying their meals, waiters hovering over their tables eager to clear the dishes, new customers coming in to replace old ones leaving. It was choreography they'd observed a thousand times before.

"Not at all. I'll start with the textbook definition. Ready?"

"All ears, Linda."

"A poison is a substance that causes a chemical reaction that disrupts normal bodily function. In plain English, it's anything, literally anything, your body reacts to in a bad way."

"That I understand. How do they work, though? I mean, what happens when a poison enters your body?"

"That's where it gets fairly complex, Kim. Do you ever read literature called a PI that comes with your medications? The Prescribing Information that the FDA makes the manufacturer put in the box the medicine comes in. You'll see words like absorption, excretion, and pharmacokinetics…"

"Can't say that I have, Linda. I never really cared how my drugs worked, to tell the truth."

"Nobody outside my office has. Anyway, these terms tell you how your body handles the medication you're taking. Just replace the word medication with poison."

"Because they're all just chemicals?"

"Exactly. Got any meds in your purse? Take one out."

"Yep." She reaches into her bag to take out the bottle of dicyclomine she went nowhere without, and handed it to Dr. Fletcher, who looked closely at the label.

"Dicyclomine. Perfect. You suffer from abdominal pain?"

"Stomach cramps, you mean? Once in a while. I started a few years ago, though I'm not sure why."

"Doctors aren't sure either, because cramps are not fully understood. See if you have the PI for this drug at home. Or if not, it's online, too. It'll tell you how the drug works, and how the human body reacts to it."

Dr. Fletcher handed the bottle back to Barbieri, who put it back in her bag. "Ever notice writing inside a black box for the drugs you're taking. Either on the packaging the drug comes in, or in the PI?"

"Sorry, no."

"It's called a 'black box warning', naturally. The FDA insists on it for drugs that can do damage even if you take the recommended dose. Like kill you."

"I'm still here, so far. Go on, Linda."

"Then there are drugs that can kill you only if you take an overdose by mistake. A good example is warfarin."

"Friend of mine takes that. Blood thinner, right?"

"Yes, an anticoagulant. It's fine, usually. Perfectly harmless. But if someone takes too much at once, he or she might suffer massive internal hemorrhaging. How's General Tso treating you?"

"Perfectly. Love it. Are we liking the beef with broccoli?"

"We are indeed. And death, either from either internal bleeding, or from regular bleeding if they get a cut. Which is how it kills rodents, by the way."

"My friend's still alive, last time I checked."

"Like ninety-nine point nine-nine percent of patients who take it. It's an incredibly tiny minority that's at risk. When I graduated to forensic pathology, I focused on suspicious deaths. The first poison I actually uncovered on a victim was hydrogen cyanide, which interferes with blood gaseous exchange."

"In other words...?"

"In plain English, Kim, it prevents red blood cells from transporting oxygen. Without oxygen the victim develops hypotoxia, which damages the liver, kidneys and lungs. If the dose is large enough, it can induce convulsions and death. In smaller doses over time, it can trigger cancer and heart disease."

"Cancer. Really?"

"Really, Kim. Cyanide is a carcinogenic, as are several other poisons, actually. Dioxin is another one. I remember one case where the deceased had cancer, and we assumed, at first, that cancer was the cause of death. We were wrong."

"What was it, if it wasn't cancer?"

"Polonium-210. Radioactive and extremely potent. We conducted a more intensive tissue analysis and discovered that the deceased had traces of it. This stuff is incredibly poisonous, approximately two hundred fifty thousand times more toxic than hydrogen cyanide."

"He was murdered. Homicide, not cancer. How'd the pathologist miss it?"

"The alpha rays were too small to detect."

"You just lost me, Linda. Sorry. So, technically he died of natural causes. But in fact, he was murdered."

"Indeed, Kim. If we'd just put down cancer as the cause of death, his murderer would never have been caught."

"Jeez. But the suspect was arrested? Where is he now?"

"She. The woman's upstate, sentenced to life without parole, which means she's going to die in a cage in a couple of decades. You've heard of fentanyl, though. Right?"

"An opioid painkiller. Sure. I covered quite a few arrests where drug dealers were selling it on the street. Strong shit."

"It's actually a synthetic opiate fifty times more potent than morphine. Incredibly lethal. And now there's a version even more potent, called carfentanil. 'Spelled 'a n *I* L', not 'a n *Y* l.' It's about ten thousand times as potent as morphine. One of our technicians at the Medical Examiner's office died after touching the deceased's skin."

"Touching? Not by inhaling it, or by getting it injected?"

"Or by swallowing it. The woman just touched the poor guy's arm. Then, osmosis takes over."

"Meaning her skin absorbed it?"

"Yes. Once it gets inside the body, blood flow or chemical pathways take it to their target–bone, liver, kidney, lungs, or skin. That's why poisoning is an especially dangerous murder weapon. There's a lot better chance of killing innocent victims."

"Yikes! I didn't know that."

"You're not alone, Kim. Most people don't. Then there are the cyto-toxins, which are poisons that attack cells to induce widespread hemorrhaging and organ damage. Snake venom is an example. Cobra or viper bites you, and you simply bleed to death. Internally."

"I'm more interested in man-made poison, Linda."

"Perfect segue, Kim. Ever hear of neurotoxins?"

"Neuro meaning, they attack the nervous system?

"You're learning, Kim. Neurotoxins prevent neurons from their normal activities. The damaged neural pathways cause cellular apoptosis. Meaning they cause the cells to die. Which leads to paralysis, seizures and death. Sometimes a really horrible death, when it's strychnine."

"That one I've heard of. Strychnine. If muscles can't work, you can't breathe and you die."

"Right. There's a cousin of strychnine, Gelsemium, made from Gelsemium elegans, or 'heartbreak grass'. It's a rare plant that only grows in Asia. Russian and Chinese assassins lace their victim's food with it."

"Chinese food." Barbieri glanced down at her half-eaten dish. "Nice."

"It's a neurotoxin that attacks not just any neuron, but neurons on the spine, which is why it causes gruesome contractions. Neurotoxins have also been found to affect the brain, causing profound depression deep enough to make the victim suicidal."

"Wait! Suicidal?"

"Yes. I understand the Russians are masters at that. They have a whole arsenal of psychotropic drugs. Powerful, mood-altering substances designed to cause such mental anguish that victims take their own lives. I haven't seen any cases at all in New York, but I've read about cases overseas. There's a poison they're been using for years, called Novichok."

"Novichok came up in some research I did a few nights ago, I believe."

"No doubt, Kim. It's becoming fairly common, unfortunately. Novichok is the name the Russians give to several binary anticholinesterase nerve agents that attack the peripheral nervous system. Binary, meaning it's made by combining two inert chemicals to make one lethal drug."

"And anticholin... something?"

"Esterase. Don't sweat it, Kim. Novichok simply blocks the nerves from sending messages, causing paralysis and death. The actual compounds are top secret because the Russians are using them to assassinate their enemies, and we don't want any Muslim or Albanian terrorists to get a hold of them."

"That's another thing I noticed in my research. The total secrecy. Once I reached a dead end, I just couldn't dig any deeper no matter how many links I followed. What about academics who study these poisons for a living?"

"Afraid not. Scientists in Moscow are constantly working on the formula to make it more lethal, and harder to identify by pathologists and by customs agents."

Barbieri waited a few moments to let that sink in.

"Scientists write about it all the time in the toxicology journals that most of my peers ignore. I'll find a couple of good articles and email them to you."

"Thanks, Linda."

"Not so fast. If you can wade through all the medical jargon and figure out what the authors are really saying, it'll scare the bejesus out of you."

Barbieri reached for the cell phone and turned off the recording app. "Not any more scared than I am right now. I think I've heard enough about poisons for one day, Linda. How about we move on to something more pleasant? You have children?"

Dr. Fletcher and Barbieri talked about family, and careers, and vacations, and politics, and movies, and theater for another half hour or so, until they'd both finished their meal and were ready to call it a night. Barbieri signaled for the check and put the cell back in her messenger bag. That hadn't escaped the notice of her two escorts, who continued observing everyone and everything around them.

As Barbieri and her guest both got up and grabbed their coats that had been draped on the chair backs, Barbieri again gave them a small wave as if to say, 'we're outta here.' Which was again picked up by her guest.

"You going to introduce me, Kim?" Dr. Fletcher whispered to her.

"Sure. Linda." When they passed the guards' table, Barbieri made the introductions.

"Carl and Connie. Linda. Linda, Carl and Connie. Linda was just giving me a lesson on how to poison my enemies." They all reached out to shake hands with Dr. Fletcher.

"Pleased to meet you, Linda." Connie said. "We're not on Kim's enemies list, are we?"

"Not both of you. What'd you guys have?"

"General Tso's chicken..." Reynolds volunteered.

"I had that! Wonderful!"

"... Szechuan shrimp," said Shelton. "Also, great."

"Okay if I join you guys for a minute?" Barbieri asked her bodyguards. She turned to Dr. Fletcher. "Hey, Linda, I'm gonna stay a while longer with these two mokes. Mind??"

"Not at all, Kim. I hope I was helpful," she said, as she shook Barbieri's hand.

"You were. We should get together again, and talk about anything besides corpses."

"I'd love that. Call me and we'll set something up," Dr. Fletcher replied. Smiling at Shelton and Reynolds, she said, "Nice meeting you both–and please keep an antidote handy when my friend here makes dinner." She then turned and made her way out of the restaurant, and as soon as she was out the door, Barbieri took a seat at her guards' table.

"What did you learn, Kim?" Shelton asked.

"That this Lebedev case just got really interesting. I think Timothy Brennan needs a heads up."

"It's really a homicide, you mean?"

"Believe so. If, in fact, it was, it's unlike any homicide I've ever seen."

CHAPTER FIFTY-TWO

NYPD Headquarters
One Police Plaza
Manhattan
Wednesday, January 13
8:00 A.M.

The drive from Barbieri's home in Brooklyn to Police Headquarters took longer than expected, because the lousy weather made traffic even worse than the usual rush-hour bumper-to-bumper near standstill.

The morning temperature had risen to just above freezing, and a cold, hard, driving rain had left her and her two guards soaked and miserable even before they got in their vehicle. After parking the Suburban at a lot several blocks away, they all sprinted over to the headquarters building, the guards more concerned with dodging raindrops than with protecting their client from any assassin suicidal enough to be lurking nearby.

They all made it inside safe and sound but drenched to the bone, took off their overcoats and dried off the best they could, and Reynolds and Shelton escorted their client through the lobby. They had all agreed their services wouldn't be needed once she got through the security checkpoint there, confident that no hitman would even get inside the fortress, much less actually get close enough to attack her.

Earlier that morning, Brennan had alerted the security staff that Barbieri and her bodyguards should be allowed in. After clearing the walk-through metal detector, the reporter nodded to her team that she was okay, took the elevator up to the fourth floor and made her way to Brennan's office. She rapped on the door and entered, and as soon as she stepped inside, she was taken aback to see Detectives Macnamee and Curley already there, huddling with their boss at his desk. *What the hell do they have to do with Lebedev? They're working on the Leotta homicide.*

She had called Brennan two days earlier, on Monday, after speaking with Dr. Fletcher, to ask him to have the Medical Examiner perform a forensic autopsy on Lebedev. She expected to be meeting just her old boy toy himself. Anticipating the result, though, and connecting a couple of dots that had until then seemed completely unconnected, Brennan had asked the two detectives he'd assigned to the Leotta case to join them.

As the host of this meeting, Brennan was sitting behind his desk, with Macnamee and Curley sitting facing him on the other side, their still-dripping raincoats hung on an old-fashioned wooden tree rack in the corner. When she entered, Brennan stood up and walked around his desk to shake her hand, then grabbed a chair that had been off to the side and placed it between his two detectives. As Barbieri added her jacket to theirs on the coat rack and began to speak, Brennan cut her off.

"Kim, your hunch was correct. You were right," he said. "Partly, anyway. The forensic autopsy found traces of a chemical in Lebedev's body that could be arsenic. Or more precisely, a new version of arsenic nobody's seen before, that stops short of killing the victim."

"Which made him so depressed he killed himself," Barbieri responded. "Another hunch, maybe."

"Plausible. But we're not convinced about that," Macnamee said. "We've gone over everything we know about this guy, A to Z and back, and our theory is that it was a staged suicide."

Curley added, "Look at it this way, Kim. Whoever killed Lebedev made it look like he took his own life."

"The murder was a long time in the works. Step one was poisoning Lebedev, which could have started months before he died. The dose was enough to sicken him, and make him depressed, but not enough to kill him right away."

"Time-released murder. Oh, my fuckin' God," Barbieri said. "It made the poor bastard so depressed, his friends and neighbors thought he was suicidal."

Curley finished the explanation. "Step two was that sometime later, some unnamed Russian gangster put him out of his psychological misery and killed him."

"So, suicide becomes a credible cause of death," Barbieri said. "Perfect crime, if you don't look too closely. Okay, so let's say he was murdered. Who do we like for it?"

She used 'we like', meaning 'who do we think did it', as she had learned years before from NYPD cops when she was with the *News*. Over time, as she became fluent in their language, the cops she met on the job accepted her into their world. In their eyes, the crime reporter had succeeded at morphing from a 'them' to an 'us'.

"Right now, Kim, we have no idea," Brennan replied. "And even if we had a suspect, there are problems. First, where's the evidence for homicide, and how do we tie it to the suspect?"

"And second...?"

"No way we prove it in court. The Assistant District Attorney I spoke to thinks we'll never be able to prove who ordered that Lebedev be poisoned, nor who actually carried it out. Not beyond a reasonable doubt, anyway. The Russians are too smart for that, no question. And besides, the perps who actually poisoned him are probably long gone, back to Moscow or Stalingrad or wherever. Another thing we'll never be able to prove is that the poison was meant to kill him."

"As opposed merely to harm him," Curley said. "Manslaughter rather than Murder One. Just enough to make him look like he could have killed himself."

"Welcome to my hall of mirrors, Kim," Brennan added.

"Okay. So, we don't know who poisoned Lebedev," Barbieri said. "Or who ordered the hit. I got that. But what's this got to do with Leotta? He was stabbed. Not poisoned."

"The killer's either multi-talented, one, or two, there could have been two killers working for the same mob boss," Curley said. "Either way, we suspect there's a connection. Motive."

"You're thinking Leotta and Lebedev could have been killed by the same hit man, or men, plural, for the same reason. Let me guess," Barbieri said, suddenly seeing the connection the detectives had already made. "Shady real estate deals? Money-laundering?"

"It's all we've got right now," Brennan replied. "Our theory is that somebody didn't want the transactions looked at too closely."

"Which is exactly what I was doing with Leotta."

"The Russkies also found out the front they used to purchase the properties, Lebedev, was ripping them off. It's a theory," Curley added.

"One of the Russians I spoke to tried to tell me Lebedev's the guilty party," Barbieri replied. "Vasily Klimnikov. I suspect the son of a bitch was bullshitting me just to save his own skin."

"Russians we interviewed gave Lebedev up, too. All of them. Which means it is probably some made-up bullshit. Some kind of concocted story to make us chase our tails. So, here's what we're thinking, Kim," Brennan said. "All the Russian buyers you've been exposing in the *Journal*, at least one must be some kind of leader of the pack."

"They might never admit to being in this enterprise together, or even knowing one another, but we're hoping one of them's a weak link," Macnamee explained.

"That never even occurred to me. That it's some kind of conspiracy."

"Or maybe organized crime," Curley continued. "Of the Russian variety. We don't know who that individual is, but we believe if we talk to all of them about the murders, one of them will get rattled."

"Maybe turn on each other. Or on the ringleader," Curley said. "Dishonor among thieves."

"Or say something they shouldn't."

"As I said, it's just a theory, Kim."

"But a sound one, its seems to me," she replied. "Coincidentally, I just told Reynolds and Shelton their job is to keep me from being poisoned to death, too." Barbieri turned to her old squeeze. "Hey, Timothy. You've seen me in this situation before, right?"

"Many times," Brennan answered.

"You ever know me to back down? Go hide in a corner?"

"Only once, with that psycho we set a trap for. Other than that, this kind of threat always just released your inner beast. All they ever accomplished was to piss you off."

"And when I got angry, I put their balls in a vise."

Brennan and Barbieri were performing this play in front of an audience of two, Macnamee and Curley, who tried to follow the plot as best they could.

"God damn right you did! Felt kinda sorry for the poor bastards, I gotta admit."

"Speaking of the psycho, how long did it take for us to trap him? Remember?"

"Six months. Maybe seven?"

"Seven. The problem was we waited for him to take the bait, and the motherfucker took his sweet time. I don't want to make that same mistake with these bozos."

"What do you propose, Kim? Go after their assassin?"

"Nope. Draw him out. Make myself an easy target, and make him act before he's ready. You said these Russians are dumb, right?"

"I did. And they are."

Well, I'll give them opportunity to prove it. I'm still the same sweet ball-clamping girl I was then, Timothy. Let 'em fuckin' try, is all I can say." The reporter checked her watch and stood up as if to leave, signaling to their audience that the play was over and it was time to head to the exits.

"Gotta end this pleasant conservation, sad to say. I'm meeting a friend in Central Park. Nice seeing you again, detectives," she said, turning to Macnamee and Curley.

"Always a pleasure, Kim," Macnamee replied. "Brennan never let on that you have this bad-ass 'hell-hath-no-fury' bitch side to you. I think I'm in love."

"It's my best asset, but I employ it only sparingly. Right, Chief?"

"For which our miscreants are forever grateful, Kim," Brennan said, walking around his desk to see her out. "Where are your bodyguards, by the way? Downstairs? I told security to let them in,"

"Right outside the checkpoint. I'm in good hands, still, Timothy." Brennan moved closer to her, as if he were violating her personal space. She did not pull back. "This is getting pretty complex, Kim. Dangerous. You've started stirring up one big, messy pot again."

"I know, Timothy. Believe me, I know." Before leaving Brennan's office, she turned once again to the two detectives still sitting near their boss' desk. "Listen. When you guys find the suspect who you like for Lebedev and Leotta, give me a heads up. Okay? I'd like a word with him about his plans for me."

"Kim, you'll be the first to know. Or the second," Curley said, nodding at her boss.

CHAPTER FIFTY-THREE

Central Park
Manhattan
Wednesday, January 13
9:30 A.M.

"It seems I cannot escape you, Kim. I'm just a man, an ordinary man, albeit a Slavic one."

"Animal magnetism, Sergei. Albeit totally one-sided. So, what brings you to New York? You'd told me back in Moscow that you have no business here."

"Things change. An opportunity came up, and I decided it required me to perform due diligence in person."

"You mean you needed to lie low for a while. Get out of Moscow and see the world."

"A woman who understands me. Why did I marry in haste, Kim? Anyway, my business here is nothing that concerns Lebedev, or therefore you."

Barbieri and Petrov were sitting on a wooden green bench in the middle of Literary Walk, among gigantic statues of Robert Burns, Fitz-Greene Halleck and other distinguished authors nobody's bothered to read for centuries. The temperature had gone way down overnight, and while the sun had been out since dawn, it hadn't had enough time to warm things up yet.

Both Petrov and Barbieri were dressed appropriately, the reporter in a down jacket and wool watch cap, and Petrov in a heavy Brooks Brothers winter coat and a hat never seen in New York except in Russian immigrant neighborhoods. A fur hat with long ear muffs called a shapka ushanka, the genuine item that could have come only from Mother Russia herself.

She had picked that location to meet because it drew a lot of onlookers—mostly buskers tap dancing for tips and street artists hustling signed kitsch—and tourists eager to dispose of extra cash, and the walk was unique. Rather than meander this way and that, like every other path in the park, the elm-tree-lined promenade was laid out in a perfectly straight north-south line. Which made it a lot easier for her bodyguards, who seemed to be just minding their own business three benches over, blending in perfectly with the passersby, to spot anyone trying to sneak up on their client and Petrov from either direction.

Their job was to find the right balance between preventing any attempts on her life and giving her the privacy that she needed to go about her life, personal and professional, and they had agreed that this was a good compromise. They were far enough away not to eavesdrop–and if they heard anything, both Reynolds and Shelton understood it was none of their business. While she and Petrov talked, the bodyguards did job one–keeping their eyes out for bad actors.

"Speaking of which, you pick up anything about the fellow following me here?" the reporter asked Petrov.

"Not much, Kim. Whoever sent him, they are much more secretive than usual. It's clear to me the Bratva wants you dead, and they will stop at nothing to make sure they succeed."

"Think I was followed here? To Central Park, I mean?" Barbieri looked around for Reynolds and Shelton, and failed to spot them. She knew in her gut they were nearby, somewhere, ready to do whatever it takes to keep her out of harm's way. *Those two sure know how to disappear on me.*

"My guess is, yes. They know everything there is to know about American security forces, and they don't think your agents are in the same league as the Brits. Scotland Yard absolutely nailed our Federal Security Service for the Skripal assassination attempt."

"Poison, right?"

"Correct, Kim. American agents they have contempt for. FBI, Homeland Security, Secret Service. To my friends in Bratva they're all amateurs, unworthy of respect."

He reached into his bag and took out an envelope. She took it and opened it, and found a photo of a man she did not recognize. An older man, she estimated, and overweight, based on his triple chin and wrinkled face.

"Lebedev?"

"Yes." She stared at the mystery man's face for a second or two, then put the photo back in the envelope, which she then tucked away inside her messenger bag.

"Okay. Thanks. So, who did they send to New York? You have names?"

"That I have not heard. They have a crew of soldiers who handle that sort of assignment, and their identities are top secret. But there is one thing, Kim. I don't know if it's a coincidence, but there's a rumor going around in Moscow that the Bratva is working with the FSB on some kind of operation."

"The one against me? Are they going to try poison on me?"

"That I cannot say, Kim. Perhaps. Perhaps not. Someone high up in the Kremlin is involved, which is a serious move by the Bratva. Putin's apparatchiks know how to eliminate problems even more than the Bratva gang members do. If the Bratva comes after an enemy, he might have a chance. Same thing if the FSB comes after him. But if one of Putin's bootlickers puts both gangs on the target's ass, he's toast."

"Or she. I might need even more security than I have right now, you're saying?"

"They'll never be enough, Kim. Look, I have to go." Petrov got up and took Barbieri's hand to help her up. As he headed south on Literary Walk, toward Central Park South, he turned back to face her. "I'll keep my ears open and let you know first thing, but be careful."

"Hold on a second, Sergei," Barbieri said. Petrov walked back to her.

"You should know by now, Sergei, that I'm not easily intimidated. That's not an asset in my profession. But this time is different. We can't be passive about this and wait for them to announce what they plan to do to me."

"You're right, Kim. Keeping my ears open is not enough. I'll contact somebody I know who's aware of these things and get back to you by tomorrow, or the day after. At the latest."

"Thank you, Sergei. If I don't hear from you in two days, expect a call from me."

As she watched him walk away, two burly men she recognized joined him, one on either side. *Valery and Gennady, his eloquent, sophisticated bodyguards from the hotel in Moscow. Where the fuck were those two cretins hiding?*

She started walking in the opposite direction, toward Bethesda Fountain, and Shelton and Reynolds fell in step alongside her. *Same question. Where the fuck were these two hiding? Were they sitting with their two Russian counterparts, swapping war stories?*

"What did you learn?"

"Congratulate me, guys. Seems I'm number one on the Russian Mafia hit parade. And you two have your work cut for you."

CHAPTER FIFTY-FOUR

Hampton Inn
Manhattan
Thursday, January 14
11:45 A.M.

Sergei Petrov was in his suite on the twelfth floor of his hotel in Manhattan's Hell's Kitchen neighborhood, just a block west of Times Square.

His accommodations, room 1246, faced the back of the building one block down rather than the avenue. It was quieter, he believed, and saved a few dollars in the bargain. The Hampton Inn was not quite seedy, but clearly aspired to be, as shown by the fraying carpeting and indifferent-bordering-on-surly employees.

Even if the hotel's guests were nouveau riche bastards, like himself, who could afford the finest accommodations in the land, they were Russian bastards first. And thus, they couldn't break the old Soviet habit of traveling on the cheap, checking into economy hotels and checking out with a suitcase full of purloined monogrammed towels, bars of soap, shampoo, shower caps, sewing kits... anything that wasn't nailed down and could be bartered at home.

Petrov was at the built-in desk in the bedroom, inches from the TV on one side and coffeemaker on the other. His eyes were glued on the spreadsheets on his laptop's display, as he scrolled down and across in between sips of tea. The two bodyguards were in the adjoining room, out of sight, but within earshot. One of them, Valery, was busy checking his cell phone, while the other, Gennady, was busy doing nothing. It was as if it was his job description, just staring into space and staying out of the way, and he excelled at it.

At precisely eleven forty-eight in the morning, Valery pocketed his phone and walked over to the bedroom door, which was closed. He knocked softly on the doorjamb to get his boss' attention and told him he was going out for a smoke and would be back in fifteen minutes. Petrov looked up at his guard, nodded okay, and went back to his laptop.

Valery grabbed his parka, walked over to the front door of the suite, unlocked it, and stepped out into the hallway. He pressed the button for the elevator, which he took down to the one. Once outside the lobby revolving door, and out on to the west side of Eighth Avenue, he reached into his coat pocket for his pack of Winston cigarettes. He took one out, lit it, inhaled deeply, and began walking up along the avenue, always crowded with trucks, taxis and delivery vans, towards the corner of Fifty-second street.

When he reached the corner, he turned around and retraced his steps, never leaving the hotel entrance out of his sight. He was never off duty, even when not at his post, simply because neither were any Russians out to murder his boss.

Valery kept up this pattern, walking and smoking, until he saw Gennady emerge from the lobby and walk to the corner of Fifty-first street, and cross over to the east side of the avenue. Valery inhaled one last time, dropped the cigarette on the ground and crushed it with his right foot, and walked off in the opposite direction.

Their assignment completed successfully, there was no reason to go back to Petrov's suite. He would not be looking up from his computer and asking himself where his two bodyguards had gone off to. Instead, they called the pay phone at a laundromat in Brighton Beach, and let it ring three times before ending the call.

• • •

Throughout her five A.M. to three P.M. shift, the maid assigned to that section of Petrov's floor had taken her sweet time cleaning rooms. She was in no hurry to see what was inside Room 1246. A few extra dollars slipped to her at the beginning of her shift had seen to that, and had bought her silence.

The maid was a stocky Latina, just short of five feet tall, with short hair dyed blonde, bright pink lipstick, and impossibly long fingernails that somehow didn't interfere with her scrubbing, scouring, and mopping. Ignoring the 'Do Not Disturb' sign on the doorknob, she let herself in and discovered about what she'd been told to expect, and to keep her mouth shut about.

There was an overturned chair by the desk, and a broken cup and saucer on the carpet. The cup had tea stains on the sides and rim. There was what looked like vomit on the carpet beside the chair. And what looked like a bloodstain pooling where she thought the guest's head had been. There had clearly been a hideous act of violence in the room, and both the hotel guest and his killer or killers were clearly long gone.

While the bribe had bought her silence, it did not change her work ethic. She did what she had been trained to do, the only thing she knew how to do to support her family. She went back out into the hall to the housekeeping cart, picked up some industrial-strength cleaning supplies, and went back into the room to perform her duties.

The maid picked up the chair the guest had been sitting on and put it back in its place beside the desk. She sprayed and wiped the vomit and bloodstains on the carpet until there was no evidence of them. She picked up the teacup and brought it back to the kitchenette, where she rinsed it out and put in on the rack to dry. The maid then eyeballed the suite to make sure she had missed nothing. She hadn't.

Her job complete, she left suite 1246, keeping the 'Do Not Disturb' sign on the doorknob and leaving the door open a crack, then pushed her cart to the next job site down the hall, room 1248.

Looking at her, nobody would suspect that the maid had seen or done anything out of the ordinary that morning. All in a day's work.

• • •

Later that afternoon, around 4:15 P.M., two other guests were in the lobby, among the many visitors to New York sitting, reading, checking maps, flipping through sight-seeing brochures and watching their watches. The men looked and dressed like ordinary American businessmen going about their business—clean cut, average height and weight, blue oxford shirts, dark slacks and white running shoes without a scuff mark on them. One had a black backpack slung over his right shoulder, while the other carried a Lands End blue canvas briefcase.

They had arrived one day after Petrov and his entourage, and both had stayed in the same room three floors down from Petrov's, number 926. Once they checked in, they stayed in their room for their entire stay, ordering breakfast, lunch and dinner from local restaurants and having them delivered to their room. They never saw Petrov or his guards and were never seen by them.

Between them, the two guests had two pieces of luggage. The one with the briefcase was pulling a standard-issue black carry on, the kind just small enough to be crammed into an airplane's overhead bin. The one with the backpack on was having a little difficulty maneuvering a large duffel on wheels built to carry many weeks' worth of clothing, electronics, accessories, sports gear, souvenirs and hotel swag.

When the two men checked out and exited the hotel, their vehicle, a black Toyota Highlander behemoth, was waiting for them at the curb, just outside the lobby door, with the cargo door already opened. The driver got out and stood by the car, eyes fixed on pedestrians heading towards him from both directions. The first man loaded the carry-on into the cargo area, and moved some boxes around inside it to make room for the oversized, unwieldy duffle. Then, both men grabbed a handle on either side, bent into a deep squat, lifted the duffle up off the ground, and heaved it into the back of the SUV.

That huge piece of luggage was filled not with clothing, electronics, sports gear or shower caps. Instead, it carried one-hundred forty-seven pounds of dead weight.

Both pieces of luggage, along with the backpack and briefcase, now securely inside the Highlander, the two guests climbed into the back seat. The driver got back behind the wheel, pulled the vehicle away from the curb, and started driving north, up Eighth Avenue toward Central Park.

Within seconds, the Highlander became invisible, swallowed up by all the other SUVs, cabs, minivans, shuttle buses, Uber cars, electric bicycles, FedEx vans, police cars and garbage trucks crawling in the same direction at the same heavily sedated snail's pace.

CHAPTER FIFTY-FIVE

10 North 10th Street
Brooklyn
Thursday, January 14
6:48 P.M.

"You guys feel like going out? I got nothing in the fridge, yet again."

"I can be persuaded," Shelton replied.

"Chinese place on Wythe looked good," Reynolds added.

"Mister Cho's," Barbieri said. "It is actually, assuming you like ultra-hot and extremely spicy. Szechuan dishes will make your head explode. I'll treat."

"Exploding body parts. I'm game."

Barbieri and the bodyguards had just got back to her apartment from *Journal* Headquarters in Manhattan, where she'd met with Fitzgerald to put the finishing touches on her contribution to the upcoming installment in the foreign money-laundering story. That was Fitzgerald's excuse, anyway. His real agenda was to find out how his rookie reporter was coping with the situation she had found herself in. Or, more accurately, had somehow put herself in.

As usual, the driver, in this case Reynolds, had let his client and his partner off in front of her apartment house, and then drove down the block to look for a spot. Which wasn't hard, considering that most of the shops near North Tenth had already closed for the night and all their clerks and baristas and sales associates had already driven back where they came from.

He wasn't concerned about parking tickets, anyway, as he was driving a company car, and he took all the 'No Parking' signs he passed as just a suggestion. Once the Suburban was put to bed for the night, anything they did afterwards had to be in the neighborhood, or at least within walking distance.

Mister Cho's being agreeable to all three, they then put on their collective outerwear–it was getting brutally cold at night, the temperature dipping well below freezing–and did their synchronized leaving-the-apartment-to-go-out routine. One guard in front, Barbieri in the middle, and the other guard in back when they were forced to walk single file, and one guard on either side when there was enough room on the sidewalk to walk three abreast.

They took the elevator down, walked out the lobby door and headed toward Wythe Avenue, the guards keeping their eyes open and their mouths shut. When they reached Mister Cho's four minutes later, they went inside and found the place already full, mostly with men and women no older than twenty-two who looked like they'd never been to any kind of basic training—much less, special forces. And so noisy it was impossible to be heard.

Shelton gave her client and partner a 'Whaddya think? Do we wait?' shoulder shrug, and got a yes gesture from both, so she gave her name to the maître' d and they all joined the other would-be diners outside to wait until it was called. Reynolds and Shelton tried to find the right balance between staying vigilant and just enjoying a night out among non-threatening youngsters, which they accomplished by tag teaming. For a few minutes, one would make small talk with Barbieri while the other kept a watchful eye on the others waiting for a table. Then, they switched roles, and Barbieri became quite good at switching conversations back and forth between them.

Once inside, though, the two bodyguards both went into on-duty one hundred percent mode. Only after eyeballing the other patrons, and sensing no danger at all from the boys and girls at tables of three, or four, or five, did they relax and just enjoy the spicy hot dishes that had steam coming out of their ears.

The two guards needn't have worried. The Bratva team had already finished the surveillance phase of their operation, and were well into their planning for the next phase: execution.

CHAPTER FIFTY-SIX

10 North 10th Street
Brooklyn
Friday, January 15
12:30 P.M.

"Shit! No answer. Shit! Shit! Shit!"

Barbieri ended her attempt to reach Petrov after the fourth unanswered ring. Two days before, the Russian businessman had promised to find out if she was on Bratva's assassination list, and then get back to her within forty-eight hours.

It was now fifty-one hours.

She tried to reach him again at fifty-one hours and thirty-five minutes, and again at fifty-two hours and fifteen minutes. Nothing. *Where the fuck is he? I've gotten the poor bastard killed? Shit! Now they're coming after everyone I know, too!*

CHAPTER FIFTY-SEVEN

FSB Headquarters
2 Bolshaya Lubyanka Street
Moscow
Friday, January 15
4:50 P.M.

"What have we got?"

"A perfect way to terminate the target, sir. She is almost guaranteed to ingest the product, and when she does, our messenger will be long gone. The target is taking medication for migraine headaches. She uses a nasal spray device that delivers between seventeen and twenty-one micrograms of product."

"The product?"

"Novichok. Our latest version."

The Federal Security Service laboratory scientist and special operations director were standing on either side of a table in a sealed, windowless room in the sub-sub-basement of their headquarters building, three stories below street level. An intact medication spray device was the only item on the left side of the table. The parts that went into it, from an identical sprayer that had been disassembled, were spread out on the right side.

Next to the table was an easel holding a large color illustration of a human nasal cavity, detailing and naming all its anatomical structures. It was the type of educational visual aid that ear, nose and throat specialists have on their examination room wall, but never actually use to help their patients understand what's wrong with them.

"We are certain she'll take the medication?"

"Inevitably, yes. Migraine is not a condition that can be cured. Only treated whenever it reoccurs. It is chronic, meaning the patient has had the condition for years, and she has been taking medication for it for years. And she will need to continue taking it in the future. Definitely."

"Treated, but not cured. Good. Four micrograms leeway. We cannot be more precise?"

"No, we cannot, but it is not a problem. In devices like this, with all nasal sprayers, actually, the patient's dexterity becomes a variable that cannot be controlled. There is no pill, or syringe, to deliver a precise dose."

The scientist picks up the device, pretends to place it inside his right nostril, and returns it to the table. "If she hasn't used the sprayer much, or she doesn't press the plunger right, she may not inspire one hundred percent of the product that it delivers. But I assure you, seventeen micrograms of this type of toxin are more than enough to kill the target. More than that does not matter."

"Overkill. Good. How does product enter the bloodstream, once it is sprayed into the nostril, I mean?"

The scientist steers the director's attention to the illustration displayed on the easel. "It is absorbed by tissue in the nasopharynx. Here. Ordinarily, the active ingredient in the migraine medication she uses, zolmitriptan, goes to the blood vessels in the brain and sensory nerves of the trigeminal system. This constricts the vessels to end release of neuropeptides, the compounds that cause the migraine."

"At that point, her headache will be the least of her problems. Vehicle?"

"That also works to our advantage, sir. The inactive ingredients in this drug are in an aqueous buffered 100 microliter solution containing citric acid, disodium phosphate dodecahydrate and purified water. We know how to tinker with the product so that none of these alters potency."

"You figured out the vehicle how? Reverse engineering?"

"Not even needed. All the product specifications are online, on the company website." The scientist took a printout of the specifications from his shirt pocket and handed it to the director. "The device is made by Amneal."

"Amneal? Never heard of them. American? German? Swiss?"

"American. They're a division of AstraZeneca."

"That name I know. They make our job so easy, I should send them a thank you note."

"Maybe when the mission is completed, sir. And send one to the United States Food and Drug Administration, while you're at it. They require pharmaceutical companies to put the technical information out there."

"Thank God for transparency. So far, I'm on board." The director picked up and examined the nasal sprayer. "Off the shelf device?"

"It's fairly standard for a prescription product." He pointed to the sprayer parts arrayed on the table. "Blue plastic body with a gray cap, and a simple plunger that delivers a single dose of medication, or whatever liquid the company puts in the sprayer."

He mimicked placing the tip of the bottle about one-quarter inch inside his nose. "All the target does, when she feels a migraine coming, is take off the cap, place the tip of the bottle in her nose, like this, and press the plunger. Fool proof. The parts are no problem for us, and we can reproduce the label as well." The director closely inspected the writing on the label. "These details matter if the target has become used to them."

"The label says five milligrams. Is that her dose?"

"It is. Five milligrams. That is the dose specified on the box her medication comes in."

"How many sprayers in a box?"

"Six, sir."

"And how many does the target have left? All six? Five? Just one?"

"That, we don't know, as of now. And we won't know until our messenger reenters the target's residence to make the switch. He has photographed the box, not the sprayers inside it. Unfortunately. We won't know how many devices we'll need until the operative opens the box up and replaces them."

"Bring six just in case. Targets never notice how many doses they have left, probably. I never do until it's too late."

"Perhaps not, but we want to make sure our sprayer is there when she has a migraine."

"Of course." He picks up the sprayer and looks at the tip, which has a tiny, almost invisible, hole on the business end. "How will our associate in New York get the product into the sprayers?"

"We've solved that as well. We will deliver the sprayers with the vehicle already inside it. After he's combined the two inert components of the product together, which makes it toxic, it is then drawn up into a syringe. The needle is inserted into the sprayer cap, and the product is injected into the device. Then he will put the cap back on, and the device will be good to go. All the tools will be prepared and ready for him."

"The label will be reproduced?"

"No need. It's on the company website as well. I printed it out already."

"Zomig."

"Zomig."

. . .

"We also tasked you with eliminating the target's bodyguards, Correct?"

"You did, sir. However, we have received no information about them that would help us tailor a lethal dose for each of them individually. However, if you think it acceptable to eliminate them only temporarily, rather than permanently, we may not need it."

"As long as you assure us that they are unable to interfere with the mission. My agent's task should take perhaps five or ten minutes. After that, it doesn't matter to us whether they are dead or alive."

'That is not a problem, sir. We've developed a new version of an anesthetic that will put our target into a deep sleep state in seconds. It's used in hospitals right now to sedate patients about to undergo surgery."

"I've had that myself. Knee surgery. But the anesthetic was administered intravenously. I remember the nurse sticking a needle in my arm. I remember seeing her press the plunger on the syringe. Then I remember waking up with a new knee."

"You remember correctly, sir. In all likelihood, the anesthetic you were given was Diprivan, the brand name for propofol. Diprivan is, in fact, always administered intravenously, and always inside hospitals. But what we've been able to do is separate the molecule, called diisopropylphenol, from the vehicle."

"As I understand it, a vehicle is just the solution the drug is mixed with, to make it easier to inject."

"Correct. In addition, it reduces the chance of infection. If the drug is not injected, however, there's no need for the vehicle. What we've come up with is a way to have the target ingest the diisopropylphenol molecule either by inhaling it, or by swallowing it. Either way it reaches the brain in seconds, and if the dose is strong enough, the target is out cold for a long, long time."

"And if it's not strong enough?"

"Then the patient just feels like he's drunk, or sleepy, or his sense of time is distorted. He will respond to commands though, which tells us he is conscious. Higher doses block the brain's ability to integrate information, and the patient does not respond to commands. If the dose is too strong, the patient can have a stroke or a brain injury—or die right on the operating table. So, we have to be really precise if we just want to make the targets unconscious."

"If they become unconscious, how long will they be out? Hours? Days?"

"That we cannot say with any certainty right now, sir, at least with human targets. We've perfected our version on monkeys only."

"OK. Got it. How will you transport this drug to New York City?"

"There's no need, sir. Diprivan is already widely available there, as is the apparatus for separating out the molecule. A heat exchanger to heat the liquid, a condenser to heat the vapor back into a liquid, and a receiver flask to collect the distillate. It's all fairly basic laboratory equipment that our technicians could easily handle, for sure."

"All we have to do is instruct our agents in New York to acquire the drug and the apparatus, and deliver them to our technicians. The drug they can get from any doctor's office, and they can order the apparatus from any medical equipment distributor. As soon as they have all the materials, I will arrange a zoom meeting with them, and walk them through the process step by step. It's all quite straightforward."

"A zoom meeting? To disable a couple of security guards? Perfect. When I give you the okay, just make sure they know how to produce doses at least strong enough to make anyone unconscious. If the anesthetic is too strong and it injures or kills the bodyguards, that's their problem—not ours. We can live with that."

CHAPTER FIFTY-EIGHT

Gorky Park
Moscow
Saturday, December 26
1:17 P.M.

Arkady Ovechkin entered the park—officially burdened with the grandiose, Soviet-era name Gorky Central Park of Culture and Leisure—from the gate on Lenin Prospect, and strolled slowly over to the skateboard area about a half mile down the walking path.

Ovechkin was just an average, nondescript, middle-aged government bureaucrat, the bureaucracy he belonged to being the FSB. He was out on a lunch break, and he looked the nondescript part. On the short side, carrying a standard, government-issue, black briefcase, and wearing a brown fur ushanka hat and a black, well-worn overcoat the weather forecast had called for.

He had a crew cut, with matching neatly trimmed mustache, on an otherwise clean-shaven face. Altogether, his gentlemanly appearance was designed not to draw attention from passersby, and it succeeded beautifully. Freezing temperatures were only a minor annoyance to Muscovites determined to get out of their overheated homes or offices. None of them sharing the park with him that day—parents, children, couples, retirees, vagrants, police officers—seemed to give him a second glance.

When Ovechkin reached the skateboard area, he cleared the light dusting of snow from an otherwise empty bench near the entrance, sat at one end and placed the briefcase at his side. Outside of a couple of skateboarding daredevils pushing each other to defy death, he was alone. He took out an apple from the left pocket of his jacket, a small pocketknife from the right one, and a paper napkin from his breast pocket.

The gentleman then went to work. He unfolded the napkin and laid it neatly on his lap. That done, he opened the knife, carefully peeled the skin off the apple and cut it into six perfectly equal slices. He was now ready for his snack.

Just as Ovechkin closed the knife and put it back in his jacket pocket, a man wearing a messenger bag over his right shoulder sat down on the bench a few feet from him, pulled the straps of his bag over his head, and placed the bag on his lap. Like the conservative Ovechkin, he dressed to impress nobody, but in a whole different way. He looked like the messenger he was, with long hair tied back in a ponytail beneath a scruffy knit cap, and equally scruffy beard, and distressed jeans torn at the knee.

The messenger turned his head toward Ovechkin and gave him a small nod, as if to say, 'I know I'm violating your personal space for a moment, but forgive me. I don't mean to.'

For maybe five minutes, the two men sat just a few feet apart, each minding his own business. Ovechkin ate a slice of his apple, and the man next to him sat with his eyes closed. A sufficient amount of time now elapsed, the man opened his eyes, reached into his messenger bag and took out a large envelope. After examining both sides of it, he opened the envelope, took out a small, unmarked cardboard box and reached over to place it on the bench closer to the FSB bureaucrat.

The box was halfway between them. Seeing that the box was within reach, Ovechkin reached out his left hand and accepted the box without comment. He held it for a moment or two in both his hands, then opened the top. The other man stared ahead.

Inside, Ovechkin found two glass vials nested on their side in molded foam padding, each about the size of an ordinary test tube used for drawing blood. Only instead of blood, each contained a clear, colorless liquid. Ovechkin looked at the man, who turned his head toward him to make eye contact.

"The product you requested. Novichok"

"Novichok. Is it the correct dose?"

"Yes. Four milligrams in total. The amount was calculated based on the target specifications provided to the Institute."

"Why two vials?"

"The product is made of two chemicals. Both are now inert, and so perfectly safe for you to handle. They become active, and lethal, only when they're combined."

"But harmless right now, you said?"

"Absolutely no danger. It is safe for our chemists to manufacture and handle, and for your courier to transport to New York. The two chemicals are also perfectly legal, in case the courier gets stopped by airport security. Each is a type of pesticide, actually."

"They're labeled 'one' and 'two.' No chemical names?"

"That is secret. The courier handling them will never know what they actually are, for his own protection. If he's caught and interrogated, he has nothing to reveal. Worst case, he'll spend ten years in an American prison, and then they'll repatriate him. He'll get a hero's welcome when he arrives back in the motherland."

"Now, if the courier knew their chemical names and revealed them under interrogation, he'll get twenty years in an American prison. And we would kill him the minute he again set foot on Russian territory."

"Understood. How does our operative combine them when they arrive in New York?"

"Instructions are in the envelope. It will not be difficult."

"But it will be lethal then."

"Lethal enough to kill in seconds. Novichok never fails. But it is perfectly safe for your operative to combine as long as he wears a mask and gloves, and as long as he is careful."

"When?"

"When should they be combined, you mean? Any time before it's ready to be delivered. There's no expiration date on Novichok."

"Got it."

"Good luck." At that, the shabbily dressed man next to the government bureaucrat pulled the strap of his bag over his head and onto his shoulder, glanced up and down the path to reassure himself he was not being followed, got up from the bench and walked away toward the Oktyabrskaya Street Metro Stop exit. He was not in any hurry, just another Muscovite enjoying a beautiful day in Gorky Central Park of Culture and Leisure.

As the unkempt man disappeared from view, Arkady Ovechkin carefully closed the box containing the two vials in their foam padding, and put the box back in the envelope. Then he put the envelope into his briefcase and closed it. He carefully put the briefcase at his side, in his field of vision and easily reachable, as he went back to the apple waiting on his lap.

His job was done, yet he wasn't quite ready to get back to his stuffy office.

CHAPTER FIFTY-NINE

NYPD Headquarters
One Police Plaza
Manhattan
Saturday, January 16
2:30 P.M.

"Hey, Rabbi. Russian mob still keeping you busy?"

"Business has never been better, Chief. What can I do for you?"

"Maxim Lebedev, a Russian walking among us. He on your radar?"

Chief Brennan had known his next step: Renewing his acquaintance with higher ups in the Organized Crime Control division of the NYPD. In his previous incarnation as a detective in Brooklyn, he had brought them into an investigation whenever a crime looked like a member of the mob did it. Whether the mob in question was Italian, or Salvadoran, or Albanian. Or Russian.

Brennan was on the phone with Sergeant Joe Eckstein, AKA the Rabbi, his main contact in the Organized Crime unit. They had had a good relationship for years, one where the Rabbi could be counted on to give him enough information to avoid wasting his time chasing down nothing-burgers.

"Maxim is indeed. He's into everything–drugs, money-laundering, tax fraud, insurance scams and Medicare fraud. America is the land of grifting opportunity for him and his comrades."

"But you never brought him in? No arrest records, far as I can see."

"Can't prove any of it, unfortunately. Not a thing. We bugged his apartment, but he said nothing incriminating. Nothing that could hold up in court, for sure. We had him under surveillance a few times, but he was a model citizen, as if he knew he was being followed."

"But we're certain he's guilty as hell. What about his unsavory associates?"

"They weren't as good at covering their tracks. They incriminated themselves plenty, and we picked them all up. They're all out on bail, as far as I know."

"So Lebedev's comrades are arrested, but he's given a pass. Possible he wanted them caught, so he could keep all the money coming in for himself? He knew they were all being watched, but didn't tell them? Let them get snatched up by us?"

"That didn't occur to us, Timothy, but—yeah. He got the NYPD to eliminate everyone he had to share his ill-gotten gains with. What's your interest in this jamoke, may I ask?"

"Lebedev's just turned up deceased, Rabbi. No sign of foul play, though. Medical Examiner said he had cancer."

"Coulda been, Timothy. They're humans, the Russian mob. They get sick and die all the time, just not fast enough for me. Wouldn't put my money on natural causes, though. Not in their line of work."

CHAPTER SIXTY

International Departures Gate
Doromedovo Airport
Moscow
Saturday, January 2
3:39 P.M.

For the security agent eyeballing foreigners and Russians flying out of Moscow, the end of her shift could not come soon enough.

Marina Gromykin was worn out from not paying any attention to the X-ray screen as what seemed like the same battered and barely usable suitcase rolled past every nanosecond. Nor from going through the motions of rummaging through suitcases and backpacks and duffel bags because she had a quota to fill.

It was exhausting work, doing nothing. Every once in a while, just to break the monotony, she stopped some poor bastard or another just because she wanted to show him who's boss. The old Soviet habit of 'why waste your energy when you're going to get paid, anyway?' was alive and well in this remote outpost of the Russian Federation.

The next man in line at her station carried only a backpack and a small piece of carry-on luggage. He put the backpack and bag on the rollers, and watched them roll toward the X-ray machine as he took off his shoes and belt. The backpack passed through first, and something on the screen made Gromykin stop the machine to study the image.

She stopped the conveyor belt, pulled the suspicious backpack off, and took it to a table behind her. There, she opened it, switched on the flashlight she used for just such life-and-death situations, and peered and pawed inside it as its owner stood by nervously. She reached in and pulled out a cylindrical metal container, which she then hefted in her hand and shook, as if to hear any forbidden liquids sloshing around.

"What is this?"

"A water bottle."

"Forbidden! See the sign!" She gestured her head toward the wall poster with an impossibly long list of items, in type too small to read from a distance, that passengers were forbidden to bring on board. She then tossed the bottle into the bin for confiscated belongings, zipped up the backpack and returned it to its rightful owner. Though the X-ray had also revealed a box with two small vials inside the main compartment, she just ignored them. The 100 euros her supervisor had slipped to her an hour earlier, during her lunch break, saw to that.

The passenger put his belt and shoes back on, strapped the backpack onto his shoulders, then walked over to the American Airlines departure lounge and made his way to the last row, as far back as he could go and still keep the boarding gate in view. Making sure there were no passengers close enough to see him, he took off the backpack as he sat down, unzipped the main compartment and took out the box inside it. The box that the security agent had been bribed to ignore.

He looked around again, turning his head one hundred and eighty degrees one way, then one hundred and eighty degrees the other way. Satisfied that no one could see what he was doing, he opened the box to make sure the vials it contained were still there. They were. He closed the box and returned it to the main compartment in the backpack. Everything in its place, he then looked at his watch and checked the departure board for the latest flight information. He had one and a half hours to kill.

• • •

Nine and one-half hours later, the American Airlines aircraft carrying the Bratva courier, and one hundred seventy-seven other non-Bratva passengers and crew, landed at Logan International Airport in Boston.

For the entire flight, he had been sitting in an aisle seat in row twenty-three, toward the back of the plane, the backpack with the precious cargo tucked under the seat in front of him. He never nodded off, nor left his seat to use the lavatory. Other than nibbling at the meals and snacks that the flight attendant handed him every hour or so, he just sat, immobile, staring straight ahead as still, and as vigilant, as a mother hen protecting her nest.

It took only a few minutes for the plane to taxi to the terminal and come to a full stop at the jetway, and the passengers heard the 'ping' sound that told them it was safe to unbuckle their seat belts and retrieve their luggage.

After waiting for all the passengers ahead of him to get their belongings from the overhead bin and make their way up the narrow aisle to the front of the plane, he grabbed his own carry-on from above, took his backpack out from under the seat in front of him, and made his way out of the plane, onto the jetway, and into the American Airlines International Arrivals terminal.

He and his lethal cargo were now on American soil.

Although the courier could not read English, he had no trouble following the images and icons that greeted him. After taking a moment to get his bearings, he made his way through the seemingly interminable concourse and outside to the ground transportation area, where the black Lincoln Navigator he'd been told to look for was waiting. He gave a barely noticeable nod to the driver standing beside it, who gave him a barely noticeable nod back. The driver looked exactly as the courier had been told to look for: an older man with an unremarkable face framed by black horn-rimmed glasses, and wearing a green velour jacket.

The courier and the driver had both been instructed not to speak with each other, and they complied. Without saying a word, the driver took the backpack from the courier and put it in the cargo area of his SUV. Then he climbed into the driver's seat and drove off toward the airport exit. The courier, now with only his carry-on bag, went back inside the terminal and made his way back through security to the American Airlines International Departures lounge. He had a return flight to Moscow to catch.

The ingredients for the most powerful poison known to assassins were now in the hands of an anonymous FSB agent, and on their way from Boston to New York City.

CHAPTER SIXTY-ONE

FSB safehouse
345 East 28th Street
Manhattan
Wednesday, January 13
1:17 AM

"Face mask, face shield, and chemical-resistant gloves all on."

"Done."

"Remove the instructions from the package, unfold them, and lay them on the table."

"Done."

"Agree to follow the instructions completely."

"I do."

The two FSB agents were following the script they'd been studying for years. The first had joined the agency just days after the second, and both were equal in rank. In the two-person drama they were now appearing in, each had an assigned role, and both were forbidden to go off script. Screwing up could be a fatal mistake, especially to themselves.

"Step one. Remove the vial marked A from the package and place it on the table," the first agent said. He was about forty years old, tall and well-built, wearing snug-fitting jeans, a plain vanilla white tee-shirt with no logo or messaging, and black running shoes. He was also protected by the same mask, shield and gloves she had donned.

"Standing up or on its side?" asked the second agent, a short, trim woman, also within a year or two of forty, with long blond hair pulled back in a ponytail. She was dressed exactly like her partner—jeans, tee shirt and running shoes—but with a different color pallet. For this perilous assignment, clothing had to have no chance of getting in the way.

They had met in Moscow as FSB rookies, and began working closely after several months in New York. Close enough to be more than colleagues, if they wanted. Which they knew better than to do. Both understood full well that in their organization, becoming a subject of gossip would be career suicide.

Whatever feelings the two might have had for each other, they were kept firmly suppressed at that moment, in that room. The stakes were simply too high to let emotions get in the way.

The two agents were in the basement of the safehouse, a small, almost-too-warm room lit only by a fluorescent light above, standing across from each other with a small table between them. On it were a set of inert ingredients that, if those agents did their job right, would combine to make a weapon tailor made to cause one particular individual to suffer a horrible death.

"Standing up," the first agent answered.

"Done," said the second agent.

"Step two. Place the syringe and the six medical spray devices next to the vial."

"Done."

"Good. Step three. Remove the vial marked B and place it on the table, behind the vial marked A."

"Done."

"Good. Step four. Unscrew the cap of the vial marked A. Repeat with vial marked B."

"Done."

"Step five. Using your right hand firmly grip vial marked B, lift it off the table, and bring it within an inch of the mouth of the vial marked A. Firmly, please. It must not slip out of your hand."

"Done."

"Step six. Tip the mouth of vial marked B and position it inside the mouth of vial marked A, so that the rim of vial marked B is within the rim of vial marked A. This is critical, as it assures none of the contents spills outside vial marked A."

"Done."

"Step seven. Now, carefully and slowly, slowly pour the liquid from vial marked B into vial marked A. Hold it in this position until one hundred percent of the contents in vial B has been transferred to vial A."

"Done."

"All the product from vial marked B is now in vial marked A? One hundred percent of it?"

"One hundred percent. Yes."

"And there is none left in the vial marked B? Zero?"

"None."

"Good. Step eight. Insert the syringe into the vial marked A, and draw all the product into it. Slowly and carefully."

"Done."

"Step nine. Remove the spray cap from the first device. Insert the syringe needle into the tip. Inject exactly 17 units into the device. Remove the needle from the device. And finally, put the spray cap back on the device."

"Done."

"Repeat step nine with the remaining five devices," the first agent instructed.

"Done," said the second agent after flawlessly repeating that step five times in a row.

"All six devices have precisely 17 units of product?"

"Yes."

"There is no product left in the vials marked A? They are completely empty?"

"Yes. Step ten?" asked the second agent.

"Step ten," declared the first agent, "is we tell Viktor the package is ready to be delivered."

The two agents then climbed up the stairs and out of the basement, after first removing their face masks, face shields, and gloves and leaving them on the floor. They had one assignment, and they had successfully completed it.

It would be up to another team of FSB agents to clean up after them, and still another team to retrieve the newly created poison delivery devices and get them to their next destination—the agents assigned to plant them inside the target's home.

With the resource development phase of the assignment now complete, it was time to enter the last remaining, and extremely critical, step.

Execution.

CHAPTER SIXTY-TWO

10 North 10th Street
Brooklyn
Friday, December 15
9:45 P.M.

Barbieri's two guardian angels remained on duty in her apartment, peering out of windows and listening for anything unusual. It was almost ten at night, near the end of another exhausting day of nothing to report.

The opera she had picked out earlier, Savirio Mercadante's *Maria Stuarda, regina di Scozia,* had gotten three thumbs down from everyone within earshot—even Barbieri had no use for it—and she turned it off after the first act.

Shelton reached for a cigarette from behind her ear and looked, hopefully, at her roomies. Both shook their heads, 'no'. She knew smoking was bad for her, and verboten by her partner and Barbieri both, but she wasn't yet strong enough to break the habit. Her job description was often 'stand around and wait for something to happen', and she found that going out for a smoke was sometimes just something to break the monotony.

"Haters. Every single one of you two." Shelton reached for her knee-length, down coat and watch cap and headed toward the door. The temperature had been hovering around thirty earlier that night, and she preferred not to freeze to death over a smoke.

"Back in ten?"

"Nine and a half at most, Connie," Reynolds told her partner..

Shelton let herself out of the apartment, took the elevator down to the lobby and walked outside and onto North 10th Street, zipping up her jacket all the way to her neck even before she stepped outside. There, she took a cigarette out of her left coat pocket, lit it up with a match held in her right hand, took one long drag and inhaled deeply. She hoped to smoke two cigarettes quickly, one right after the other, before heading back to all the excitement awaiting her upstairs in Barbieri's apartment.

It wasn't nearly as cold outside as she'd feared, and as she walked up the block, she glanced up and down the street, looking for anything suspicious. Nothing caught her eye. Just a couple strolling down the block, away from her, and a woman across the street carrying a shopping bag of what looked to be Chinese takeout while struggling to get her keys out of her purse.

Her radar still on, the guard turned at the sound of a car engine coming down the block. She looked out on the street to see a neon yellow SUV approach Barbieri's building, then keep going without even slowing down. Another false alarm. She finished the first cigarette, dropped it, watched it as it fell to the ground and set off a small spark, and crushed the ember with the toe of her shoe. One smoke down, one to go.

Smoking let her think for a few moments about something else besides keeping Kim Barbieri alive. She was still on duty, but she was offsite. Her guard was down. She had forgotten, intentionally, the cardinal rule of bodyguards-manship, which was that she had three people to protect–her client, her partner, and herself.

Shelton lit her second cigarette as she walked back and forth, continuing to be alert for anything suspicious. When there was nothing left to that cigarette, she dropped it and again watched it as it hit the pavement. But before she could crush it with her shoe, she felt some kind of cloth pressing against her mouth and nose.

She struggled, but pressure on both the front and back of her head kept the cloth in place. Seconds later, she lost control of her body and dropped to the ground, paralyzed. Unable to move a single muscle, she felt her body being dragged, limp as a rag doll, into the open side doors of a van parked nearby.

When she came to, several minutes later, Shelton discovered she was lying down on the metal floor of some kind of truck. Maybe a panel truck, or a delivery van. She tried to move her arms and legs, to see if she could somehow bang on the floor or sides of the vehicle, but she was immobilized from head to toe. With every part of her body seeming to be taped into submission, she was more mummified than bound and gagged.

All this highly trained bodyguard could do was lie still and think about the danger she had put herself in. And put her partner and the client she was supposed to protect in as well.

. . .

"Where the hell is Connie?" Reynolds asked Barbieri while checking his watch. "It's been eleven minutes. No, twelve."

"Maybe she struck up a conversation downstairs. Happens."

"Not on the job, it doesn't. That's not Connie's M.O."

Reynolds reached for his two-way radio and pressed the Push-To-Talk button. "Connie."

Hearing nothing, he told Barbieri, "I'm going downstairs to look for her. Stay right here."

"Yes, sir."

Reynolds grabbed his leather jacket and watch cap from the rack in the entryway, walked over to the front door to her apartment, opened it and poked his head out. Sensing no danger, he walked out into the hallway toward the elevator, yelling into his two-way radio as he did.

"Connie! Come in! Come in! Connie!"

The repeated attempts to reach his partner momentarily distracted him from taking in his surroundings. Just then, perhaps four feet from the elevator, he felt a metal object pressed against the back of his neck, pointing upward toward his brain. He'd always imagined what it would feel like to have a gun barrel jammed into his back, or into his neck. Now he knew.

He heard a man's voice from behind him, in what seemed to be a heavy Eastern European accent. Which made him realize the Russians had come to fulfill the promise their teammate had made to Barbieri at the restaurant.

"Your partner Connie is unable to respond right now. Face the wall, please. And listen."

Reynolds complied. He could not see who was jamming the gun into his body.

The man holding the gun reached into the guard's belt, took away his weapon, and put it in his own jacket pocket. Then he pressed the elevator button, and the door opened instantly. The man already waiting inside the car walked out onto the floor, and stood against the wall, inches from Reynolds' face.

"You will come with us into the elevator. You will stand between us. If anyone else comes into the elevator as we descend, you will not say a word. If you do, your partner will be killed. Understood?" This assassin's accent was Russian, but not as heavy as his colleague's accent was. As if he had lived in the States a lot longer, and learned to speak more like an American.

"Yes. Understood. Yes."

"When we get down to the lobby, we will all walk out the doors and into the street. If you try to escape, both of you will be killed. Understood?"

"Yes. Completely."

"Good. Go."

The two assassins turned Reynolds around, but stood facing forward, allowing him just a profile view of their faces by shifting his eyes right and left. The three entered the elevator, and turned to face the elevator door as it closed. The first man pressed the button for the lobby, and the elevator went down. All three kept their eyes on the floor indicator lights at the side of the door, watching them switch off and on every three seconds as the car descended to the lobby.

When the car reached the lobby and opened its doors, they walked out in single file, with Reynolds in the middle. This again meant he could not see the bad guys' faces, just the back of the head of the man ahead of him. And nothing of the man behind him.

After opening the lobby door, they made a left turn and walked down the block, still in single file. Just then, at the sound of a car engine getting louder, Reynolds turned and felt one hand pressing the back of his head forward, and a second hand pressing a cloth against his mouth and nose.

. . .

Barbieri realized the mistake Reynolds had made as soon as he closed the door behind him. *He left me alone here! I've got to leave!*

Despite that realization, she stayed still, temporarily unable to think clearly enough to come up with a plan. But after thirty seconds, it came to her. She opened the door a crack to avoid making a sound, just as the elevator arrived at her floor and the doors opened. That was the moment Reynolds and two Russian thugs entered the elevator, and left her field of vision. Her plan was abandoned as quickly as it had been formed. *What the fuck do I do now? Think! Stay calm! Think, damnit!*

She reached for her cell and called 911.

"What's your emergency?"

"A man is being kidnapped."

"Location, ma'am?" Barbieri gave her address.

"Can you identify the victim, ma'am?"

"Yes. Carl Reynolds. He's a security guard assigned by my employer to protect me."

"Your security guard is the victim?" the 911 dispatcher asked, incredulously. "Can you identify the kidnappers, ma'am?"

"No. They may be Russians. I believe they're Russian. Russian, definitely."

"Russians, ma'am? Please do not move, ma'am. A car is on its way." *Fuck that. I'm not staying here.*

She peeked out the door again, and did not hear the elevator moving. *It's still in the lobby. I've got maybe forty-five seconds. Run, damnit!*

Still inside her apartment, Barbieri carefully closed the door and made sure the lock clicked shut. She grabbed her coat and wallet, and again unlocked and opened the door and peeked out into the lobby. *Still no elevator. Good.* She tiptoed over to the stairwell door, pushed it open, entered the stairwell, and ran down the stairs all the way to the lobby level.

When she reached it, she waited inside the stairwell door. As soon as she heard the elevator doors close and the elevator motor hum, she opened the door, exited the stairwell and made her way to the building's service entrance, which was below street level and obscured from view by a low brick wall. She waited there, silently, unsure of what do to do next.

Twenty seconds later, at the sound of a siren coming down her block, Barbieri emerged from behind the wall and got ready to flag the radio car down.

. . .

As the stairway door on Barbieri's floor closed behind her, the two Bratva gangsters who had ambushed Shelton and Reynolds came around from the hidden part of the L-shaped hallway. Both wore black facemasks and latex gloves. One of them carried a box in his jacket pocket. The other quietly took a lock pick kit out of his pocket, unzipped it, and started to jimmy the lock on their target's front door as his fellow goon acted as a lookout. Twenty seconds later, the first Russian heard a click as the tumblers fell into place, and turned the knob. The door opened and they quickly and quietly tiptoed in.

The assassin with the box made his way straight to the bathroom while his partner in Russian crime stood by the front door, which had been left open a crack, and stood just inside, listening for the elevator.

Neither man spoke. The killer with the box turned on the bathroom light and opened her medicine cabinet above the sink. On the second shelf, he found the box he was looking for, in an upright position so that the name Zomig could be easily read. The box had already been opened, which meant there was no need to open it and reseal it after he was done. One possible error avoided.

He took out the box and lifted the flap on the side, and found four unused devices, in two rows of two, lying on their side. He took all four of the sprayers out of the box and put them in his left front jacket pocket. Then, he reached for the box inside his right front jacket pocket and took four lethal sprayers out. He then placed them inside the box that had been in her medicine cabinet, in two rows of two, closed the flap, and put the box back where he had found it on the shelf, in the same upright position with the name Zomig facing out.

Their job done, the assassination team shut the light, exited the apartment, and closed the door behind them. The breaking and entering mission took all of forty-five seconds, and had been observed by no one.

The men then took the staircase down, removing their masks and latex gloves and putting them in their jacket pockets as they hurried down to the lobby. At the bottom of the stairwell, they turned toward the service entrance. At the sound of the siren, however, they stopped short. They reversed direction, left the building through the lobby door and started walking down the block, just two men in no particular hurry.

The hitmen walked five blocks, toward Driggs Avenue. Without stopping, one of them took the four Zomig devices the target had not used out of his pocket and tossed them into the first garbage can he saw. He then tossed the two remaining lethal devices in the second can they saw. Finally, they both tossed their masks and gloves in a third garbage can, careful not to leave any fingerprints on any of the items.

The evidence against them now gone, they hopped into the car idling at the corner of Driggs and North Tenth Street. The driver shifted the gear from 'park' to 'drive' and drove toward the bridge that could take them out of Brooklyn and into Queens, toward JFK airport.

On the way to the airport, the Bratva member who had planted the lethal devices in her medicine cabinet reached into his pocket for his cell and informed his aider and abettor that he needed to call their handler back in Moscow. With the phone on speaker, he let the handler know that his boys did good and were on their way home. And that they will soon be available for the next termination.

He then turned off the cell phone and ejected the SIM card, and then kept the now unusable device in his hand until they reached the middle of the Kosciuszko Bridge over Newtown Creek. There, as the driver slowed the car down to about five miles per hour, the Bratva killer opened his window and tossed the phone far over the railing into the putrid stench below.

The car then resumed its normal speed, on the way to Kennedy airport, as the phone hurtled down toward a horrible death inflicted upon it by the raw sewage, pesticides, arsenic, cadmium, chromium, lead, mercury, cesium-137 and other corrosive goodies that had been dumped into the creek since forever.

CHAPTER SIXTY-THREE

10 North 10th Street
Brooklyn
Friday, January 15
10:19 P.M.

At the sound of the siren and the sight of the flashing lights, Barbieri popped up from behind the wall near the service entrance, ran out to the street and waved down the patrol car racing up her block. *If those mother-fuckers are still here, let 'em try something now! Motherfuckers! And where the fuck did they take Reynolds and Shelton??!!*

The radio car rolled to a stop just a few feet short of where she was standing, and the officer driving the patrol car turned the engine off and shut the siren, but left the flashing lights on the roof on. Two officers opened their doors and emerged from the car, one a petite, dark-skinned African-American woman and the other a stocky, white woman with what looked like a crewcut under her cap.

To Barbieri, their roles seemed to be 'good cop' and 'bad-ass-mother-fucker-looking-for-any-excuse-to-beat-the-piss-out-of-some-worthless-piece-of-shit cop.'

After they confirmed that Barbieri had dialed 911, introductions were made and the reporter gave them a full account of all the events of the last few minutes. The bodyguards in her apartment. The disappearance of the first bodyguard, Connie Shelton, and the kidnapping of the second, Carl Reynolds. Her sneaking downstairs when she thought the coast was clear.

Prompted by the 'good cop', Barbieri ended her recap by relating why she needed bodyguards in the first place, and when she was finished, the two officers took out their flashlights and started walking up and down both sides of the block, shining their lights down alleyways, behind bushes, up the sides of nearby buildings, and inside vehicles parked on the block. Rather than trail them, Barbieri stayed by their radio car.

In the middle of the block, the white officer stopped conducting her search when she came upon a gray van, with no windows other than the windshield. The sides and back had no signs on them indicating the business it belonged to.

She stood in front of the vehicle, aimed her flashlight inside through the windshield, and spied what looked like two bodies lying on the floor. When the light struck them, she could see that both started squirming, but were not going anywhere.

She then called over her partner, who had made her way down toward her from the other side of the block. When she reached the van and peered inside, both officers drew their weapons and pointed them toward the vehicle, and the white officer cautiously pulled on the back door latch.

The door was unlocked. The African American officer, with Barbieri a safe distance away, climbed into the back of the van and checked the two victims, one male and one female, lying on the floor. Seeing that they were alive and apparently unharmed, she pulled out Reynolds first, then Shelton.

Neither cop said a word, but they both understood how to handle the bodyguards. Working together, as a team, they stood Reynolds and Shelton against a nearby fence and unwound all the tape they had been bound with, and as soon as they were able, Reynolds and Shelton stretched out and massaged their newly liberated body parts.

Barbieri came over to join the party, but chose not to interfere with the officers doing their job. From years of experience covering arrests of assorted scumbags, shitheads and dirtbags for the *News*, she knew better than to get in the way of cops on duty.

"You got any IDs?" asked the African-American cop. Both guards took out their wallets from their back pockets, with Shelton having to fully unzip her down coat to reach it, and handed them to her. She eyeballed the ID cards, looking back and forth between the photos and guards' faces, to see if there was a reasonable resemblance, then handed them back.

With Shelton's coat open, the white cop noticed her weapon tucked into her waistband.

"Your kidnappers overlook something?"

"I guess they did. Maybe the coat hid it."

"Or they were too stupid to look. I'd bet on the latter."

"You know this lady?" she asked Reynolds, nodding toward Barbieri standing nearby.

"Kim Barbieri? Yeah. We were supposed to protect her from some angry Russians."

"Good job. Miss Barbieri, you can have these two back, if you still want them."

"Are they okay?"

"You two hurt anywhere?" the white cop asked. "Injured? Maimed? Stabbed?"

"No."

"No."

"Appear to be," the white cop said to no one in particular.

"Police get the guys that did this to us?" Reynolds asked.

"Not yet. We will," the African-American cop replied. "First, we're going to get you to a hospital just to confirm you're alive and well. Doubt our supervisors would take our word for it. Detectives will get your statements there, while the emergency room doctors confirm neither of you is deceased."

Resigned to undergoing several hours of interrogation and examination, the kidnap victims huddled with Barbieri while waiting for the ambulance to arrive. The two cops, meanwhile, wrote up their reports on their incident reporting app on their iPhones. Until the police found their kidnappers, there was nothing Shelton and Reynolds could do but lick their deep psychological wounds.

The reporter knew she wasn't going back to her apartment, or spend even a second anywhere, without police protection, so she took out her cell and called Brennan. After hearing her account of that evening's excellent adventure, he asked Barbieri to hand the phone over to one of the officers. After exchanging pleasantries, he identified himself and then informed them he was on his way to the scene of the crime, and they must wait there until he arrived.

The two officers' job was done, and normally they would radio in that they were ready for the next nine-one-one call. But not this time.

This time, they would have to wait a while longer. They wouldn't be free to go until Chief Brennan said they were.

CHAPTER SIXTY-FOUR

International Departures Terminal
John F. Kennedy International Airport
Queens
Saturday, January 17
7:00 A.M.

After the heavy snow that had begun falling at midnight caused a brief delay for de-icing, the Aer Lingus Airbus A340 jet bound for Shannon Airport in Dublin, Ireland, pushed away from the terminal at seven in the morning. Departure was just fifteen minutes behind schedule.

On board were two hundred and ninety-seven passengers, most Irish nationals returning home, American corporate types on business trips to Ireland and the UK, or American tourists eager to explore the Emerald Isle. Among the exceptions were two men with South African passports, in seats 14a and 27b, who were flying to Dublin in order to catch a Lufthansa Airlines connecting flight to Berlin, Germany one hour after their arrival at Shannon. Within forty-five minutes of landing in Berlin, they would take a second connecting flight, on Aeroflot Airlines, to Moscow, Russia.

The South African passports the two men were carrying were forgeries, products of the Russian security service, FSB. Their photos were valid, but nothing else was. Their identities were fake. Their personal information was fake. Their visa stamps were fake. Their passports were so expertly crafted, however, that the men sailed through one security checkpoint after another, on every leg of their itinerary, without raising a single suspicious eyebrow.

The assassins who had picked up where the team that assembled the lethal devices had left off, and planted them inside the box of Zomig sprayers in Barbieri's medicine cabinet, had completed their assignment as well.

It meant nothing to the Bratva gangsters whether the target was killed that day, or months later. And it meant nothing to them if their identities were somehow revealed to American authorities in the future. Before the day was done, they would be back on Mother Russia soil, well out of reach of both the New York Police Department and the Federal Bureau of Investigation of the United States Department of Justice.

Once back home, they would begin enjoying the BMWs, luxury apartments, and other fruits of their lethal labor. That was the deal they'd made with their Bratva bosses, and they kept up their side of it, without question.

CHAPTER SIXTY-FIVE

NYPD Headquarters
One Police Plaza
Manhattan
Saturday, January 17
11:00 A.M.

Barbieri and her ex-boy toy, NYPD Chief of Detectives Timothy Brennan, were directed by security to what seemed to be a not-quite-abandoned office, bare except for four beat-up office chairs that somehow hadn't made their way to the dumpster dumped out back on Pearl Street, just outside the service entrance of the lower Manhattan building.

He had driven with her back to his apartment in Staten Island the previous night, after giving the two cops who'd responded to this apparent kidnapping the third-degree, and taken her with him when he drove to One Police Plaza the next morning.

On entering the office, she was surprised to find the two detectives assigned to Leotta's murder, Macnamee and Curley, already there and going through their notes. *What are they doing here? They adding Reynolds and Shelton to Leotta and Lebedev now?*

"Connie and Carl... where are they?" she asked the detectives, more concerned with her bodyguards' well-being than in any attack by Russian gangsters on her. She and Brennan both took chairs across from Curley and Macnamee.

"Still at Woodhull Hospital, just for observation," Curley replied. "We interviewed both of them while they were there, me and Macnamee, and neither of them gave us much. They're okay. Not to worry." Only Curley spoke. Her partner and Brennan remained silent.

"Whatever drug they got that knocked them out, it wore off in maybe ten minutes. Toxicology will tell us what it was, some day. So, Miss Barbieri, can you go over the events leading up to your call to nine-one-one? We know you gave all the information to the officers on the scene, but if you wouldn't mind...?"

The reporter gave the detectives a brief summary, skipping over the events they already knew about–her investigation of Russian money-laundering through real estate, and being followed and then threatened by some anonymous Russian gangster. She recapped what had happened to her bodyguards the prior evening, with Shelton not returning and Reynolds getting alarmed. Him going out to search for her, and being forced into the elevator by two goons she did not recognize. End of story.

"That when you called nine-one-one?" Macnamee asked.

"Yes."

"Then what did you do?"

"I decided I couldn't just sit in my apartment like a fuckin' idiot. I'd been told by the nine-one-one dispatcher to just sit tight, but I wasn't about to wait for the Russian killers to come back. Like Reynolds had told me to do. I just couldn't. What if they had a key? The Russians, I mean. What if I could keep them from killing him and Shelton? Distract them, I don't know. I went into the stairwell and walked maybe ten flights down to the service entrance, and hid until I heard the radio car."

"You mean the siren? Not the radio car per se?" Curley asked.

"Yes. The siren," Barbieri replied.

"You didn't see anyone outside? Reynolds, or Shelton or the two kidnappers?"

"No. Sorry."

"No need to apologize, Kim." Brennan said, interrupting the questioning by Curley. "You did not hear them, either?"

"No."

"And the van where they were tied up? Did you see it from where you were hiding? Or notice anyone near it?"

"No. Not from the position I was in," Barbieri said. "It was hidden from view by the wall outside the service entrance to my building."

"Do you know if they got into your apartment after you left it, Kim? Was your door lock forced in any way? Was anything missing?"

"I didn't go back there to check. When Brennan here came to the rescue, I left with him. Again, sorry."

"Again, Kim, no apology needed," Brennan offered.

"And I haven't been back there since last night."

"But we have, Kim," Brennan said, choosing that moment to tell her about the investigation he'd begun hours earlier. "The team from the Crime Scene Unit I sent to your place—they found nothing. No sign of forced entry, nothing knocked over, and no sign of anyone rummaging through your stuff."

"Okay," she said. "But did they even look for any kind of poison? Russians are using it more and more to get rid of anyone on their shit list."

"They did, and came up empty," Brennan replied. "The team took swabs from counters and door-knobs, a few other likely places, and sent them to the lab. Could be a day or two before we're notified. The Crime Scene Unit guys also examined the van where Shelton and Reynolds were found. Nothing yet. Whatever they used to knock them out—not a trace was found. We couldn't even find a VIN number or their license plate. The van may as well have come straight from the mystery machine factory."

"So, two Russian mobsters kidnapped and hog-tied your two guards," Macnamee said to Barbieri. "And made no attempt to kill you? Is that your theory of the case?"

"Looks that way. Maybe they saw me leave the apartment and go downstairs, and decided not to attack me there."

"Or the whole time the Russian Mafia was just sending you a message," Curley said. "Back off or you're dead."

"Just me, you mean? Or the whole team working on the story? Editors? Fact checkers...?"

"Just you." Curley said. "You're the one that's made yourself a big fat pain in their collective asses."

Chief Brennan, who had been sitting throughout the interview, stood up and started pacing around the room. The detectives and Barbieri looked at him as he did so, as if that would help them follow what he was saying.

"Macnamee. Curley. This stinks to high heaven."

"It does indeed, Chief," Curley replied. "This attack, if that's what it was, was too easy."

"What do you mean, Timothy?" the reporter asked Brennan.

"We'll let you know after we've looked into this a little more closely." He then turned to his detectives. "Guys, I think Kim's given us all she knows. Let me have a few moments with her, if you don't mind."

"What you're saying, Timothy, is we should get off our collective asses and knock on some doors," Macnamee said to Brennan. As the two detectives got up and left the office, Curley said, "Okay, jefe. We have two perps unknown out there somewhere. We'll head back to her apartment house, see if anyone saw anybody do anything to anyone."

"Interview Shelton and Reynolds first." Brennan ordered. "Rule either of them out. Or both of them. Or neither of them. And get back in here the second you find out anything. Please."

"Will do," Curley replied, as they left the office and headed down the hall.

"So, Macnamee, who do you like?" Curley asked her partner, out of earshot of their boss.

"Reynolds. You?"

"Fifty bucks says it's Shelton," Curley said. "There's something hinky about her."

"If there is, I haven't seen it. Reynolds stinks to high heaven in my book. You're on."

• • •

As soon as the two investigators left his office, Brennan gave Barbieri a big old bear hug. She started to bring her arms around him, but stopped. She left them hanging by her side while he kept holding her tight.

"I really stepped in it, Timothy. Haven't I?"

"You did, Kim. But it's OK. We won't let anything happen to you. We won't let those Russian motherfuckers anywhere near you again. Besides, I like pulling up my big boy shorts and acting like a real detective."

Barbieri and Brennan unembraced, and they sat down facing each other just a foot or so apart.

"Like riding a bicycle, I bet. I've got to get back home, though. I have things I need to get."

"You're not going home anytime soon, I'm afraid. Not until we know for sure the assassins have picked up their AK forty-sevens and gone home."

"So, I'm in the Reporter Protection program now? Where am I going into hiding?"

"Tonight, my place again. You'll be safe there, especially as long as I'm there, too. Then we'll make another call to your boss at the paper and find you a safe house. Somewhere the Russkies won't ever find you."

"What about Reynolds and Shelton?"

"You'll be assigned a different team of bodyguards when the time is right. Fitzgerald'll see to that. It's all arranged, Kim. Neither your employer nor I are going to let you get killed."

"Evens the odds against me at least, Chief. You told Fitzgerald that Tim and Connie are okay."

"He already knew. Connie called him before I had a chance. I could tell he was not pleased with them, which is why the paper's reassigning them, and you won't see them again, probably. At least not when they're on duty. They'll come over to your apartment at some point to get their gear, but you won't be there to greet them."

"Shit. It's not their fault. When you speak to Fitzgerald again, tell him I want them back."

"Why?" Brennan asked, rising from his chair and pacing like a caged panther. "Because you like them? Kim, who or what your boss does to keep you in one piece is his call. Emotion should play no part in it. Until he finds a new team for you, you and I will be joined at the hip. Figuratively speaking, this time. You'll be safe. You have my word."

"You're right, Timothy. But... shit."

"Besides, there's something about those two rent-a-cops we don't like."

"You don't think...?"

"I do. All three of us do. Me, Macnamee and Curley. Let's get going."

CHAPTER SIXTY-SIX

19th Precinct Station House
East 67th Street
Manhattan
Tuesday, January 19
3:45 P.M.

"So run this by me again, Connie. What made you leave Kim's apartment and go outside the building?"

"I told you. To get a smoke. Kim didn't allow anyone to light up in her place."

"What time was that?"

"I told you that, too. About ten, I think. Maybe a little before."

Detective Curley and Connie Shelton were in Interrogation Room A at the station house. Shelton was sitting at the square table in the middle of the room, while Curley paced back and forth in front of her. Shelton, being off duty, was wearing jeans and a blue sweatshirt, and had no makeup. Curley, being on duty, was dressed in just about the same 'who-gives-a-shit-how-I-look?' uniform of the day.

"Okay. Got it. So, why didn't you just go out in the hallway to smoke?"

"Could've, I guess. But that might have pissed off the other tenant on her floor. We're one really despised minority, smokers. Honestly, though, I wasn't thinking about them. I just don't mind the cold weather at all."

"Not in a coat like yours, for sure. When you went down, were you armed?"

"Glock nineteen. Don't leave home without it."

"Okay. So, you take the elevator down and now you're out on North 10th. Then what?"

"Then I lit a cigarette and walked slowly up and down the block, just puffing away and killing time. Didn't notice anything that shouldn't have been there. When I put out that cigarette, I lit up another one. I'd told Kim and Tom I'd be back in ten minutes, so I had time for another smoke."

"Got it. Then what?"

"Then nothing. I kept walking and smoking till I finished the second smoke and tried to put the cigarette out with my shoe. Next thing I know I feel like I'm breathing in some chemical. Never smelled anything like it. Then when I come to, I'm wrapped up like Hannibal Lecter and some cop's dragging me and my partner out of a van that I don't remember getting into."

"Got it. Your weapon? You had it on your person when you were found? Is that right?"

"Right. Just me. The Glock nineteen was still in my holster. They took my partner's, though. Don't know why."

"Neither do we. Your holster was tucked in your belt. Right? Which hip? Left?"

"Behind my back. I'm right-handed."

"And your coat was zipped up, Connie? Which means you couldn't reach it fast. Like if you saw something suspicious."

"Guess not. You're right. Maybe because grabbing a smoke meant I was off-duty..."

"You're never off duty."

"Or maybe I just wasn't thinking."

"No, Connie, you weren't. Did they frisk you? Pat you down?"

"If they did, I wouldn't know, would I? I was fuckin' out cold."

"That's the other thing that doesn't add up. You seemed to go out of your way to make yourself vulnerable. One. And two, you weren't disarmed by them."

"Wait. Don't tell me you think I had something to do with this. Like it's an inside job?"

"We don't. Not yet, anyway."

"Not yet? I'm under investigation!!"

"Let's just say we've got a big, fat, loose end that needs to be tied up."

"What loose end?"

"The Russian jamokes who want to kill Kim got both her bodyguards out of the picture way too easily, way we see it. You stepped outside just in time, and they took you out. Like they were expecting you."

"You think we abandoned her on purpose? Both me and Carl? Is that it?"

"And neither of you was hurt by them. Drug just knocked you both out for a time."

"Detective, look. Me and Carl had nothing to do with the Russians. You can investigate us all you want, and you won't find any evidence linking us to them. None. Because there is none. Maybe we were careless, I'll give you that."

"Or derelict. What about Carl? You sure he wasn't in on this?"

"One hundred percent. The guy's honest to a fault. Beyond question. Detective, I know you have a job to do. Go look at my cell phone records, my emails, my calls, my written reports. Financials. Where I've been, and who I spoke to. I'm innocent here."

"Okay, Connie. Would you mind sticking around for a while? My partner and I will want to interview you again after we brief each other. Okay?"

"To see if there are any inconsistencies between me and Carl. I got it. I'll just go out and grab something to eat, and come right back. Want anything?"

"Nope. We're good."

· · ·

At the same time that Detective Curley was with Shelton in interrogation room A, Detective Macnamee was questioning her partner in room B. If either of the two bodyguards was in cahoots with the Russians—or if both were—the thinking went, interrogating them separately opened up the possibility that one of them would slip up and make their investigation a snap.

"You think I had something to do with the Russians, Detective?"

"Not at this point. Any reason I should?"

"No. Honestly."

"Okay. You and your partner are on duty in Kim's place and she goes out for a smoke. She does that often?"

"Can't help herself. She's tried to quit, a few times, but…"

"Both you and Kim wouldn't let her smoke inside."

"We didn't tell Connie to take it outside. She already knew how we felt, and she went outside on her own. Said she'd be back in ten."

"But she wasn't? Back in ten."

"That's when I tried to find her. She's always been super-punctual. I also tried reaching her on our walkie-talkie, but I was getting the silent treatment."

"So, what happens next? You grab your coat and leave Kim's apartment and walk toward the elevator. She was still home, right?"

"Right. She was. I told her to stay there. Soon as I'm out the door, I felt a gun barrel on my neck."

"Understood. That when they took your gun?"

"Yes. Out in the hall. One of them disarmed me."

"There were two of them?"

"I saw two men. If there were others, I didn't see them. They warned me they'd kill Connie if I didn't do what they said."

"They both had Russian accents?"

"I think so. Maybe Ukrainian. And one accent seemed to be thicker than the other one."

"But you understood both of them?"

"Perfectly."

"What did they tell you to do, Carl?"

"Cooperate. Just do as they say, or they'll kill Connie and me."

"They took you down in the elevator. Then what?"

"We walked outside the building, me between the two of them. I felt some kind of fabric or mask press against my face. Inhaled some awful odor. That's it. That's all I remember till the cops came for us."

"Sounds like they were real pros. You never saw these guys before, right?"

"Never."

"Did Connie?"

"Not that I know of. Ask her."

"We will. Look, Carl. We're a little suspicious here, to be honest. The Russians set a trap, and you and your partner fell right in. And, neither of you was killed. Why? How? And, the person you're guarding, their target, nothing happens to her, either. So, the Russians actually got you out of the way, but failed to kill Kim, anyway. Or weren't even trying to. And then they disappear. Gone. None of this makes any sense."

"I wish I could help you, Detective. I know my partner was missing. I know I went out to find her. I know I was kidnapped at gunpoint. That's it. Nothing more."

"Okay, Carl. You can go. We'll be in touch."

• • •

Two hours later, Connie Shelton was being double-teamed by Detectives Curley and Macnamee.

Curley had briefed him on her interrogation of Shelton, and on her suspicions about Shelton's weapon. The three of them were inside Interrogation room A, with the detectives sitting across the table from Barbieri's bodyguard. The down coat she'd worn during the attack was on a hook on the wall. And at Macnamee's request, she removed the gun from her holster and handed it to him. It was now in a cabinet against the wall behind him.

Their goal was not to make her think she was a suspect in this case, but that she was there simply to provide a more complete picture of the events. If it reached a point where she clammed up and demanded to see a lawyer, they wanted it to be later rather than sooner.

"Connie, we're going to go over some of the same things I asked you about before. Not to trip you up, but because when we went back and reviewed what you'd told us, it raised a few more questions that you can help us answer. No worries. Okay?"

"Okay. Sure."

After a quick rehashing of the events before Shelton went outside for a cigarette break, Curley and Macnamee got to the subject of her weapon.

"Ok. You go downstairs and you're still strapped. Right? You don't remove your weapon when you're in Kim's apartment."

"Never when I'm up. Only when I retire for the night. And even then, I leave the Glock nineteen right on the nightstand. That's how we were trained."

"Got it. You put on your down coat that's knee-length, right? You zipped it all the way up?"

"Not until I was in the elevator. I knew it was fuckin' cold outside."

Macnamee took Shelton's weapon in its holster out of the cabinet and handed it to her. "Would you mind placing this behind your belt and putting your coat on now?"

In response, Shelton stood up, put the holster in her waistband, then walked over to the wall and took down her coat and put it on. She left the coat open.

"And please pull the zipper all the way to your chin."

"How's it look on me? Not bad, right?" Shelton asked after closing her coat.

"Actually, it looks tight on you, Connie. Now, if you wouldn't mind, pull out your weapon liked you'd do if the situation called for it. You're defending a client from a maniac waving a knife, maybe."

Shelton complied, reaching for her pistol, taking it out of the holster, and gripping it tightly in her hand–but only after taking the several seconds needed to open her coat first.

"That's the thing, Connie. The coat's preventing you from reacting fast."

"Like I told you before, I wasn't thinking. Maybe I was just rusty, because I never had to grab my weapon in a hurry before. Not once." Shelton put the gun back in the holster, then sat back down at the table across from the detectives.

"Maybe. We've all sometimes screwed up, but usually not when we're on the job. Then there's the second thing that makes no sense at all, which is why the Russians didn't disarm you. I mean, if you're kidnapping someone who you know's got a weapon, you want to take it away from him. Right?"

"I see your point, Detective. But I was knocked out. I don't remember if my kidnappers frisked me or not. Of if they did, did they even realize the weapon was there? It was in the small of my back, which is totally hidden by this fuckin' Pillsbury doughboy coat I'm wearing."

"Point taken, Connie. But it could be interpreted like they weren't worried about it. Your weapon, I mean."

"You mean I was in on this whole thing? What the fuck..."

"We don't know enough to make that determination. But you gotta admit, this looked way too easy. Suspiciously so. Look, Connie, you're not a suspect as of now, and we have a lot more questions that only the Russians can answer. If we ever find them."

"Connie, if we can rule you out, we will."

"Detectives, I got nothing to hide. Check everything, like I told you before. Everything. I'm not stopping you."

"We will, Connie. Please don't leave the area for a while, okay? We'll be in touch."

The interview over, Shelton grabbed her coat, exited the interrogation room and left the station house. Macnamee and Curley went back to their desks, went online and got to work on their suspect's financials.

CHAPTER SIXTY-SEVEN

NYPD Forensic Toxicology Laboratory
Jamaica, Queens
Friday, January 22
10:23 A.M.

"We figured out how Reynolds and Shelton were both knocked out, Detectives. The Russians forced them to ingest the drug propofol. You've heard of it...?"

"Propofol? Wasn't that...?"

"What killed Michael Jackson? It was indeed. Propofol's an anesthetic, used mostly to sedate patients before surgery. To help the gloved one get a full eight hours of sleep, his doctor injected him with what turned out to be an overdose of the drug. Enough to knock Jacko out for good, evidently."

"But the Russians, they just put a mask over their faces. They didn't inject the drug."

"It's designed to be injected into your body. That's how propofol's made. Only the Russians have, apparently, figured out a way to make victims inhale it through their nose and mouth. Never been ingested that way before, as far as I know."

Detectives Macnamee and Curley were in the NYPD Forensic Toxicology Laboratory meeting with Jeffrey Schmidt, one of their scientists working on the Barbieri case. They had ordered blood samples from

Shelton and Reynolds to be sent to the lab, to see if they could figure out what drug the Russians used to put the two bodyguards out of action.

Schmidt was on the short side, looked to be about thirty-five, and had a full beard that overflowed onto the top of his white lab coat. He, Macnamee and Curley were sitting in a circle by his worktable in the lab, surrounded by vials, devices, clamps, pipettes, burners and other lab equipment neither detective had seen since high school.

Schmidt had given each a printout of his findings, which the detectives glanced at from time to time as they talked.

"So, their kidnappers didn't really intend to kill them."

"Evidently not. Just sedate them for a short time while they went after their real target. Not to get too technical, detectives, but propofol easily crosses the blood-brain barrier, so it goes to work right away to depress higher brain functions like motor control, conscious thought, memory, and sensory perception.

"Long-hand for 'putting them under'."

"Exactly. And I mean fast. In one study I found, as doctors were injecting it, they asked patients to count backwards from ten. Ten, nine, eight... Almost nobody made it to four."

"So, after getting the bodyguards to inhale this drug, the Russians had more than enough time to tie them up and dump them in the back of the van," Curley stated.

"Absolutely," Schmidt replied. "Just as important, propofol wears off fairly quickly, so Reynolds and Shelton were fully conscious by the time the police officers found them. A single dose lasts only maybe five minutes. Meaning that the recovery period for patients sedated with it is very short, and they're fully awake faster."

"So, by the time the cops found Reynolds and Shelton in the van, they were no longer under the influence," Macnamee said.

"Seems so."

"Anything else?" asked Curley.

"Not yet. We're still trying to figure out how the Russians converted an intravenous drug into an aerosol drug. That was a new one for us."

"Reverse engineering?" Curley asked.

"That's what we're attempting as we speak. The officers who caught the case didn't happen to find the mask the kidnappers used on them, did they?"

"Unfortunately, no," Macnamee answered.

"Didn't think the Russians would leave that behind. Too much to hope for. All the companies that make propofol make it in liquid form that goes into the patient's vein. It can go all at once by injection or slowly by infusion, but either way your blood takes it to your brain, and nighty-night. Nobody makes it as any kind of mist that the patient inhales. And right now, we don't understand how it enters your bloodstream from your nasal cavity. Yet."

"So, how the hell did the Russians make it?"

"No idea. Truthfully. We've already contacted a couple of companies that manufacture propofol. Maybe they can figure that out."

"Think they'll help us?" Macnamee asked.

"I wouldn't hold my breath, Detective. These drug manufacturers aren't too forthcoming with their trade secrets."

CHAPTER SIXTY-EIGHT

NYPD Headquarters
One Police Plaza
Manhattan
Saturday, January 23
7:00 P.M.

"So, nothing?" Chief Brennan asked.

"Not a damn thing, Timothy," Macnamee replied. "Me and Curley interviewed both Reynolds and Shelton. We talked to their bosses at the paper. Then we looked at every financial record we could get a hold of on them both. There's nothing that ties either of them to the Russian mob. No sudden windfalls. No expensive trips to Fiji. No holes in their stories. Nada. For either of them. If they're involved, they're doing a great job of covering it up."

The two detectives were in Brennan's office in lower Manhattan, reporting on everything they knew about the kidnapping at 10 North 10th Street in Brooklyn. Their coats were draped over their chairs, the office warm enough to make them forget New York was in the middle of a cold-snap.

"Damn. I liked Shelton for this," said Brennan.

"We did, too. Me more than him," Curley said, nodding toward her partner. "When Shelton was kidnapped without putting up a fight, she said she was just negligent. Neither of us believed her, and we dug as deep as we've ever done to find something on her. But we found nothing that proves otherwise."

"We found out how they were knocked out, at least. Propofol." Curley added.

"That's what the Russians used? An anesthetic? Damn."

"No idea how they got it, though. It's never used outside an operating room, we were told."

"Back to square one, then. If those two weren't involved, then the Russians were just damned good. Which, in my experience, they've never been. So, they kidnap and then drug and then bound and gag Kim's bodyguards and then dump them in a van, but otherwise leave them alive and well. And then they leave the body they're guarding untouched. What's wrong with this picture? Did they go through all that with no purpose at all? And where the fuck did those motherfuckers disappear to?"

"We've gotten nowhere on any of this, Jefe. Zippo."

"And nothing that proves our theory of the case, either. That this kidnapping and Martin Leotta's murder and Lebedev's were part of the same Russian operation, or were perpetrated by the same perpetrators."

"We're running on empty. Leotta's killer and Lebedev's are still out there, and we have no more leads to follow. And we're nowhere on tying the cases together either, Timothy. Total dead ends. The only thing we can do is keep knocking on doors."

"Agreed. Knock away. Find something, anything to clear these goddamn cases, and gimme evidence that'll hold up in court. Or these Russian shitheads will get away with murder. Murders. I don't like open cases, and neither do the higher-ups I report to."

"Understood, Timothy."

"And I don't have to tell you guys that we're going to have another killing on our hands if we keep dropping the ball here."

CHAPTER SIXTY-NINE

Gorky Park
Moscow
Tuesday, February 7
3:00 P.M.

The three Bratva capos were sitting on benches on either side of a concrete table that doubled as a chessboard. Totally oblivious to the cold, they were looking at their individual laptops reading the same article in that morning's *Wall Street Journal*.

The article was more of the same in that it revealed more details about more luxury real estate purchases slash money laundering operations in the States that Bratva was involved in. Except that the name of one reporter was different.

"Who the fuck is this Cynthia Powell person? We know anything about her."

"She's the new cunt that the paper replaced that old cunt Barbieri with."

"We're already working on making sure Powell's buried next to Barbieri. We're finding out where she lives. Her work phone number. Her cell phone number. Email address. Home address. We'll get them all, just like we got Barbieri's."

"And then order the guys in Brooklyn to expedite her termination."

"Send those bastards a message. Why the fuck would they assign a new reporter to a story that got another reporter killed?"

"And what kind of reporter would take that job?"

"A suicidal one."

"We'll do what we can to make it an assisted suicide."

"They think they're better than us, the Americans. But they're not."

"Heartless bastards."

. . .

Cynthia Powell did not exist.

It was the alias that Barbieri's editor, Thomas Fitzgerald, had given her so that she could continue investigating the Russian money-laundering without fear of turning up deceased under mysterious circumstances.

The *Journal* had assigned Barbieri a new team of bodyguards, both men this time. Rather than let them dictate terms of her house arrest, as Reynolds and Shelton had, she trained her new minders to give her a little extra slack when she went out on errands. Just enough to tempt any Russians lurking nearby to jump the gun and try something doomed to fail.

The paper had also gotten a new, furnished apartment for her, in another Brooklyn neighborhood far, far away from her old one. It would be only a temporary home until she could find a place of her own. She wrote one hundred percent of her stories from there, going from working remotely to working even more remotely.

Becoming a full-time work-from-homer definitely had one advantage. She could take a get-out-there break whenever she felt like daring any assassins to attack. *Come and get it, bitches!*

Despite her best duck decoy imitation, though, the assassins who'd waylaid Reynolds and Shelton seemed to have dropped any interest in her. Or they moved on to their next victim. *I had no trouble at all getting men to notice me before. Now, nothing. I don't exist. All those charm school lessons ain't worth squat now.*

The bankers and realtors Barbieri recently interviewed were all new to her. None of them would recognize her, because none of them had ever seen her before. By now, she had made the transformation from rookie investigative reporter to hard-nosed, take-no-prisoners inquisitor able to break through the mystery inside the riddle inside the enigma of each Russian money-laundering scam.

Fitzgerald saw no need for her to do any more 'show and tell' presentations for him or his team, and the articles she continued to send in breezed through all the editorial and fact-checking gauntlets the *Journal* imposed. She was an even better investigative reporter than Fitzgerald had expected she would be when he'd brought her on board.

Though she never again set foot in the paper's headquarters, Barbieri had arrived–under an assumed name, for sure, but she had definitely earned her paycheck at the paper.

CHAPTER SEVENTY

10 North 10th Street
Brooklyn
Thursday February 9
10:25 AM

Brennan had driven Barbieri over the Brooklyn Bridge, whose entrance ramp was just a couple of quick left and right turns outside Headquarters, to her old apartment in Williamsburg. He'd made a few calls to some friends in high City Hall places, and arranged to keep paying the rent so that her apartment would stay under her name.

She had not been back there since the kidnapping, making herself quite at home in the new, permanent home she'd found, along with new furniture and a whole new wardrobe, all courtesy of the *Journal*. But none of the meds and lotions she'd abandoned weeks before at her old place.

"What if we don't catch them?" She asked him, employing the term 'we' as opposed to 'you'. She wanted to get them as badly as the cops did. "What if we never catch them? The Russians, I mean. Much as I'm liking this 'you-wanna-piece-of-me?' bullshit act, I can't do it forever."

"We'll catch them," Brennan assured her. "I've put some damn good men on it. And those stupid bastards will make a mistake. Guaranteed."

"I believe they will as well. I'm counting on it, in fact."

"They're stone-cold killers. Thugs. Mercenaries with no soul. But they're still idiots. Dumb pieces of Russian shit no smarter than dumb pieces of American shit. So, they'll make a dumb-ass mistake whether or not you walk around with a neon sign saying 'Here I am, Boris'."

Brennan slowed down as the car entered North 10th Street. Seeing no empty spots, he pulled up to her old building, double-parked, and turned the engine off.

"Wait till I check things out."

"No problem, Captain. Them Russians may be stupid, but I sure ain't."

He got out of the car and looked up and down the block. Two radio cars were also double-parked on the street, just a few feet from her building, and four uniforms were outside the building's front door standing guard.

The brass at headquarters had assumed that the Russians were not aware that Barbieri had been moved to a new apartment, and Brennan ordered the commander of the local police precinct to keep up appearances by assigning officers there twenty-four-seven. He was eager to comply, because unsolved crimes made his precinct look bad to the brass, and would give them the excuse they need to send him packing.

The officers on duty there had already been fully alert, eyes darting this way and that, but snapped to attention when they noticed the Chief of Detectives pulling up. Satisfied that there was no danger, Brennan walked around to the other side of his car and opened the passenger-side door for her.

"All clear?" she asked.

"All clear. Let's make this fast, Kim. Our luck, this could be the one day the Russkies decide to come back and finish the job."

"I could only hope."

They walked together, almost joined at the hip, to the front door of her apartment house, and Barbieri took out her key fob and opened the lock. Before going in with her, Brennan turned to an officer he'd seen before, who was standing beside it.

"See anything or anyone suspicious?"

"No, sir."

"Right answer, officer."

Barbieri and Brennan walked across the lobby to the elevator, and the door opened right away for them. When they got to the top floor, they rushed down the hall to her front door. She inserted the apartment door key, which she had already pulled out from her purse while in the elevator, and inserted it into the lock. Then she hesitated.

"My luck, they're inside waiting for me."

"They aren't. If they'd even driven down the block, they would've seen they were outnumbered by all the cops outside."

"And my life is sure as hell not worth a suicide mission. But, as you keep telling me, they're not in Russia's Mensa affiliate." She then turned the lock and pushed the door open, and they entered the apartment.

As they stepped into the hallway and she turned on the light, both Brennan and Barbieri gave the kitchen and living room the once over to see if anything was out of place. Nothing was, or at least appeared to be.

"I'll only be a few minutes, Captain. I just have to go to the bathroom and sort through all the damn medicines I've been taking, and we're done."

"You've got half a minute, Kim. Go."

• • •

As soon as Barbieri began walking toward her bathroom, Brennan called out to her.

"Hold it a second, Kim. You know what? Forget all your meds. Just grab the one or two bottles keeping you alive. Better to get out of here fast."

Barbieri stared back at him for a moment, wondering about his change of heart. She thought the best thing was to agree with him, then take everything, anyway.

"Okay. It'll take just a second. If you ever needed a pill in a hurry, you'd understand."

Barbieri entered the bathroom, turned on the light and opened her medicine cabinet. She grabbed a few of the over-the-counter items from the bottom shelf and dumped them in her purse. Then she took the prescription drugs and put them in her purse as well. *If I don't get a migraine from this, it'll be a miracle.* As she took the box of Zomig sprayers off the shelf, though, something on the label caught her eye.

On the bottom flap, next to the letter and number code, was a barely visible message. EXPIRATION DATE; 110121. *That's two months ago. Shit!. Screw this! I haven't had a migraine in God knows how long. If this assassins coming after me bullshit didn't give me a migraine, nothing will.*

Although she had no intention of using an expired medication, she tossed the box into her bag anyway, just in case her insurance company puts up a fuss when she tried to refill it. She then shut the bathroom light, and returned to the living room, where she found Brennan staring out the living room window.

"Done. Anything?"

"Nothing."

"No time for my clothes?"

"Sorry, Kim. We're outta here. Besides, leaving all your clothes here gives you a great excuse to go shopping and fill up your closets again."

He unlocked and opened the front door and they stepped out into the hall, shutting the door behind them, and walked the few steps to the elevator. While they were waiting, though, the trash chute caught her eye. *I've survived without it for a couple of years. A few more days won't kill me.*

Barbieri reached into her bag and took out the box of Zomig sprayers. She then pulled down the door to the chute, tossed the box in, and let the door close. She listened to the sound of the box hitting the sides of the chute as it fell, and landing with a small, almost inaudible thud at the bottom. Out of sight, out of mind. At that point, the elevator reached her floor, the doors opened, and she and Brennan got in.

"You're right, Brennan. Fuck 'em. Why keep making myself a target? Why give them the pleasure?"

CHAPTER SEVENTY-ONE

Odessa Laundromat
512 Brighton Beach Avenue
Brooklyn
Wednesday, February 27
1:15 A.M.

After locking up the laundromat for the night, the almost-retired Bratva assassins Vasily Klim and Grigory Gryshin headed back to their respective homes in Brighton Beach.

Klim's home was right around the corner, on Brighton 5th Street, and he reached his front gate at 1:17. Gryshin's home was a few blocks further away, on Brighton 11th Street. Other than themselves, both streets were completely empty. The temperature had dipped to just ten degrees that evening, making it simply too cold for anyone in their right mind to venture out.

At 1:17 in the morning, as Klim was about to open his front gate, he felt a needle being stuck into the back of his neck, just below the brain. Three minutes later, at 1:20, a needle penetrated the back of Gryshim's neck, also just below the brain.

Less than a second after the solution in the syringe was sent into their body, their brains stopped sending signals to their muscles, which then ceased functioning. Both men collapsed and lost consciousness. About fifteen seconds later, their diaphragms stopped, fluid filled their lungs and mouths, and they started vomiting.

Both old men were now totally paralyzed. They stopped breathing. They went into convulsions. Less than two minutes after being injected, they were both dead. Klim at 1:19 A.M., and Gryshim at 1:22 A.M.

Their missions accomplished, both of the assassins who'd ended the lives of Klim and Gryshin disappeared into the night. They reappeared in Moscow, just twenty-seven hours later.

The two bodies remained where they fell, completely unnoticed, until residents walking to the subway five hours later noticed them and called nine-one-one.

To the first responders dispatched to each scene, the victim appeared to be just an old drunk who'd stayed out too long and frozen to death. Having no desire to suffer the same cryogenic fate themselves, they hustled the body into the ambulance and sped off to the Medical Examiner's office in Flatbush.

Novichok, and Bratva, had claimed their latest victims.

• • •

Kim Barbieri was almost certainly dead—or at least was no longer sticking her nose where it didn't belong—but the scandal involving Bratva money-laundering was clearly not going away. Quite the opposite. The latest article by the *Journal* reporters did what it was supposed to do. Exposing more of their luxury apartment purchases and triggering investigations on their most recent deals by the New York State Attorney General and the United States Department of Justice. The Russian mafia was now on their radar.

Although the operation targeting Barbieri was successful, the threat to Bratva's illegal income stream was very much alive and well.

In the eyes of senior Bratva leadership, the operation had become a fiasco of the first order. That was unacceptable to them, and they had to make their displeasure clear. They needed to send a message.

The Bratva CEOs and CFOs who had ordered the assassination in the first place could not, of course, blame themselves. That does not follow bureaucracy failure guidelines, which call for assigning blame to peons far below them on the org chart.

They settled first on the two men who led the New York end of the operation. The message was sent. Do not fuck with our bottom line. And the Bratva members who had heard through the grapevine of Klim and Gryshim's untimely deaths understood it perfectly.

Those bargain-basement Bratva thugs who'd only followed orders all got to enjoy the lifestyle of the Russian rich and famous for a while. But it was short-lived. They were all soon dead as well.

The man in the gray cap who'd first tailed Barbieri got a bullet to the brain as he was watching his new BMW 330i being pulled through a Moscow car wash.

In a New York parking garage, the man and woman who'd combined the Novichok ingredients to make it lethal were found dead in their car, after exhaust fumes that were supposed to go out the tailpipe somehow made their way into the passenger compartment instead.

The bodies of the two men who'd kidnapped Reynolds and Shelton and then placed the Novichok in Barbieri's bathroom were found floating in the Moskva River. Minus their heads and hands.

Regardless of how they were murdered, in the CAUSE OF DEATH field in their autopsy reports the coroners all entered the same word: 'UNKNOWN'.

THE END

ABOUT THE AUTHOR

Sid Meltzer took a couple of worthwhile detours on his way to becoming a crime novelist. He started out as a New York State Probation Officer, a job that helped him see things from a criminal's point of view, and let him peer into their minds' many dark alleys.

Working with the ethically-challenged prepared him well for the caliber of people he met in his next career—advertising—where he learned how to craft stories that hook readers in and keep them engaged.

Murderer from Moscow is his second *Kim Barbieri* thriller.

NOTE FROM SID MELTZER

Word-of-mouth is crucial for any author to succeed. If you enjoyed *Murderer from Moscow*, please leave a review online—anywhere you are able. Even if it's just a sentence or two. It would make all the difference and would be very much appreciated.

Thanks!
Sid Meltzer

We hope you enjoyed reading this title from:

www.blackrosewriting.com

Subscribe to our mailing list – *The Rosevine* – and receive **FREE** books, daily
deals, and stay current with news about upcoming
releases and our hottest authors.
Scan the QR code below to sign up.

Already a subscriber? Please accept a sincere thank you for being a fan of
Black Rose Writing authors.

View other Black Rose Writing titles at
www.blackrosewriting.com/books and use promo code
PRINT to receive a **20% discount** when purchasing.